The Luck of the Paw

Susan C. Daffron

An Alpine Grove Romantic Comedy

Book 9

Published by Magic Fur Press
An imprint of Logical Expressions, Inc.
P.O. Box 383
Ponderay, ID 83852

The Luck of the Paw

ISBN: 978-1-61038-044-7 (paperback)
       978-1-61038-045-4 (EPUB)

Like all of my books, *The Luck of the Paw*
is dedicated to
my husband James Byrd,
my best friend and biggest supporter.
Thanks for everything!

Books by Susan C. Daffron
The Alpine Grove Romantic Comedies
Chez Stinky

Fuzzy Logic

The Art of Wag

Snow Furries

Bark to the Future

Howl at the Loon

The Good, the Bad, and the Pugly

The Treasure of the Hairy Cadre

The Luck of the Paw

Daydream Retriever

The Hound of Music

The Jennings & O'Shea Mysteries
Sensing Trouble

Sensing Secrets

Sensing Truth

Chapter 1

Edible or Not

"Gizmo *no!*"

The small shepherd-collie mix grabbed the manila envelope in Mia's hand, bolted through the door, and proceeded to heave up more partially masticated garbage all over the postage-stamp-size lawn outside the Airstream.

Mia wanted to scream. How much garbage could one small dog eat? A Technicolor array of foulness already covered the entire long, narrow floor of the vintage trailer.

Momentarily stunned, Mia swiveled, followed the dog outside, and grabbed his collar, pulling him back toward the steps in front of the metal door. In the neighboring trailer, Mrs. Grafton peeked out from behind a lacy curtain. Mia looked up and waved sheepishly at her.

Although the message on the answering machine said Mia's regular veterinarian was closed for some type of employee training, canine digestive indiscretions didn't observe holidays. Mia closed the dog into the tiny bathroom at one end of the Airstream and surveyed the damage. With only forty-two minutes to deal with cleanup, walk Gizmo, and get back to work, Mia needed to move fast.

The floor wasn't looking too good. On her way back inside, she picked up the sodden manila envelope she'd dropped. Gizmo had torn and eaten half of it, so the contents were leaping out of their nine-by–twelve confinement. Yuck.

Picking up the edge of the envelope with the tips of her index finger and thumb, she tossed it into the little kitchenette sink. Right now, she had bigger issues to deal with than junk mail.

Disturbing retching noises came from the direction of the bathroom while Mia worked on scrubbing the floor and returning the bits of debris to the garbage. What if there was something really wrong with Gizmo? This was shaping up to be Mia's worst birthday ever. And that was saying something.

Mia dropped the sponge into the sink and grabbed the phone book. Time to reach out to the 24-hour emergency vet. If Gizmo was seriously ill, Mia had to do something. After an unpleasant negotiation with a churlish receptionist, the woman finally agreed to let Mia drop off Gizmo on her way back to work. It was entirely possible that Mia's credit card didn't have enough left on it to actually pay, but she'd deal with the ugly financial ramifications later.

The trip to the vet was predictably unpleasant, but at least Gizmo was safe and in good hands for the moment. Mia returned to her desk and had just settled in with her headset so she could power through more tedious stacks of paper when her boss, Lenore, walked up and tapped the top of her cubicle wall.

Mia looked up and slowly pulled off her headset. "I know I was late. I had to take my dog to vote...I mean to the *vet*."

Lenore scowled. "You realize that punctuality is one of our seven key values here at Round House Distributing. We take it very seriously. Being on time reflects your integrity, dependability, and respect for others."

"I know." Mia tuned out while Lenore droned on about the virtues of promptness and employee dedication. You just never knew when there might be a data-entry emergency.

Everyone needed to be very, very sure that the carrots and celery were correctly accounted for at every moment of every day. What if one of those rascally vegetables ran away? Or got lost? What would we do? Sheesh. They were distributing vegetables to grocery stores, not analyzing the intricate nuances of nanotechnology.

Lenore raised her voice. "Mia! Are you listening? You know that we are submitting the Scarlet Nantes for the 1996 taste-test awards."

"Of course I'm listening. The carrots taste good and returning late from lunch is bad."

The line of Lenore's red lipstick puckered into a pursed frown. "Are you being smart with me?"

"No."

"You will need to make up those extra minutes tomorrow."

"Right. I'll tell my dog not to get sacked...*sick* again." Mia made a serious effort not to roll her eyes. Like that would work. Gizmo wasn't great at following instructions. The sad truth was that Mia had no business even owning a dog, but when he'd appeared at the trailer park, wandering around looking for food, she'd taken him in. Every once in a while, she'd encounter a battered copy of one of the thousands of flyers she'd put up all over the vicinity. She'd called animal shelters, vet clinics, and notified anyone else she could think of, but no one had claimed him. Now she couldn't imagine her life without Gizmo's goofy presence in it, even if his unfortunate habit of getting into things he shouldn't was likely to bankrupt her.

After Lenore finally ran out of lecturing steam, she gave Mia one final stern glare and left the cubicle, Mia put her headphones back on, turned up some heavy metal for mood music, and began typing. As the strains of AC/DC surrounded her, the tune "Problem Child" seemed particularly appropriate. It was Gizmo's theme song, after all.

After grabbing her time card and punching out, Mia stopped by the emergency vet to pick up Gizmo. The good news was that he had a clean bill of health. The bad news was that Mia's credit card was declined, just as she'd feared. She'd known it had to be pretty close to the limit, but it never hurt to try.

After quite a bit of negotiating with the receptionist while Gizmo worked to tie his leash around her legs, Mia managed to convince the woman to let her make payments for the remaining charges that couldn't go on the credit card.

With a sigh, Mia exited the clinic with Gizmo and loaded him into the back of her 1978 Datsun B210 that she referred to as Dottie. The car was harvest gold, rusty, and slower than a great-grandma wading through molasses. Mia could drag-race cement mixers from a standing stop and lose. The car was embarrassing, but at least the trailer park was close to work, so Dottie didn't have to work hard. It was a good thing, since sometimes the old car got a little cranky on cold mornings.

Undaunted by his unanticipated and expensive excursion to the veterinarian, Gizmo was raring to go home. He ran back and forth across the dirty beige vinyl seats from one window to the other, sticking his nose out, enjoying all the scents of fertilizer, dirt, hay, and agribusiness wafting through the windows. The air was probably redolent with pesticides too, although Mia tried not to dwell on that idea.

The Central Valley of California was full of agriculture, manufacturing, and oil-refining businesses. Everyone always said the area had a peculiar stink, but Mia had lived in Windiberg her whole life, so she never noticed it. As she drove, her thoughts drifted to the subject of money as they so often did. The kitchen cabinet was stocked with a couple boxes of macaroni and cheese, so dinner was covered. But how was she doing on dog food? Did she have enough left to make it to payday?

It was so annoying that she kept getting turned down for raises. You'd think that after three years, she'd at least get a cost-of-living adjustment. But no. What a bunch of cheapskates. She could apply to receive a discount on bulk carrots though. Unless you were Bugs Bunny, it wasn't much of an employee perk.

Sadly, Gizmo would probably love to dig into one of those gigantic twenty-five-pound bags of carrots. He'd eat them. Just like he ate everything. The animal was a walking furry garbage disposal. And yet she loved him.

Mia looked over her shoulder at the dog's happy face. He had pretty black and brown markings with a white blaze on his chest. His long silky fur probably came from his collie heritage, but it was hard to say what breed contributed to his ears. She'd named him Gizmo because his ears and dark brown eyes made him look like one of the mogwais in the movie *Gremlins*.

After she'd realized Gizmo was staying for good, Mia had gotten him fixed, so it was unlikely he would spawn an army. But giving him a moniker based on a creature that could destroy an entire town might not have been the best idea. Dogs had an unfortunate habit of living up to their names.

~

Mia returned to her Airstream, which was located deep within the Edgewood Paradise Estates. The pretentious name was probably designed to make the trailer park sound a lot nicer than it actually was. The word "Edgewood" implied trees, not a bunch of RVs and single-wide trailers jammed right up next to each other on asphalt pads. Mia knew more about the toilet habits of her neighbors than was probably good for her mental health. On the other hand, the rent on her trailer was cheap and the park allowed dogs.

She took Gizmo for a long walk around the neighborhood with a special tour of the dusty weed-filled vacant lot next door. The hope was that a little extra time among the dried-out vegetation would inspire Gizmo to completely clear out his digestive tract. Sharing two-hundred square feet of space with a dyspeptic flatulent dog was never any fun.

They returned to the trailer and Gizmo settled in on the long couch that ran along one side. Mia pulled the manila envelope out of the sink, and a pile of postcards fell onto the floor along with a white envelope. She bent to collect the colorful cards before Gizmo could get to them. The postcards were old and many had images of pretty scenery. The photographs certainly weren't taken in Windiberg because they were full of picturesque mountains, lakes, and evergreen trees.

With a small shove, she encouraged Gizmo to move down to the other end of the couch so she could sit next to the tiny table. She spread out the contents of the envelope, which included fifty-two postcards and a white letter-size envelope with the words "Good luck" typed on the outside. She peered inside the white envelope and pulled out a stack of lottery tickets. There were a few Fantasy 5 tickets and scratchers. Who would mail her lottery tickets? She stood up and pulled the mangled manila envelope out of the sink. Gizmo apparently had consumed the return address, but it had definitely been sent to her. She turned the large envelope over in her hands and stared at her address, which was typed neatly on the front.

She sat back down next to Gizmo and looked through the postcards. She flipped over one of the cards and the back said she should see some little town called Alpine Grove. Wherever it was, the place was certainly scenic.

All of the postcards were addressed to her father back when he'd lived at home, right before the divorce. The postmarks were from the seventies, when Mia had been in third or fourth grade. Each card had a little note and was signed "CA."

Who or what was "CA" supposed to be? California? Initials? Did her father have a lover she hadn't heard about? Her parents' divorce had been nasty and Mia's familial relationships took the word "estranged" to a new level.

When her father had taken her dog away back then, it was unforgivable. He said Rusty was going to a good home, but even as a little kid, she wasn't naive enough to believe that. Maybe people thought it was silly to be so upset about a dog, but she had felt betrayed and confused. Worst of all, she'd missed Rusty. She cried every night for weeks when she went to bed. His big furry body wasn't sprawled out on the throw rug where he was supposed to be. One night, she couldn't stand it anymore and she heaved the old rug out the window during a thunderstorm. It wasn't the dog's fault her parents got divorced.

No one would tell her why her parents split up, but Mom's new husband was an obvious clue. Mia had detested Howard with a fierce passion and had left the house the day she graduated from high school. That was a day she wished she could forget.

Mia stroked the silky fur on the back of Gizmo's ears. "What do you think, Giz? Why would someone send me old postcards?" The dog lifted his head and the tip of his tail wagged slightly.

It was time to deal with dinner, so she stacked the cards in a pile and vowed to read them later. Deciphering the scrawling handwriting could take a while, and she was hungry.

Mia set the water to boil on the hot plate, opened the blue box, and pulled out the packet of powdered cheese sauce mix. Gizmo looked on with interest as she drained the pasta and added the margarine and milk to create the sauce. She sat back down at the table and handed him a yellow-orange noodle, which he gobbled down with enthusiasm.

She took bite of the macaroni and sighed. There was only one box left in the cabinet and she could squeak a couple of more meals for Gizmo out of the bag of kibble. But there was no way she could put off asking for a raise any longer. Tomorrow, she'd talk to Lenore about it. This time for sure. After being late today, the timing wasn't great, but tomorrow was a new day. Mia would just have to march into Lenore's office and make her case. It had been so long, and she did her work without complaint. She *deserved* a raise.

Gizmo put his head on her knee and looked up at her with his soulful brown eyes. Mia ran her fingertip down his muzzle. Dog food was expensive and the latest veterinary adventure was more evidence that if Mia were brutally honest with herself, she couldn't afford a dog.

As someone who could barely feed and shelter herself, did she even deserve a dog? It would be far better for Gizmo if Mia gave up and just found him a new home with a nice family that would give him lots of treats and expensive dog food.

A tear slid down her face and she leaned down to rest her head on his back. The idea of handing Gizmo off to someone else was too awful to contemplate. He was her best friend in the world. How could she bear to give him up?

With a final sniff, she patted his back. "I promise that tomorrow I'm going to go get that raise. We'll celebrate with a big new bag of dog chow. You'll see. It's going to be great."

Gizmo stood up, wagged his feathery tail a few times, and jumped down from the sofa to the floor, looking expectantly at the door.

Mia brushed her palm across her cheek to wipe away the tears. "You're right Giz. I need to stop sitting here feeling sorry for myself. Let's go for a walk. Everything will be better in the morning. Tomorrow we'll get up, and I'll go to work and get us that raise. Just you watch! I'll be the new me. Eloquent, forceful, and professional. Lenore won't know what hit her."

Gizmo danced around in a circle, enthusiastic about the idea of a walk and more dog food. Mia bent to clip the leash onto his collar. Who was she kidding? Why should this job be different from any other? If history was a precedent, she was going to shyly slink into Lenore's office, stand there feeling uncomfortable, and then blurt out something completely bizarre or stupid. Lenore would glare at her, say there was no way they could possibly give her a raise, and Mia would finally have no choice but to skitter out of there in extreme mortification.

She followed Gizmo down the steps and shut the door behind her. Asking for a raise might not be a great idea. Maybe it was best not to rock the boat. Mia had actually managed to stay at this job for a while. It wasn't very difficult and she was basically comfortable there. Not getting fired for a change had a lot to recommend it. Her stints in retail and food service had shown that dealing with the public was not a good idea. Data entry was boring, but at least she didn't have to talk to anyone, which was perfect for her.

Mia looked past the lights of the trailer park toward the huge metal buildings that made up the industrial complex where Round House Distributing was located. Maybe she could find a way to trim expenses even further. How many miles was it if she walked to work? If she sold Dottie, that might give her enough to pay the vet bill. Of course, if Gizmo ate something else he shouldn't, she'd never be able to *get* to the vet.

Thinking about money all the time was so boring. She'd been over these arguments a thousand times in her head and written countless entries in her journal about her struggles with money.

Tomorrow, she'd ask for a raise. For *sure* this time.

～

The next morning, Mia awoke to the sound of Gizmo's sharp barking. She sat bolt upright and covered her ears. "Gizmo, stop that!"

The dog was running back and forth down the narrow length of the trailer barking like crazy. Mia crawled out of bed and looked out the window. She grabbed Gizmo's collar, "Sit! What is going on with you?"

The dog's goofy ears drooped and he looked suitably chastised. Mia stroked his head. "It's a little early, but I guess we can go out for your walk. Just be quiet for a minute while I get dressed. I'm sure Mrs. Grafton heard your little outburst and she'll probably file another complaint. Please don't get us thrown out of here."

Gizmo wagged happily and wandered around Mia as she donned jeans and a t-shirt. She clipped the leash onto his collar. "Okay, let's go."

She opened the door and almost tripped on a newspaper. Gizmo tried to snatch it from her hand as she picked it up and she threw it inside the trailer before shutting the door behind her. "Sorry, Giz, no more paper for you. It's not food and I can't afford any more of your adventures in creative consumption."

The stroll through the neighborhood was peaceful. No one was up yet and everything was quiet and still. It was Mia's favorite time of day. From here, it was all downhill toward another dull stint at work. But she was still determined to ask for that raise. Today was the day. She was *not* going to chicken out this time.

They returned to the trailer, Mia fed Gizmo, and she settled in with a bowl of store-brand Cheerios. The newspaper wasn't hers, but whoever was supposed to get it undoubtedly wasn't awake yet, so they probably wouldn't mind if she read it while she had her breakfast. She'd fold it back up nice and tidy and give it to the manager on her way to work. No one would be the wiser and she'd get to relax for a few minutes.

The thin newspaper was filled with local agricultural happenings and a few snippets of state and national stories culled from the newswires. Carrot prices were down and farmers were cranky. That was probably bad news for Round House Distributing too. What if she got laid off? That would be ironic. Go in to ask for a raise and get fired. Mia held her spoon aloft for a moment and sighed. Even *her* luck wasn't *that* bad, was it?

She scanned through the horoscopes. According to her horoscope, she should spend her money in a non-frivolous way and put her plans for the future on hold. What money? What plans? Dog food for Gizmo wasn't exactly frivolous.

She took another spoonful of cereal and glanced at the crossword. Below it were the lottery numbers for Fantasy 5. For the first time in her life, she had tickets, so she may as well check them against the numbers. Didn't one of the tickets have a ten on it? Mia moved to reach for the pile of postcards that she'd set aside the night before.

Pulling the envelope out of the stack, she went through the lottery tickets, comparing them to the numbers in the newspaper. Three of them weren't even close, but then she paused. Both the ticket and the paper said "11 24 30 09 10." Mia put her hand up to her face, covering her mouth.

She'd won. She actually *won the lottery*.

Leaping from the chair, she put the lottery ticket on a shelf in a cabinet as far away from Gizmo as possible. The dog jumped up around her, ready for action and the possibility of another walk. Mia put her hand on her chest. If she hyperventilated and passed out, she'd never get the prize money. "Gizmo, I think you're about to get the biggest bag of expensive dog food ever!"

Mia's hands were shaking as she changed her clothes and got ready for work. This was unbelievable. How did you go about claiming the money from a lottery ticket? She reached up, grabbed the ticket, and read the back. It said she should sign the ticket and call an 800 number. Lenore was going to have to get over it, but this was one personal call that Mia was going to make on company time.

She carefully put the ticket into her pocket and hugged Gizmo goodbye. "Be good Giz. I've hidden the garbage way, way up high. So take a nap, okay? I'll see you at lunchtime."

Mia got into Dottie and mustered the old Datsun up to speed, so she actually arrived at work early. Her heart was racing and she kept touching her pocket to see if the lottery ticket was still there. What if she lost it?

At her desk, she dialed the number on the back of the ticket and spoke to a woman with a cheerful voice who said that the fastest way to claim the money was to visit one of the lottery offices that were located throughout the state. After getting directions to the closest one, Mia walked to Lenore's office and tapped on the door jamb.

Lenore looked up from her pile of papers and took off her reading glasses. "Yes, Mia. What can I do for you?"

"I need to take a personal day to drive to Fresca—I mean *Fresno*." Mia tried not to let her voice quaver. Why did she always screw up words when it was important?

"What on earth do you need to go there for? Are you in some type of trouble? You're already behind on your hours."

"I'm not in trouble, but I'd rather not say. It's personal—and it's just one day."

"I suppose. But you need to find someone to cover for you, and today you must be sure to make up the hours you missed yesterday. We are behind."

"All right. I'll do that. Thank you. Have a day!" Mia moved to leave and stopped when she realized what she'd said. "I mean have a *good* day."

Lenore scowled and put her glasses back on. Mia put her hand in her pocket to touch the ticket again. She didn't know how much she'd won, but winning the lottery might mean she could leave this place forever. No more data entry. She could sell her horrible car. Maybe the trip to Fresno would be the last time she'd have to spend half the journey coaxing Dottie up to freeway speed. What an amazing notion. Maybe she could get a car that could handle long trips. She could travel! Go anywhere and do anything. How long did it take to get lottery money? Hard-core gamblers probably knew these details, but Mia had no idea.

For Mia, the rest of the day passed in a daze. She got caught up on work and spent a lot of time calling around the office trying to convince one of her colleagues to cover her shift the next day. Describing her trip as an "emergency" was probably a bit of a stretch, but it would be worth it.

At last, after a considerable amount of begging, she finally was able to cajole Tony into taking on her data entry with the promise that she'd pay him back by working for him the next time he had a hot date. Tony thought of himself as an exceptional Lothario, and he warned her that payback would be soon. He had his eye on a woman down in purchasing and firmly believed there was no possible way she could resist his charms.

With any luck, Mia would no longer be working at Round House Distributing by the time that poor woman agreed to subject herself to a date with Tony. By then, Mia would be long gone. She'd be somewhere. Anywhere other than here.

While she was typing in data about carrot prices, purchases, and locations, Mia let her thoughts wander. What would it be like to leave this place? How would that feel? Walking into Lenore's office and saying, "I quit. You can take this job and shove it." Just like the song. A little smile crossed her face as she imagined Lenore's confused expression. What a magical moment that would be.

~

The trip to the lottery office was long and dusty as Mia drove across miles upon miles of flat, dull farmland. After the first half hour, even Gizmo was bored. Dottie didn't move with great speed and the people in the other cars on the highway noticed. A few people felt compelled to emphasize their irritation at the B210's slow pace with elaborate hand gestures. Mia stared straight ahead, trying to ignore the automotive animosity that surrounded her.

Finally, she made it to the lottery office and parked in an underground parking garage. After admonishing Gizmo to be good and suggesting he enjoy a nap in the shade, she went inside to discuss her new-found wealth. By the time she returned to the car, she was so overwhelmed, she needed some time to collect her thoughts. She got into the car and sat staring straight ahead, silently processing the information. Gizmo leaped around in the backseat, and finally she turned and smiled at him. "Guess what, Giz? We're rich!"

Mia had known that matching all five numbers would be a good thing, but not *that* good. Signing the forms almost seemed like a dream, with the clerk's voice acting as the soundtrack while she collected the signed paperwork and explained how Mia would receive her winnings. The money would take a month to process, so the woman suggested that Mia not quit her job immediately. Mia was disappointed, but it made sense. Making all those lovely quitting fantasies come true would have to wait.

The clerk had given Mia a brochure with frequently asked questions for winners. In the car, she took a few minutes to read it over while Gizmo looked over her shoulder. Because her name was part of public record as a winner, it would be newsworthy, so she should expect some publicity. It also pointed out that she might want to get a financial advisor and included repeated warnings that winners not make any quick, rash decisions or put too much trust in others.

Mia put the flyer aside and turned the key in the ignition to start Dottie. There was a lot to think about. Reading between the lines, it sounded like winning the lottery was not going to bring out the best in other people. But any negatives were outweighed by the thrill of quitting her job. Mia could do whatever she wanted. The idea was utterly mind-blowing.

No more living in the Edgewood Paradise Estates. For the first time in her adult life, it would be financially feasible for Mia to consider leaving the area entirely. At last, after years of being trapped in her hometown, she could finally get out. Where should she go? Maybe she could travel and look for a new home. Somewhere far, far away from where she'd grown up. Someplace with trees and mountains. No more flat farmland for her. And no more carrots.

Never again having to hear about the tedious rivalry between her high school football team and the team at the school in the next town over made Mia a little giddy. The constant rah-rah school spirit was vomit-inducing, since high school had been a miserable time for Mia. Being a quiet, socially bizarre freak meant she'd spent a lot of time alone.

At the time, she'd hated almost every aspect of her life— her family, herself, and the horrid town she lived in. She'd dyed her hair jet black, which, combined with her entirely black wardrobe and raccoon-esque eyeliner, made her look like she was the carrier of a terminal disease or the guest of honor at a funeral.

In retrospect, it shouldn't have been a surprise that virtually everyone had avoided Mia. It was better that way. Because of all the stress, anger, and general malaise of high school, that was when she'd started having the problem of saying the wrong words when she was nervous.

Mia had always been soft-spoken, and when she had to do an oral report, hecklers would shout from the back of the classroom that they couldn't hear her. During her freshman year, one evening at dinner, her mother asked about her day and Mia had complained about her dislike of speaking in front of other people.

Howard, her mother's husband—Mia couldn't bear to ever call him *stepfather*—had constantly teased her about her appearance and told her she was too wimpy. Then one night she'd asked him to pass the box of Ritz crappers, instead of crackers, and after that his torment became incessant. For the next three years, every single time she got near him, he made some joke about those tasty crappers. He just couldn't let it go.

Then one fateful day in biology class, it happened again. Mia got so flustered when the teacher asked her a question about a one-celled organism that Mia had blurted out that "bacteria are one-celled *orgasms* without nuclei." The whole class roared with laughter to the point that she'd wanted to crawl under the desk and die.

In English class, she'd had to do an oral book report and she'd referred to it as a boob report about The Great Goatsby. *Goatsby?* Every time she thought about it, she relived the mortification. Where had goats and boobs come from? It was like her brain had a complete meltdown.

Mia became so terrified that she'd transpose or misuse words, the problem kept getting worse. It felt like almost every time she opened her mouth, something strange came out. She hid in empty classrooms at lunchtime, so she wouldn't have to deal with the awkwardness of having no one to sit with.

Once she finally graduated, the embarrassing verbal incidents declined a bit, probably because she avoided people as much as possible. Being away from Howard's sarcastic, nasty sense of humor helped too. But her lack of oratory skills meant her forays into gainful employment were often short-lived. It had taken only two days to discover she had no future in the food-service industry. Her stint at the Dairy Queen was cut short when she said "Here's your Diet Cock" to a customer.

Working at a call center hadn't worked out much better. Her supervisor had received complaints after Mia said, "How can I hate you?" to a number of people attempting to order new telephone services.

Fortunately, Windiberg had lots of manufacturing jobs, which involved less human contact. For several years, Mia had worked in a factory, standing for hours at a heat-sealing machine. The company distributed all kinds of store-brand nuts and candy. It was the yucky generic stuff that hung on racks in plastic bags at the grocery store. She'd learned that the fake, no-name M&Ms were nowhere near as good as the real brand-name chocolate, but someone had to put those cheap knock-offs into the bag and seal the top. That person was her.

Sometimes Mia still dreamed about working there. She could feel the pedal under her foot, the thump of the candy falling into the bag, and then the hissing noise the sealer made as it affixed the label onto the top of the plastic baggie. The smells of burning sugar and nut oils filled the warehouse, because sometimes a worker missed and caught some food in the heat sealer. Even now, the scent of melted licorice gave her a raging migraine.

The job at Round House Distributing had been a step in the right direction. At least she got to sit down. And except for when people burned popcorn in the microwave, the building generally smelled better than a factory. Given her skills, or lack of them, the data entry job was really the best she'd been able to do. For a long time, she believed she'd be able to get ahead a little financially and take some college classes, but it had never happened. Life was expensive.

Mia shook her head and put down the brochure next to her in the passenger seat. Money wasn't going to be a problem anymore. And that was nothing short of a miracle. Over the years, she'd tried to remain grateful for her job and not complain too much because things could have been a lot worse.

Even when things were bad, she'd always had enough to eat and a roof over her head. The Windiberg library also provided countless hours of joy for her. Books were free and she'd read her way through almost every section of the library. Novels, health, finance, psychology, and anything else that happened to catch her eye. It cost nothing, and after a few unfortunate book-shredding incidents, she'd set aside a special cabinet just to store her books away from Gizmo's teeth.

Going forward, everything would be different. In the last twenty-four hours, Mia's future had changed completely. She had no idea what might be next, but it would certainly be different from what she'd experienced so far.

Mia turned and looked at Gizmo, who was sitting expectantly in the backseat. "Here's to bold new adventures, Giz! Let's go home."

~

Mia had a lot of time to think on the drive back home from Fresno. The prospect of leaving everything she'd ever known was both exhilarating and terrifying. She had a month to get everything in order before she hit the road to discover her new life.

She ticked off items on a mental to-do list. She needed to give notice on the Airstream and sell her things, but because the Airstream mostly had built-in furniture, there wasn't much. The few photographs and mementos she wanted to keep could fit in a car. Selling her junky housewares and knickknacks might give her enough cash to buy food and make one of her veterinary payments. She also could go to the doctor, get her eyes checked, and see the dentist. It had been a long time since she'd visited any medical establishment, and the bills for those visits wouldn't arrive until after she had the lottery money. Once she had the money safely tucked away in her bank account, she could pay off the rest of Gizmo's vet bill, sell Dottie, and get a new car.

The next few days at work were strange. It was distracting to have a huge secret that she couldn't tell anyone. All she could think about was the fact that she'd actually *won*. It didn't seem real. Then one evening after work, there was a knock on the door. Mia peeked out the window. It was Mrs. Grafton, who never dropped by her trailer with good news. Usually, she was on a mission to complain about Gizmo.

Mia grabbed Gizmo's collar and opened the door.

Mrs. Grafton stood at the bottom of the stairs with an uncharacteristic sappy smile on her face. "Oh Mia! How is my favorite neighbor?"

"I'm, uh, fine. Is something wrong?"

"No, not at all! I just wanted to stop by and bring you these blueberry muffins I made." She held out a plastic container. "I thought you might like them. I brought a couple of dog biscuits for your sweet little dog too."

Mia pulled Gizmo back and gestured toward the trailer. "Thank you. There's not much room, but please come in." What was going on? Mrs. Grafton disliked her and absolutely hated Gizmo. The last time they'd spoken, she'd referred to Mia as a "trashy slut" and Gizmo as a "mangy cur."

"Thank you, dear. I'll just put them on the counter." She set down the muffins. "Do you have a second?"

"Okay." Mia closed the door and sat down on the long sofa. Gizmo leaped up next to her.

Mrs. Grafton settled into the chair at the tiny table and readjusted her skirt and her thighs to center them on the chair. "I read about you in the paper. Aren't you excited?"

Mia narrowed her eyes. The woman's sudden change of heart was starting to make sense. "I don't have a subscription to the paper."

"Mia! You won the lottery, for heaven's sake."

"I know."

"So what are you going to do with the money?" Mrs. Grafton clasped her hands together as if she were praying to the gods of chance. "I am so envious. You know how hard I work."

Actually, Mia had no idea what Mrs. Grafton did, beyond complaining, snooping, and spying on the neighbors. "I suppose."

"Well, we have a family situation and my dear daughter has asked me for a loan. It kills me to have to turn her down. She's a dancer and she needs money for surgery."

"I'm sorry to hear that. Is she okay? Did she hurt herself?"

"Not exactly, but she needs to invest in her career. We've always been so close, you and I, so I was thinking you might want to contribute to her cause. She's very talented, you know."

"It will be a few weeks until I receive my winnings." Mia stroked Gizmo's head. He was being such a good boy. "I don't understand. Why does your daughter need surgery?"

Mrs. Grafton leaned forward. "It's a competitive business. All of the dancers need to improve on what nature gave them. If you don't get augmentation surgery for the girls, you can't compete."

"The girls? Wait…you mean a *boob job*?" Mia flashed back to her book report fiasco. Yes, she really meant boob this time. "Are you seriously asking me to *invest* in your daughter's breast-augmentation surgery?"

"Why yes, dear. That's what I said. She needs it to further her career. Insurance doesn't cover it, and it's so unfair that she can't write it off either. I mean, it's a work-related expense! But she's not self-employed, so the accountant said the deduction wouldn't fly. And Deb would certainly pay you back. With interest too. She'll be getting much better tips, and I know you'd make back your investment in no time."

Mia shook her head. "I don't think so. Thank you for the offer. But right now, I, um, have some things I need to do. I have to get up at sex…I mean *six* tomorrow morning."

Mrs. Grafton stood up. "Well, just think about it, dear. It's an extremely wise business move. We could work out the details so you could double or triple your money. I wouldn't steer you wrong. You'll thank me in the end. Deb is very gifted."

Mia stood and held onto Gizmo's collar. "I'm sure she is. Thank you for the muffins."

"Return the plastic container when you can. And do let me know when you're ready to invest!"

Mia closed the door, turned to the counter, and opened the muffin container. She broke a muffin in half, took a bite, and looked at the dry, crumbly core. Yuck. Gizmo wagged happily as she handed him the other half. "Since you don't have the most discriminating palette, it's yours."

Gizmo made a few hacking noises, but managed to choke down the muffin. He looked up eagerly. Mia shook her head, put the lid back on the container, and stuffed it into the micro-fridge below the counter. "I don't think so. No more cement muffins for you. After your last digestive disaster, I think you need to pace yourself."

Gizmo settled back down on the sofa and put his head between his paws with a sigh.

Over the next few days, it became apparent that the word was out about Mia's good fortune. At her doctor's office, the receptionist told her about a fantastic new product that she distributed. It was a new type of makeup and Mia could get in on the ground floor just by holding parties for her friends.

Mia didn't want to point out the fact that any friends she'd had moved away long ago, so she just nodded politely as the perky woman explained all the "science" behind the new product line. The whole thing sounded like a more complicated version of Avon or Amway, neither of which Mia had even the remotest interest in selling.

Finally, the doctor was ready to see her. After being weighed on the huge industrial scale that always made her at least five pounds heavier than any other scale, she had to strip and wait around snuggled up in a gown, attempting to cover up and not freeze while sitting on crinkly paper.

Sitting and waiting for the doctor was part of the process. As if getting her downstairs poked and prodded in incredibly uncomfortable ways wasn't bad enough, they made you wait so you could dread and dwell upon the special feel of the speculum for a little while longer.

Why did they call them stirrups, anyway? Was it to make a pelvic exam sound like more fun? Horseback riding might be fun. Being checked inside and out down there was not.

Doctor Isaacs was a tall, chatty woman who in any other context Mia might actually enjoy talking to. As it was, they usually ended up talking about films. Or the doctor talked, anyway. Movies were expensive and Mia didn't have TV, so she hadn't seen a film in years. During the exam, the doctor talked about the movies she'd seen while Mia stared at the ceiling, pretending to be somewhere else.

Mia turned at the tap on the door. Dr. Isaacs walked in and grinned. "I saw your name in the paper. You won the lottery!"

"I guess everyone knows."

"Lie back and put your feet in the stirrups. Wow, those are great socks!"

"Thank you." Mia closed her eyes. Was it over yet?

"So what are you going to do with all that money?"

Mia opened her eyes again. "I'm not sure. Maybe travel? I've never been, well, anywhere, really."

"That sounds wonderful. To infinity and beyond!"

"What?"

"Oh, it's a line from movie. Please scoot down a bit farther, could you?"

Mia did as instructed and readjusted her feet in the stirrups. "So, have you seen anything good lately?" Mia put her palm on her forehead. Could she be more of a moron? The doctor was staring down her hoo-ha. "I mean movies. *Films*! When I'm here, you always talk about films."

Dr. Isaacs put her hand on Mia's knee. "Relax Mia; the speculum is more uncomfortable if you tense up. Oh, and yes, I saw *Toy Story* the other day with my daughter. Tom Hanks is great. He does the voice for a little cowboy toy. Oh and there's Buzz Lightyear, who is an astronaut action figure."

"Sounds fun." At this point, Mia would have agreed with almost anything to get this exam over with.

The doctor patted her knee. "All done. You can sit up now."

Mia slid to the end of the table, sat, and looked at the doctor. "I'll probably be moving, but I'm not sure where yet. I've been seeing you for a long time. Can I call you for a referral to another doctor?"

"Just give the office a call when you get settled and we'll give you some names and transfer your records." The doctor put her hand on Mia's forearm. "I hope you find what you're looking for and can leave everything that happened here behind you."

"Thank you. I do too."

Chapter 2

On the Road

A few weeks later, the day Mia had been dreaming about finally arrived, and she closed the door of the Airstream for the very last time. The lottery winnings were safely nestled in a special new bank account, she'd traded in Dottie, and finally left her job behind.

She had calculated her two week's notice so she'd have a few extra days to donate the last of her belongings to thrift stores and clean out the Airstream before she took off on her trip. Most of the items had come from thrift stores to begin with, so in Mia's mind she was just returning them to their ancestral home. Some other struggling unhappy teenager or twenty-something setting up her home could have them now. It was odd to think that she wasn't "in her twenties" anymore. Shouldn't she have her life figured out by now?

Everything Mia owned was loaded in the shiny new 1997 Toyota RAV 4 that she'd purchased. When she told the guy at the dealership she was paying cash, she thought he might faint. He was significantly less impressed with her trade-in, and was willing to give her the princely sum of only $150 for poor old Dottie. The forest green RAV didn't have a name yet, but Mia figured that after some time on the road, they'd bond and inspiration would strike.

She'd purchased the RAV because the rear seats folded down, which gave Gizmo lots of room to hang out. However, for this trip, she'd left the backseats up so he could ride there and not be located among the boxes filled with things he might regard as edible. Along with her belongings, Mia had stocked up on road food, maps, and travel guides, so having a new car with space was helpful.

After spending lots of time staring at the postcards that had come with the lottery tickets, Mia wanted to see Alpine Grove. The notes on the postcards were difficult to read, but intriguing. Why was this "CA" person writing to her father? What did it mean? Was he the one who'd sent the postcards to Mia? If not him, then who? Was her father actually *in* Alpine Grove? She hadn't heard from him in twenty years. Why now? After all these years, did he still remember her birthday? Was he aware that she'd won the lottery with one of the tickets he sent?

Questions about the odd package swirled in her mind. The ruminations were a nice distraction from larger, more complicated questions, like what she was going to do with the rest of her life. Mia hoped that the road trip would help her figure out what she wanted. Now that she had money, she could do almost anything. But that led to an uncomfortable question. What *did* she want to do?

For years, she'd been completely focused on what she *had* to do, so she hadn't spent any time thinking about what she *liked* to do. The focus on earning enough to continue to live independently with food and shelter had quashed any desires or dreams for the future.

Even after taxes were taken out of her lottery winnings, Mia had enough to live on for quite some time, almost no matter what she decided to do. As long as she didn't fall prey to one of the many scammers trying to part her from her new-found wealth, she'd be fine.

One happy side-effect of leaving her home town would be ditching her telephone number forever. The calls from people who wanted to "help her manage her money" had gotten so completely out of hand that she'd stopped answering the phone and had turned off the ringer. At work, people who had never talked to her before stopped by her desk to tell her sob stories about sick relatives who undoubtedly didn't exist or terrible and expensive problems she could help resolve with a sizable donation.

It would be such a relief to go somewhere where no one knew who she was. After living in an arid area her whole life, Mia yearned to see water. First, she was determined to see the Pacific Ocean and drive up the coast. Then maybe work her way to Alpine Grove and see some of the places on the postcards before winter arrived. If the postcards were any indication, Alpine Grove was pretty and located near a huge lake—another large body of water. Whether it was the ocean or a lake, it didn't matter. The main goal was to get away from endless flat farmland.

After dropping off the keys to the trailer with the manager, Mia got into the car and looked over her shoulder at Gizmo, who was enjoying the little nest she'd created for him with his own doggie bed. He looked almost as pleased to be leaving as she was. They both had troubled pasts here that were best forgotten. When she'd taken him in, Gizmo had been an extremely skinny, matted, little stray. She reached back over the seat to stroke his head. "Are you ready, Giz?"

As she passed the sign that said "Leaving Windiberg," Mia let out a whoop and Gizmo woofed a vote of support.

She was finally getting out of here for good and she was never coming back. Everything that had happened with her mother and Howard was behind her. Outside of Windiberg, no one knew about them or that she now had money. No one cared. Maybe she could leave all the anger and guilt behind and finally move on. The road stretched in front of her like an oasis. She put a CD into the player and cranked up some tunes to accompany the turning point in her life.

Several hundred miles later, Mia finally reached the coast. The closer she drove toward the Pacific Ocean, the more cars there were. Traffic had slowed to a crawl many times, but at last they'd reached the edge of the United States with nothing except the wide expanse of the Pacific before them.

Mia parked the car in a public parking lot and got Gizmo out of the backseat. He sniffed around the asphalt while she just stood and stared out at the waves. A few surfers were sitting on their boards, bobbing like colorful corks in the water. A large wave formed behind them and almost in unison, they scrambled to attention in their efforts to catch the curl.

Mia smiled. Her mother would have loved this sight. When Mia was a little girl, Mom had spun wild, elaborate tales of mermaids and sea monsters who lived in the sea. On her good days, no one was more creative, flamboyant, and funny than Elaine Riggins. One of Mia's favorite memories was of her mother dancing around the living room, singing along to an old Beatles eight-track. She would pause only to wait for the player to clunk to the next track and clap her hands in glee when the music started again. Her skirt had swirled around her as she cavorted around, lost in her own joyous world of music and lyrics.

Had Mom ever seen the ocean? Maybe she hadn't. Maybe she'd had the same longing to see water that Mia had, and that's why Mia would find her standing at the sink, sobbing uncontrollably while doing dishes.

After years of reading library books related to psychology and mental health, Mia finally understood that her mother had probably suffered from bipolar disorder. In some ways, it had been a relief to have a definition and an explanation for why her mother hadn't been able to handle many of the day-to-day realities of living her life. The diagnosis offered an explanation for the manic highs and lows. But it didn't make it any easier for Mia to accept everything that had happened.

There were times Mia would wake up from a dream crying, realizing that she no longer remembered what her mother's voice sounded like. In the dream, she kept wanting Mom to turn to her and say "I love you, sweetheart," but she never did. Other dreams were more about the rage Mia felt toward her mother for not being normal and dependable like other parents.

A crunching noise came from near her feet and Mia looked down. "Gizmo! What are you eating?"

The dog quickly gulped down whatever he had discovered and wagged his tail, obviously pleased that he'd devoured his parking lot prize before Mia noticed.

An old man wearing a straw porkpie hat got out of a car farther down the row and shouted, "Hey lady, can't you read? Dogs aren't allowed here!"

Mia waved at the man and gathered the leash in her hands. "Sorry, Giz, time to get going. We'll find a dog-friendly beach somewhere. I promise."

~

Mia had scoured her guidebooks for motels that would allow dogs, but there weren't many, so it was looking like she might get to know Motel 6s rather well. All of the motels in the low-budget chain were pet-friendly without exception, but the travel guides were largely silent about which beaches and parks permitted dogs.

After driving along the coast in stop-and-go traffic for a while, looking for a beach with dogs happily romping on it, Mia gave up and drove to the Motel 6. Apparently, this one had the distinction of being the first one, which opened back in 1962. The motel was within walking distance of a beach, but not one where Gizmo was allowed. Oh well.

After unloading her things and Gizmo from the car, Mia sat at the end of the bed stroking the fur on the dog's head. All of the anticipation of getting ready and leaving was behind her. Day one of driving had been tiring, but uneventful, so at this point the journey was a success. Now it was time to find food. She gave Gizmo's ears a final scritch. "Okay, let's go for a walk and see what awaits us out there."

After clipping a leash onto Gizmo's collar, Mia grabbed her key and a baggie and shoved them in her pocket. They walked away from the motel, toward the beach. After crossing a busy road, they began walking along the long sidewalk dotted with palm trees that ran between the beach parking lots and the road. The lots were full of vans and trucks with surfboards attached to or sticking out from them in one way or another. After watching so many TV shows filmed in Southern California when she was little, the environment almost didn't seem real.

The late afternoon sun on her shoulders was relaxing and Mia wanted to stop time, to ensure she never forgot this moment. For the first time in what seemed like forever, she was truly happy. Just walking with Gizmo on the sidewalk alongside the beautiful ocean was amazing. Although she had no idea what would happen next, right now was feeling pretty terrific.

Mia bought a fish taco from a walk-up taco shack and sat on a bench to eat it, sharing a few bites with Gizmo. Then they slowly meandered back to the Motel 6 to settle in for the evening. She reentered the room, fed Gizmo his bowl of kibble, and curled up on the bed to read. It had been a great day.

Mia opened her eyes at the all-too-familiar sound of canine regurgitation. She rolled over and felt around the nightstand, looking for her watch. Three in the morning? Ugh. Another hack came from the direction of the bathroom and Mia jumped out of bed. "Gizmo! What are you up to?"

She stopped in the doorway. Gizmo was in the center of what looked like a toilet paper explosion. Bits of white paper were everywhere. Some of it was shredded, some soggy, and some just strewn like streamers around the small tiled area. "Oh Giz. Why do you do this?"

The dog wagged his tail and spewed out a wad of paper like a spitball, which landed on the tile with a splat.

Mia shooed the dog out of the bathroom and began scraping up the paper residue from various surfaces and heaving them into the small plastic garbage can. Her next stop needed to be a pet store. There had to be some way to confine Gizmo so he couldn't eat his way through every place she stayed. If she were banned from Motel 6s, it would completely derail her road-trip plans.

A crash came from the other room and Mia started to stand up, but clunked the top of her head on the sink. "Ow!"

The Venetian blinds from the motel window were sprawled across the floor next to Gizmo, who seemed extremely eager to go outside, dancing around near the doorway. Mia grabbed his collar. "Gizmo! Hold on. Sit!"

The dog sat for half a second, then resumed his anxious cha-cha around the door.

She turned, grabbed her jeans from the chair, and yanked them on. "Hold on. I'm working on it."

Finally, she had pants on herself and the leash on Gizmo. She grabbed the room key and hurried outside into the darkness. Gizmo yanked her toward the closest patch of grass, and as soon as his paw touched green, he assumed the position. Mia made a face. That was one bad smell and she didn't have a baggie this time. At least it was dark. Maybe no one would notice that gargantuan pile on the lawn. She mentally apologized to her fellow travelers and vowed to return with a baggie in the morning, once the sun was up.

Having completed his mission, Gizmo turned around and trotted happily back to Mia. She stroked his head. "I guess you feel better now, huh?"

They returned to the room and Mia locked the door behind them. She attached Gizmo's leash to a chair near the bathroom, so she could keep an eye on him while she cleaned up the rest of the toilet-paper disaster.

After she was done, she attached Gizmo's leash to the nightstand and crawled back into bed. She pointed her finger at him, "You lie down right *there* and go to sleep."

Looking momentarily distressed at the firm tone, the dog spun around and curled himself into a ball with his nose behind his tail.

Mia squeezed her eyes shut, trying to take herself back to that sensation of happiness and peace she'd felt walking along the sidewalk next to the beach earlier. Life on the road might require a few more adjustments than she expected.

Over the next week, Mia logged many miles as she worked her way up the California coastline, stopping at various Motel 6s along the way. She acquired an x-pen, which helped keep Gizmo in one place, although he did manage to sneak a pillow off the bed and chew it up one night. The next morning when they checked out, the manager had not been amused, and Mia sheepishly paid for the damage and moved on.

Although she saw many wonderful sights, she learned that driving every day and figuring out how to get food when you have a dog became exhausting over time. Drive-through fast food was starting to bring her down, and she could order delivery pizza only so many times before she was completely sick of it.

At the Monterey Motel 6, she was lying on the bed eating chips and watching the TV news. A freak October storm had dumped more than a foot of snow in the mountains near Lake Tahoe. Mia sat up and handed Gizmo a chip. If she wanted to see Alpine Grove, it would probably be a good idea to get there before the snow arrived. She had no experience with winter driving, so she thought it would be best to see the place while it was still fall. Once she'd satisfied her curiosity about the postcards that were addressed to her father, she could head back south and maybe travel east. If she went far enough, she could go see Disney World. Why not?

She handed Gizmo another chip. "What do you think? Wanna see a big lake next?"

Gizmo wagged his tail and Mia smiled. Even though he had a bit of an eating disorder, Gizmo was an easygoing travel companion.

~

A few days later, Mia wound the trusty little RAV up the mountain road toward Alpine Grove. After due consideration, she'd decided to name her little green steed Flicka, since they were likely to have many adventures together, just like the horse and the boy in the book.

As the road ascended in elevation, she turned off the air conditioning and opened a rear window so Gizmo could enjoy the fresh, pine-scented air. The dog snorted and snorfled happily as some particularly good scents hit his nostrils. Mia giggled. All those breezes probably led to doggie information overload.

She slowed as she entered the main street of the small town. It was lined with brick buildings that had cute little shops, restaurants, and real estate offices. Several couples were walking on the sidewalk and groups of people stood chatting companionably in the sunshine. An ice cream cart with a festive umbrella had a sign proclaiming it was the last day of the season for ice cream. Mia parallel-parked next to it and purchased an ice cream cone. She got back into the car, broke off a piece of the cone for Gizmo, and handed it to him. Bending to look at the map spread out on the passenger seat next to her, she determined that the lake was south of town. Maybe she'd missed the turn. With so much open space around here, she might be able to find a spot where she could take a longer walk with Gizmo. After so much road time, the poor guy could probably use some exercise.

She drove north out of town and turned around at a motel and RV park called the Enchanted Moose. The sign proudly proclaimed that it had no vacancies. Oh well, that place was out. She drove back through town and made her way toward the lake.

There weren't many roads signs and no indication of where the lake was located. Mia turned left on one of the unlabeled roads. She'd been driving for a while and the lake was gigantic, so it had to be somewhere close. The road wound through fields edged by forest, and a few houses started appearing. As the houses got more expensive-looking, Mia figured she must be on the right track.

The road curved around another bend and then opened up to a jaw-dropping lake vista. Continuing to meander high above the brilliant blue lake, the road hugged a hillside that dropped down to the shoreline far below.

The car thumped as the pavement ended and the road transitioned to gravel. Mia slowed the car, driving carefully and taking brief glances at the phenomenal view. The houses along the road had been built into the hillside, seeming to cling to it. Many had huge panoramic windows, so from inside it must seem like you were flying over the lake. Wow. Talk about the high-rent district. This place was about as far from a derelict trailer in Windiberg as you could get. Apparently, this was how the other half lived.

Mia turned her attention back to Flicka. Something felt funny with the car. The ride felt odd and there was an extra thumping noise. Did her brand-new car *already* have a flat tire? She slowed down and steered the car past a driveway to an empty spot along the road that didn't seem to be part of someone's front lawn. Pulling over, she stopped the car and looked out at the lake. It would be only a matter of time before someone built a house on this lot. What a view. She turned to look at Gizmo. "Just a sec, Giz. I need to check on something."

Mia got out and walked around the car. Sure enough, the left rear tire was flat. She crouched down to look at it more closely. The silver head of a screw was visible and presumably the rest was embedded in the tire. When had that happened? Fortunately, the RAV had a full-size tire hanging on the back door, but she was going to have to move a lot of stuff around to find the jack. Ugh.

She opened a rear door to access the backseat. "Okay Gizmo, we have a problem. You need to get out. Let's go for a little walk, and then I'll deal with the tire." Gizmo hopped out daintily and sniffed the ground. "Sorry. For once, we're in a place with no garbage for you to eat."

Gizmo went about his business while Mia gazed out at the lake. A sharp bark came from the hillside below them and she looked down. A small pudgy white poodle mix ran up, making a wide range of yapping noises as it ran, until it spotted Gizmo. With wide eyes, Gizmo looked up at Mia in confusion, and then wagged his tail at the stocky little dog. The smaller dog play-bowed and wagged her stubby tail at Gizmo, who sniffed politely.

Mia crouched down and held out her hand. "Hey, little dog. Where did you come from?"

The dog gave up on its burst of ferocity and rolled over on its back for a tummy rub. Mia smiled. "Wow, you're a real killer, aren't you, little girl?"

From below a male voice shouted, "Lulu, where are you? This isn't funny! Come back here."

Mia, Gizmo, and the dog that presumably was named Lulu, turned to look toward the voice. A man scrabbled up the hill and grunted as he crawled up over the edge on his hands and knees. He sat back on his heels and looked at Lulu. "Come here, baby. You scared me!"

The little white dog ran over to him and he clipped a leash onto the dog's collar.

Mia held up her hand in greeting. "I guess Lulu is your log?"

Pushing his brown hair back from his forehead, he stood up. "Log? Wait, what did you say?" He readjusted his wire-framed glasses. The thick lenses emphasized his brown eyes, which were so large and round, they were almost cartoonish.

Mia tried to force herself to stop thinking about all the bug-eyed characters on *The Simpsons*, so she wouldn't blurt out something completely inappropriate and bizarre. At least the guy didn't have mustard-colored skin anyway.

She watched as he stood up and pointed at the poodle. "Lulu is yours?"

"Yes. Thank you for keeping an eye on her. I didn't think she'd run up the hillside like that. Normally, she's a lazy slug."

Mia smiled weakly, "But she's adorable. All round, curly, and mute...I mean *cute*."

He held out his hand. "My name is Chris, by the way."

"I'm Mia." His hand was soft and his clothes were brand-new and expensive, if the little logo on his polo shirt was any indication. Climbing up cliffs was probably not generally part of this guy's normal daily routine. She gestured toward her own wagging dog. "This is Gizmo. I hope we're not trespassing, but my tire…it's flaccid."

He raised his eyebrows as he glanced at the RAV4. "I've never heard that word used to describe a tire before."

Mia put her hand to her cheek, which was now extremely warm. Her face was undoubtedly a fantastic shade of red. Why did she bother trying to talk to anyone? She was such a lost cause. "I uh, um, yes, the tire is flat."

"Do you need help?"

"I can change the tire, but if you could hold my dog's leash for a second, that would be great. I need to unload stuff to find the crack…I mean *jack*." She gestured toward Gizmo. "He's not familiar with the area and I don't want him to get lost. The car is new and I'm not sure where the jack is stored. I need to look at the manual."

Chris took the leash from her with a smile. "So what brings you to Alpine Grove?"

Mia walked toward the RAV, opened the rear door, and began rummaging through the compartments in the back. She didn't really want to get into the whole story about the lottery tickets and postcards with someone she didn't know. "I saw pictures and it looked pretty here."

"It is! I've visited a number of times and I love it. This summer has been beautiful and now all the leaves are turning. Lulu and I have done some hiking. There's a trail along the lake that's easy and flat."

"I guess she's not a big walker." Mia walked around to the passenger side of the car, opened the door, and began moving things around so she could get into the glove compartment and find the manual.

"Lulu is getting older and she isn't a big fan of exercise. That's why I couldn't believe it when she hauled her little body all the way up that steep hill. I assumed I'd have to carry her up."

Mia rummaged around and finally extracted the RAV manual. It was time for Flicka to reveal where her jack was located. Holding up the booklet and flapping it toward the road, she added, "You probably have stuff to do. I'm fine. You don't have to stay."

"I'm not going to just leave you here." He readjusted the leashes in his hand. "The least I can do is hold your dog. Where do you live?"

Mia looked up from the manual. She'd found the tire iron in a bag located in one of the compartments in the rear of the vehicle, but the jack was under the front passenger seat. Setting the book aside, she stood up and kneeled next to Flicka. "I'm in the process of moving."

"I guess that explains the packed Toyota."

"Yes, it does." Mia rummaged under the seat and touched cold metal. What an odd place to put it. She held up the scissor jack. "Found it!"

He smiled. "So where were you coming from?"

"Well, Windiberg originally, but we've been traveling for a little while now."

"Really? Windiberg? I went to high school there."

Mia grabbed the instruction manual from the passenger seat and walked toward the back of the car. "Me too."

"When did you graduate?"

"1984."

Chris moved nearer to her. "Me too. I guess that means we went to school together."

Mia stopped to look at him more closely. "What's your last name?"

"Blanchard. What's yours?"

"Riggins. I sort of remember you, I think. But you look really deficient...I mean *different*."

"I don't remember anyone named Mia."

"Well, it's short for Amelia. And back then, I called myself Amanita for a while."

"Really? The poisonous mushroom girl? That was *you*?"

~

Mia crouched down to look for the spot where the jack was supposed to go under the car. She'd driven hundreds of miles to get away from Windiberg and managed to find probably the only person in teeny-tiny Alpine Grove who went to school with her. What were the odds? Probably about the same as winning the lottery. Hmm.

She looked up at Chris and pointed at the underside of the car. "Do you think that looks like the picture in the manual?"

He crouched down next to her. "Yeah, see that indentation in the metal? That's the lift point where you're supposed to put the jack."

"It works for me." Mia grabbed the tire iron and began loosening the lug nuts on the tire. She stood up, put her foot on the iron, and held onto the roof of the car. Finally, the nut gave way. "Why do they always put these on so tight?"

Chris shook his head. "You were that girl who always wore black. And your hair was different. It was black, stiff, and spiky. Kind of like Elvira."

"Wearing black doesn't automatically mean you look like Elvira." Mia did *not* want to talk about high school. She moved the tire iron to the next lug nut. "Your glasses are different now too, you know." She didn't want to mention the fact that those hideous huge black frames had been almost as horrifying as her Elvira motif. At least Chris had filled out, so he didn't resemble a turkey vulture anymore.

"I think I was in your biology class."

Mia cringed mentally. Of course he was. Naturally, she was doomed to meet someone who had witnessed one of her most humiliating moments. "I don't remember."

"I was sorry to hear about your mother and that man. I guess he was your stepfather?"

"That was a long time ago." She was definitely not getting into *that* topic with this guy.

"I was in college and my mother sent me the big newspaper article after the investigation was complete."

"Could you pass me the handle for the jack?"

Chris bent down and handed her the metal rod. "Mom said you were in my class, but I couldn't remember who you were."

"That's not a surprise, since I'm sure they didn't refer to me as Elvira in the article." Mia hooked the jack handle into the scissor jack and began cranking the handle, probably more forcefully than she needed to. Spinning it was more tiring once the jack made contact with the car. She continued slowly turning the handle until the flat was far enough off the ground so she could pull off the tire and replace it with the spare.

Chris said, "I can take the tire off the car if you want. You must be tired."

"It's fine." Mia yanked the wheel off the car and dropped it on the ground with a thud. "I've done this a lot on another can...*car*."

"You had to change tires?"

"Retreads are cheap, but they don't last." Mia walked to the back of the RAV and removed the plastic tire housing.

"Retreads? I didn't know you could still get those."

"There was a place in that old industrial park on the west side that sold them." Mia removed the cover and rolled the spare tire over to the side of the car.

"I haven't been back to Windiberg in a long time. My parents moved after my sister left for college."

"It's the same." Mia hoisted the tire onto the car and stood up. "I'm never going back."

"You sound pretty sure about that, but you never know. Maybe you'll get homesick."

"Not going to happen." She crouched down and began hand tightening the lug nuts. "I've left there for good."

Chris picked up Lulu and stroked her head. "Where are you moving to?"

"Could you hand me the tire iron?"

He put Lulu back down and gave Mia the tire iron. "Are you moving for a job?"

Mia stopped turning and glanced at him. If Chris knew about her mother, maybe he knew about the lottery too. If he asked her for money, she was going to scream. Why couldn't people just leave her alone? "You sure ask a lot of questions."

"I'm just making conversation while I'm holding your dog, since you seem sort of upset. Are you okay?"

Gizmo made a hacking noise and yakked up a piece of pine cone. Mia glared at Chris. "Could you make sure he doesn't get at anything else? Gizmo tends to eat…everything. He's not very picky."

"Eww." Chris pulled Lulu away from the well-masticated pieces of cone. "Let's move over here, you guys."

Mia tightened down the last nut and turned the jack handle to lower the car to the ground. She put the tire iron and handle back into the little tool bag and stood up. "I think I'm done. Thanks for holding Gizmo."

"Where are you staying?"

"I'm not sure. The only place I saw near town was full."

He nodded. "Yes, that's the Enchanted Moose and there's some big convention or something tonight. Plus, half of it is under construction. Lulu and I are staying there because they take pets. I don't think anywhere else does though."

"That figures." Mia jammed the little tool bag back into the side compartment in the rear of the RAV and lifted the boxes back into place.

"What do you mean?"

"I had some…particles…I mean places…here I wanted to see, but it doesn't matter. Maybe we'll just keep driving." She lifted the flat tire onto the back door of the car and reattached the cover.

"You don't have to do that if you don't want to. There's a dog-boarding kennel, and it's really nice. Lulu stayed there for a couple of days when I had to fly back to San Francisco."

Mia looked up at the sky. "It's getting late. Maybe I'll look into that. I'd rather not drive too far until I get my tire repaired."

Chris handed her Gizmo's leash and pulled out his wallet. "I have the number." He handed her a sticky note with a phone number scrawled on it.

"Thanks." Mia looked down at the note. Taking a couple of days to investigate the places on some of the postcards and getting her tire fixed would be easier without having to worry about Gizmo. "I guess I could go back to town, find a pay phone, and call them."

"Give Kat my name. She's really nice. They just opened the place, so I'm sure they'll have room for your dog."

"Okay—well, thanks again. I should get going." She opened the door to the backseat of the RAV and encouraged Gizmo to hop in.

Chris stepped forward. "Wait! Don't go. I mean, maybe while you're here, we could do something. Like, eat. You know, like, dinner."

Mia closed the door of the RAV and turned to face him. Was he actually asking her out? Really? What was his deal? It wasn't like she was encouraging him in any way. Maybe he did know about the money. Or had heard more stuff via the Windiberg rumor mill. "Why? It can't be to relive old times. You don't even remember me."

"I told you, I *do* remember who you are now. You're Amanita!"

"My poisonous mushroom girl years are worth forgetting, at least to me." Mia moved toward the front of the car. "I need to get back to town now."

Chris reached out to touch her arm and Mia was so surprised she jerked it away from him. He gave her an imploring look. "I don't know anyone here and it sounds like you don't either. It would be nice to have someone to talk to, even for one evening. Maybe we have more in common than you think."

Mia paused before reflexively saying no. With those big, round eyes staring at her, turning him down would be like kicking a puppy. Chris had been a completely harmless nerd in high school and maybe even as unhappy as she'd been. Playing off his last name, the jocks had called him Blanche Dubois, which couldn't have been enjoyable. High school might have been horrible for him too. "All right, I guess so."

"There's an Italian place in town. Maybe we could meet there tonight. Say seven?"

"All right. I should know by then if the place for Gizmo will work out."

He pulled a business card out of his pocket and wrote on the back. "I'm in room one fifty-six at the Enchanted Moose. If something happens and you can't make it, just let me know."

"Okay, I guess I'll see you later." Mia got into the RAV, wishing she hadn't said yes. Oh well, too late now. But he'd given her a way out. She could just leave a message and forget about the whole idea.

Chris waved goodbye and then started walking with Lulu toward the next driveway as she did a three-point turn to return to town. The first thing she needed to do was find a place to stay.

Chapter 3

Wag on Inn

Back in Alpine Grove, Mia stopped by a motel called the BH12. They had rooms available and the nice woman at the front desk let Mia use their phone to call the boarding kennel about Gizmo.

The owner, Kat Stevens, said they had space and gave her directions. Even though Mia's visit might end up being outside their pick-up and drop-off hours, Kat said it was okay to bring Gizmo.

After the flat tire, Mia had been feeling discouraged about her stay in Alpine Grove, but maybe her luck was changing. As much as she loved Gizmo, dealing with him in a motel room was complicated. And it would be nice to eat something other than drive-through fast food. Maybe she'd take Chris up on his dinner offer after all. He seemed sort of lonely, which was an emotion she could relate to.

The dog-boarding kennel was located north of town. Mia drove the RAV out of Alpine Grove up the highway and turned onto one of the back roads that meandered into densely forested areas. The trees in the area were amazing. Vegetation-wise, it was about as far from Windiberg as she could get. The fall colors were stunning and leaves flitted merrily across the roadway.

At last, Mia reached a driveway with a sign that said Wag on Inn. The gravel driveway wound through a section of forest filled with enormous trees. Mia didn't know what kind they were, but they were gigantic. Maybe sequoias? Whatever they were, the trees had to be old.

The driveway continued to weave around the massive evergreen trees until finally Mia stopped at a gate. A log house sat beyond the gate and a sign indicated she should turn left toward the kennels.

Following the instructions, she parked in front of the kennel buildings and got out of the car. Gizmo stood in the back with his nose pressed to the partially opened window, snuffling madly. Mia took a deep breath. It did smell really good here. Like a bottle of Pine Sol, but not fake.

A sign attached to the kennel building said to ring the buzzer. Mia pressed the button and a few moments later, a woman emerged from the log house at the end of the driveway. That must be Kat. Mia watched as the petite woman came closer, her long dark braid swaying back and forth behind her.

Kat waved as she walked up to the car. "Hi, you must be Mia."

"Yes, and that's Gizmo jumping around back there."

"Wow, those are some great ears he's got. Do you want to let him out?"

Mia nodded and extracted the exuberant dog from the back seat. "He's pretty expired about this place."

Kat tilted her head and Mia blurted out, "I meant *excited*. Gizmo is still very much alive."

"I noticed. Dogs do seem to like it here. I didn't realize it when I moved in, but to a dog, the smells of the forest are thrilling. When I walk them, I wonder about all the incredible information they must be discovering."

Mia looked up at the trees. "It's so beautiful here. You're so plucky to be able to live in a place like this."

"I've never thought of myself as plucky before."

"I meant *lucky*." Mia gestured in exasperation and turned toward the car to get the bag with Gizmo's chew toys. "Like I said on the phone, Gizmo is pretty obedient, but he tends to try to eat everything. You'd think I never feed him, but I promise I do."

"I'm sure it will be fine." Kat put her hand on Mia's arm. "Are you okay?"

Mia stopped fiddling with the bag and looked at Kat. She had striking deep blue eyes. "You're the second person to ask me that today." Pretty much everyone thought Mia was weird. Why should this woman be any different?

Kat shrugged. "I'm not trying to be nosy. Well, okay, maybe I am a little bit. You just seem kind of nervous. Don't worry about Gizmo. He'll be fine."

"I need to get my tire fixed and other stuff, but I feel funny about leaving him. I don't think we've ever spent a whole day apart since I found him."

"There's a tire place near the Kmart on the highway." Kat pointed at the RAV. "Your Toyota looks new. Do you like it? At some point, I really want to get a car. Another winter of driving my fiancé's old truck may push me over the edge."

"Oh, I love the RAV! Flicka is so much better than my last car. The flat tire wasn't her fault. I guess I ran over a nail or something."

"Aww, you named the RAV Flicka? I loved that book."

Mia smiled. "Me too. After my last car, I wanted a trusty steed, instead of a clucker…*clunker*."

Kat laughed. "Hey, I want a clucker! A chicken-mobile! That's awesome."

"No, it's not! I'm sorry I'm…well…I have this problem. Sometimes I say weird things. The wrong words just come out of my mouth before I realize what's happening."

"It's no big deal."

"I wish I could make it stop. Most people think I'm some kind of wacko." Mia shook her head. "It started in high school, and whenever I meet new people it comes back again."

"I can sympathize. I hated high school. I think the last day of senior year ranks up there as one of the happiest days of my life."

Mia smiled. "Me too. Even though this trip has been fun, it has also been stressful. The managers of every Motel 6 I stayed at are probably comparing notes about the strange woman with the dog that eats motel rooms."

Kat bent to pet Gizmo. "Oh, you would never do that, would you?"

"He would, but I'm still going to miss him so much."

"After you deal with your errands, you're welcome to stop by for his walk if you want."

Mia looked into Kat's eyes. "Really? I'd love that, if you're sure it's clay."

"Well, it will probably be dirty. Dogs are like that."

"I meant *okay*."

"It's fine. I'm sure I'll be procrastinating on writing my article anyway. If you like dogs, get ready to meet a lot more of them." Kat paused. "Are you sure you're okay? I'm not normally a huggy type of person, but you really look like you could use a hug."

Mia raised her eyebrows. "I don't know. I guess so."

Kat stretched out her arms. "It's okay."

Mia wrapped her arms around the shorter woman, resting her head on her shoulder. She was overwhelmed with the urge to weep, for no apparent reason. No one had hugged her in a long time and it felt so good.

Kat patted her back and released her. "Better?"

Mia nodded. She did feel better. "Thanks."

"Gizmo and I will see you tomorrow then. You have my number if anything comes up and you can't make it."

"I'll let you know." Mia crouched down to give Gizmo a last bit of affection. "Promise me you'll be good, Giz." The dog wagged his tail, seemingly oblivious to what all the fuss was about.

Mia got in her car and started back to town. As she wove her way through the trees again, she thought about the fact that for Kat, walking dogs was her job. She actually got paid to walk happy canines through the forest.

It was certainly a far cry from data entry about root vegetables. Being able to hang out with dogs all day would be a dream come true for Mia. Except you'd still have to talk to dog owners all the time, which wouldn't be good. At least Kat was a lot more forgiving of Mia's odd speech patterns than most people were. And she was excellent at hugging.

At the end of the driveway, Mia stopped and turned back toward town. People in Alpine Grove certainly were friendly.

~

Kat got Gizmo settled into his kennel and fetched him some water. She opened the chain-link gate and walked inside. "Here you go. I'll take you out for a walk in a few minutes. Then dinner later. You'll notice that there is nothing you can chew up here, so fun time chowing down on motel rooms is officially over for the time being."

Gizmo wagged his tail and Kat ruffled his ears. "You have the best ears. I just love them. I bet all the girls tell you that."

After cuddling Gizmo a bit more and tending to the beagle in the next kennel, Kat walked to the house, went up the front steps, and opened the door to go inside. Joel was in the kitchen, leaning over with his arm resting on the refrigerator door, examining the contents within. The dogs were downstairs in the daylight basement barking to let everyone know that an interloper had invaded their space. Kat glared down the stairs. "Quiet! It's me." The five dogs stood staring up at her, wagging and panting.

Joel shut the refrigerator and turned to face her. "How's the new dog?"

"Gizmo is really cute with the most amazing, huge, adorable ears. Apparently, he likes to eat things he's not supposed to, but here he's not going to have the opportunity to consume much other than his chew toys and dinner."

"That's by design."

Kat wrapped her arms around his waist. "I know! Aren't we smart?"

"Not smart enough to have remembered to go to the store. I think we need to get more organized about grocery shopping. We have no food. Dinner is looking bleak."

"We had food the other day."

"And then we ate it."

"I was going to go shopping over the weekend, but then that beagle came in. I didn't feel like dragging all the way to town after that."

"I know the feeling."

"Then on Monday I had to talk to my editor and complain about the software."

"I had that conference call with the guys in Las Vegas." He gave her a kiss. "So we have now chronicled exactly *why* we have no food, but it doesn't solve the problem of dinner."

"It's getting late and I'm hungry. I don't want to go to the store *now*, do you?"

"No, but I think we have to thaw out zucchini bread for dinner. With a side of dilly beans and canned zukes."

Kat giggled. "Aren't you glad I did so much canning last summer?"

"I suppose. Maybe dilly beans and rice? There might be something else in the pantry. We need to set up a weekly schedule for shopping. Scrounging up something for dinner is a pain when we have no food."

"You're going to get all analytical about this, aren't you?" Kat followed him to the pantry and peered around him. "Do we have to have a schedule?"

"The spontaneous approach to acquiring food doesn't work when you live this far out of town. What I'd really like is to just call for pizza and have it magically appear on our doorstep."

"Pizza sounds fantastic, but we'll get pizza delivery out here sometime this side of never."

He turned and handed her a can of garbanzo beans. "I know. But a guy can dream."

"Garbanzos? Dinner is getting more creative all the time."

"Have some water chestnuts too."

Kat glanced down at the cans in her hands. "I guess we need to improvise again."

"How long is the new dog with the big ears staying?"

"Probably a couple of days." Kat walked over to the counter and began measuring out rice. "His owner's name is Mia, and she seemed really upset about leaving him."

"People always are, aren't they?"

"I guess, but she was different. I honestly thought she was going to cry. She was all nervous talking to me. I guess she has trouble talking to people. It reminds me of me."

"You talk to people all the time. Sometimes you even yell at them."

"I know. But I used to be really shy. And she has sort of a weird thing where she says the wrong word."

"Like stuttering?"

"Not really. She doesn't say the word she means to say."

"You mean malapropism?"

"Exactly! I couldn't remember the name for it, but she seems really embarrassed about it. I guess it started in high school." Kat gestured toward the window. "Which I completely understand. I was a basket case in high school."

"So you've said."

She reached over and tickled his waist. "Hey, not everyone can be the brainy track star. Some of us were mutants back then, just waiting for the awful high school experience to finally be over. I'm probably scarred for life."

"Maybe, but you seem a lot happier now than when I met you." He walked to the refrigerator, pulled a package of celery out of a drawer, and made a face. "I'm afraid the celery is dead."

"I guess it can be slated for burial in the compost pile." Kat picked up a knife. "You're right. I am a lot happier. Mia reminds me a little of me a year ago. Kinda lost and anxious. Bluffing her way along, hoping no one will notice her. That was definitely me."

Joel leaned over and kissed her cheek. "I noticed you."

Kat put down the knife, stood on tiptoes, and kissed his lips. "I know, and I'm glad, because I definitely noticed you too. And not just because you're cute. You were nice to me during a really confusing time."

"Fixing stuff does seem to score major points with you."

"True, but when you asked what had happened that made me so insecure and you said you could be yourself around me—I think that's when I started to fall in love with you. It was surprising since we hadn't known each other long, but I felt the same way. When we're together, I'm just me."

"It's easier than being someone else."

"You know what I mean. When I was talking to Mia, I felt like maybe she has some stuff she's getting away from. She looked so sad that I gave her a hug."

Joel looked up from his chopping. "That's not like you. Normally, you restrict your hugging to me."

"I know. But she looked like she needed one."

"Everyone has a past. Maybe she has family or work problems. Do you know why she's in Alpine Grove?"

"I'm not sure. I got the impression she's going through some type of transition. Her car was packed full of stuff.

Maybe she left her job and is moving. I know quitting my soul-sucking cubicle job improved my mood. But then I had that whole lack of money problem."

"Speaking of work, how did installing the new beta version of the software go?"

"Let's not talk about that. There are large companies whose names I shouldn't take in vain. I mean, I'm writing a book about their software, so I have to remain all rah-rah positive about the company, right?"

"I suppose so. Saying the program is a piece of crap probably won't help your book sales either."

"Exactly. Maybe beta version seven million and twelve will fix some of the bugs. They keep reassuring me that it's going to get better."

Joel turned and smiled at her. "Didn't you know? Those aren't bugs, they're features."

"Very funny. Spoken like a true programmer. All I know is that I'm tired of installing software, trying to figure it out, and then watching it crash."

"Wait until you start writing the book. That's when the real fun begins."

"And when the real whining will start. You'll still love me when I turn into a crybaby author, right?"

He smiled. "I will. But while you're writing and swearing at your computer, I might spend some extra time out in the forest with the chainsaw, chopping firewood."

"That's probably not a bad idea."

~

Mia drove back to Alpine Grove and checked into the H12 motel. It was nicer than a Motel 6, but not by much. At least it had a mini-fridge, so that was something. The ugly plaid bedspreads were not appealing, but the room did have a decent shower. After a long day that included changing a tire, the warm water was welcome.

After she'd cleaned up, Mia spread out her meager wardrobe options on one of the beds. Almost everything she owned was filthy. A couple of the Motel 6s had laundry facilities, but most of them didn't. Once she was settled somewhere, now that she wasn't broke, she probably should invest in some new clothes. Before she left, it didn't seem worth it because it would be more stuff to pack. Plus, it wasn't like she was going to dress up for a road trip.

She found an iron in the closet and pressed an incredibly wrinkled skirt and blouse that she'd used for her job interview at Round House Distributing. It had been a while since they'd seen the light of day and the fabric looked like it had been dropped in a river and crumpled up into a little ball. Ironing had been problematic in the trailer and it wasn't exactly on her list of favorite things to do. But with more space and an actual ironing board, it was oddly relaxing to methodically remove the deeply entrenched wrinkles.

By the time she finished ironing and had gotten dressed, she had just enough time to walk over to the restaurant. It was a beautiful, crisp fall evening and leaves fluttered along the sidewalk in front of her. When she reached the restaurant, Mia opened the door and walked inside. A man with short brown hair dressed in a suit was deep in conversation with the hostess.

The blonde woman gestured toward the room, "Larry, please go back to your table. I'll be with you in a moment." She turned and smiled at Mia with obvious relief as the man walked away from the hostess stand toward the dining room. "Welcome!"

Mia smiled. "I'm meeting someone named Christ."

"Like Jesus? Wait. What? What did you say?"

"I mean *Chris*...Chris Blanchard."

"He's right over there." The woman pointed toward a table near a large stone fireplace in the dining room. The hostess was undoubtedly relieved that Mia wasn't having some type of funky religious experience right here in the middle of her restaurant.

Mia thanked her and walked away. Thank goodness the restaurant was dimly lit and the whole world couldn't tell she was blushing like a complete idiot. The air was scented with mouth-watering Italian spices, tomato sauce, and garlic. Mia's stomach growled. If the food tasted as good as this place smelled, she was in for a delicious dinner.

Chris was studying the menu and glanced over at her as she walked up to the table. He stood up, looking startled. "Mia! You look...wow...really pretty."

Mia settled into her seat. It would be a novelty to eat without Gizmo panting on her for a change. "Thanks for inviting me."

Chris handed her a menu. "This whole thing is in Italian and I'm trying to figure it out."

"Well, I don't speak the language either, so I can't hurt you."

Chris glanced up from the menu with a quizzical expression. "Okay."

"*Help*! I mean *help*." Mia put her face in her palms, rubbed her eyes, and then looked up. "I'm sorry. By now, you must think I'm a real nut job."

"Don't worry about it."

Mia smiled and pointed at the menu. "I know what rigatoni and gorgonzola are. Pasta and cheese sounds good. I bet it's a lot better than the stuff in the blue box."

"No doubt. Here's something with spaghetti. I know what that is." He leaned across the table. "I hate asking people to translate in a place like this because it makes me feel stupid and unsophisticated."

"I'm glad I'm not the only one who suffers from waiter fear."

"I won't tell if you won't."

Mia laughed and put down her menu. "Your secret is safe with me. I'm going with the pasta-and-cheese thing."

They ordered by pointing at items on the menu, rather than actually attempting to speak Italian. Chris said, "I guess since you made it here, you found a place to stay."

"Yes, and the woman at the boarding kennel was just as nice as you said she'd be. I miss Gizmo, but it makes me feel better knowing he's in good hands. And it feels so luxurious having a motel room all to myself."

He took a sip of water. "I guess you've been traveling for a while?"

"A couple of weeks. It's fun, but all the draining is tiring."

"Driving?"

"Yes. Sorry...again." Mia didn't want to talk about the fact she had no idea where she was going next. People didn't tend to take trips to nowhere. Unless of course they had oodles of time and money because they'd just won the lottery. "So I was wondering why you were crawling around a hillside in Alpine Grove."

Chris pulled off his glasses and set them on the table. "I was so surprised to find you there, I guess I forgot to say. I was looking at the house site."

"Are you building a house? That's a beautiful spot!"

"I know, but it's not for me. It's for a client. I'm an architect."

Mia took a drink of water to stall for time, suddenly self-conscious about her lack of career. If she acted interested, maybe he wouldn't ask what she did. "So you said you flew to San Francisco. Is that where you live?"

"Near there, in Oakland. I work for a firm downtown. What do you do?"

The waitress arrived with their salads, sparing Mia the need to divulge the fact that she was unemployed. She jabbed at a leaf. "Do you like being an architect?"

He looked down as he attempted to skewer a cherry tomato. "Yes, for the most part. I'd better love it, after all the higher education I endured to get my degree."

"Where did you go to college?"

"I got a BA, then a Masters in Architecture at UC Berkley. I've been working at the same place for six years now, but sometimes it feels like I've been there forever."

Mia chewed her lettuce. This was getting more interesting. She had lots of experience with job dissatisfaction. "So are you saying you don't like your job?"

"No, that's not it exactly. I mean, I love architecture. It's fascinating, and I enjoy seeing a project come from nothing but an idea and turn into a major part of people's lives, like their home or office. But the firm I work for, well, I like that a lot less. And being here has made me wish that I didn't have such a long commute too."

"The daily grind can be hard."

"I also wasn't enjoying the types of projects I was working on, which is why I'm here. The firm has taken on a bunch of work doing large-scale retail buildings, but what I'm doing here is a small single-family residential project, which is the type of work I prefer." He leaned forward. "You didn't say what you do."

Mia held her fork in mid-air. Crap. He remembered. "I'm in between jobs."

"Is that why you're moving?"

"Yes." Mia stuffed the lettuce into her mouth. Indirectly. Finding a job was part of the process of maybe finding some type of life.

"Where are you moving to?"

"I'm not sure yet."

Chris leaned back in his chair. "So you're just traveling? Wow, that's so cool. I'm envious. Some days, I'd love to just walk into my boss's office and say 'take this job and shove it,' but I can't."

Mia tried not to laugh out loud. She'd had almost the exact same thought when she realized she could quit. "I didn't say those words, but I can tell you that the day I gave my notice was a *very* happy day."

"What are you going to do next?"

"I suppose in elementary school when people asked you what you were going to be when you grew up, you said, 'an architect,' didn't you?"

"Yes. What did you say?"

"Catwoman, but it didn't work out."

Chris laughed. "Too bad. You'd look great in that outfit."

"As you know, I am a fan of basic black."

The waitress brought their main dishes and Mia dug into her pasta. It was delicious. Chris was obviously enjoying his spaghetti dish too. He held up a forkful. "Do you want to try this? It's really good."

"Sure. I can give you some of my fancy mac and cheese too."

They spooned some pasta onto bread plates and exchanged them. She smiled. "This is good. It's different than plain old spaghetti with sauce from a jar."

"I know."

"What are the little things in there?"

"I have no idea. It's yummy though."

Considering she'd had to divulge her unfortunate state of unemployment, Mia was enjoying herself. The food was excellent and Chris was actually funny in a self-effacing way. It was nice to find someone who wasn't obsessed with his job, for a change. Everyone at Round House Distributing had always been so serious about work. And they were dealing with *carrots*, for heaven's sake. It wasn't exactly rocket science or related to life-and-death situations.

Chris set his plate aside, "I'm full. Do you want the rest of mine?"

Mia gave him a "pass it over here" gesture. "Sure. That stuff is great."

He ordered a cup of coffee while Mia finished off the spaghetti. "Do you want coffee too?"

"No thanks." Mia leaned back. "I can't remember when I've eaten that much. Because of Gizmo, I've been eating on the run or skipping meals. I don't think I've eaten anything all day except some crackers in the car."

"No wonder you were hungry." He took a sip of coffee. "I want to apologize for what I said earlier. I don't think you look like Elvira."

"Well, I know I did then. It's no big deal." Mia put her hand to her stomach. All of a sudden, her digestive system was staging a major rebellion. "I, uh, need to...ladies broom!"

Chris stood up as Mia launched from the table toward the rest rooms at the back of the restaurant.

Mia barely made it into a stall before losing the contents of her stomach. The last time she'd felt like this was when she was fifteen and Mom had made that special dinner for Howard. At the time, she'd been convinced that her mother had tried to poison her so Mia would get out of the way and Mom would have more "special time" alone with Howard.

Mia sat on the floor and closed her eyes, leaning her head back against the wall. She'd been having a good time too. Presumably, Chris wasn't trying to kill her. And if by some miracle, he didn't think she was weird before, he certainly did now.

~

A few minutes later, Mia opened her eyes at a knock on the bathroom stall door. The heels that belonged to the hostess were in front of the stall. "Are you all right in there?"

Mia moaned as she wiped her mouth and stood up. "Be right out." She rested her hand on the wall to steady herself and flushed the toilet. This was probably what dying felt like. She slid the latch and opened the door.

The woman's eyes widened. "Oh my goodness—you look terrible! Should I call 911?"

Mia shook her head. "No, it's okay. I think dinner disagreed with me. It's not your foot...*fault*."

"Your boyfriend is outside the door. He sent me in here to check on you because he's very worried."

"Not my boyfriend." Mia staggered to the exit, grabbed the handle, and opened the door. Chris was standing outside, his eyes even rounder than usual. He handed Mia her purse. "Oh my God, what happened? Are you okay?"

Mia nodded, afraid to speak. Being upright was causing her stomach to flop around again. Chris put his arm around her shoulders while Mia focused all her energy on not throwing up in front of an entire restaurant full of people. That was a new level of humiliation she could do without.

The hostess followed them toward the front door. "Please come again!"

Outside the restaurant, Mia took a deep breath, letting the cold air fill her lungs. It was a relief to be away from the scents of food.

Chris said, "Hold on for a second. You're shaking." He took off his jacket and put it around her shoulders.

Mia mumbled her thanks as they continued down the street toward the H12.

Chris squeezed her shoulders slightly and bent to look at her face. "Do you need to rest? You're as white as a ghost."

"First Elvira, now Casper. Nice."

"That's not what I meant. What happened?"

"I don't know. All of a sudden, I felt bad. Really, *really* bad. It was like something that happened a long time ago when I got food poisoning from something my mom made."

"What was it?"

"Oysters. It was this special meal and I ruined it for her." Mia glanced up at him. "I didn't do it on purpose, although she thought I did."

"I'm sure you didn't. Are you allergic to oysters?"

"I don't know. I never had them again. Just the thought makes my stomach turn." Mia waved her hand weakly. "Let's not talk about it."

"While I was sitting at the table waiting for you, I paid for dinner and the waitress asked me about the meal. She said that the spaghetti allo scoglio…um, I'm probably saying that wrong, but whatever it is…the sauce was made from a mixture of shellfish."

"I'm so sorry about this. I think I'll feel better if I lie down."

"We're almost there. Which room are you in?"

"Twelve. On the end." She pointed toward the motel. "My car is out front."

They walked through the parking lot and stood in front of the door. Mia rummaged through her purse for the key and turned to Chris. "Thanks for dinner. And sorry again."

Chris angled his head to examine her face. "You're so pale. If you're having some type of serious allergic reaction, I should take you to the hospital."

"Even though I feel like I want to die, if it's like the oysters, I'll be okay by tomorrow." Mia leaned on the door heavily. "I think I need to go to the bathroom again, so um, thanks, but I really have to go now."

Chris pushed the door open and followed her into the room. "I think I should keep an eye on you."

"Whatever you want. I'll be right back." Mia scampered off to the bathroom, slammed the door, and stood motionless, trying to determine what her insides were going to do next. This was so incredibly embarrassing. She slid down to the floor and closed her eyes. After a few moments, it seemed like her stomach had calmed down a little. Realistically, after the episode in the ladies room, there couldn't be much left *in* her stomach anymore. She took a deep breath, stood up, and rinsed her mouth out with some toothpaste. She wasn't exactly minty fresh, but at least she felt a little bit less revolting.

When she opened the door, Chris was sitting hunched over at the desk with his hands clasped in front of him between his knees. He jumped up. "Are you okay? I really think you should go to a doctor."

Mia made her way over to the bed. "I just need to lie down." She crawled onto the bed, rolled onto her back, and put her arm over her eyes. Being horizontal was definitely better.

The bed moved and Mia moved her arm, glancing at Chris. "What are you doing?"

"Keeping an eye on you, remember?"

"That sounds boring."

"It's okay." He reached across her and grabbed a book from the nightstand. "I'll read this."

"Do you read romance novels?"

"Not usually. What's it about?"

"This woman is an art dealer who has nightmares from something bad that happened in her childhood. She goes back to her hometown and meets a guy who undoubtedly will help her solve the mystery. I'm not sure, since I'm not done with it."

He held the book out to her with his finger marking a page. "Is this where you were."

Mia leaned to look. "I think so."

Chris got up, threw the bedspread over Mia, and tucked her in. He crawled back onto the bed next to her and put his arm around her, so her head was resting on his chest. "Close your eyes and relax."

Mia snuggled into the covers next to him, hoping that the sick, shaky feeling in her stomach would subside. Chris began reading the novel out loud. She closed her eyes, enjoying the sound of his voice, which was soothing and resonant. She hadn't noticed it when she was talking to him before, but Chris had a great radio voice, so it was like listening to an audiobook.

It was probably wrong to be curled up with a guy she hardly knew like this, but at the moment, she felt too awful to care. As her system slowly recovered from the indignities committed against it, Mia relaxed and focused on the rhythm and intonation of Chris's voice as he read.

～

Later, Mia jerked awake, momentarily disoriented. Where was she? The light was still on and Chris had obviously fallen asleep next to her. He groaned, sat up straighter, and gazed down into her face. "I'm so glad you're still alive. I didn't do the greatest job of keeping an eye on you."

Mia moved to sit up. "I think I'm going to live. Thanks for reading to me."

"That's a pretty good story. You'll have to let me know what happens when you finish it."

"I will." She glanced at the clock. "It's kind of late. I'm sorry I got so sick and kept you here. At least I didn't barf on you."

He turned to look at her. "You don't need to keep apologizing. I had a great time. Well, not the part where you got sick, but I enjoyed having dinner with you. And just hanging out reading the romance book was nice too."

"Is your dog okay back in your room? Gizmo would have eaten half the furniture by now."

"Lulu has a little sky kennel with a bed it in that she loves. I fed her dinner and I'm sure she's completely crashed out. She's slowed down as she's gotten older."

"Maybe Gizmo will settle down someday. That would sure make my life easier."

"I'm sure once you've moved and gotten settled he'll do great." Chris took off his glasses, put them on the nightstand, and slumped down closer to her. "I think the whole getting sick thing interrupted what I was trying to say, but I feel bad for saying you looked like Elvira. I think you're really pretty and I'm sorry I didn't recognize you at first. I had no idea your hair was this auburn color."

Mia smiled. "Well, it's not always this red. It's been a lot of different colors over the years. After my Debbie Harry bleached-blonde phase, my hair was so crispy fried from all the peroxide and nasty chemicals, I let it go natural for a while. It's kind of a dark blonde, but I wanted a change so I tried henna. It's easier on my hair than dye."

"Much better than the black." He pushed a long strand back over her shoulder. "And less spiky."

"My hair gel days are behind me, along with a lot of other things."

"I know what you mean. I'm guessing you didn't like high school much either. At some schools being a nerd might be okay, but it definitely was no fun at Windiberg High."

Mia raised a fist. "Go Trojans. Kill the Crows!"

"Yeah, that's right up there on the list of things I don't miss: the stupid fifty-year football rivalry. Why do people care so much? I mean these old men would get in fist fights about it at the grocery store. You'd think they'd have something else to think about by now."

"I'm glad to know it wasn't just me. It's such a relief to be away from there."

"When did you change your name back?"

"After high school. Putting Amanita on your resume doesn't tend to improve your employment prospects. The people who know it's a deadly mushroom think it's creepy. The people who don't know what an amanita is just think you have a strange name and that it might make you a little warped."

"Did you go to college somewhere?"

She lifted her head to look at him. "No. You know what happened with my mother. I lived in Windiberg my whole life. Up until a little while ago, I'd never left town."

"Sorry, I didn't mean to bring that up again."

Mia sighed. "It's okay. In a way, it's kind of a relief that you already know about the whole mess. But yes, a murder-suicide in the family tends to derail a young aspiring college student's plans. But it wasn't like I was desperate to go. Teachers don't like it when you refuse to speak in class, and my grades were terrible."

"So what did you do after graduation?"

"Got various jobs. If it was a minimum-wage job in Windiberg, I probably tried it. I got fired a lot. I'd mix up my words and say something bizarre or insulting to a customer and they'd complain." Mia raised her eyebrows. "It probably won't come as a shock when I tell you that customer service is not my forte."

"Maybe not." Chris grinned at her. "But you do seem to be feeling better. What was the job you were doing that you were so happy to quit?"

"Data entry at Round House Distributing."

"You mean the carrot place?"

"It's not as exciting as it sounds." Mia moved her shoulders in a halfhearted shrug. "But I could pay my rent. Usually."

"I guess leaving rent behind made it possible to travel? Or do you have savings? I've been trying to do that, but I'm really bad with money. Everything in San Francisco is so expensive."

Mia sat up a little. "Oh come on, architects have to make serious money. Those jeans and polo shirt you were wearing probably cost more than I spent on food last month."

"No wonder you were hungry. Wait! You dodged my question again. How can you travel? I really want to know. I'd give anything to quit my job at this point. Well, assuming I don't get fired first." He scratched his chin. "Wow. I really wish I hadn't just told you that."

"It doesn't sound like you like your job. Maybe getting fired wouldn't be so bad." Mia poked his forearm with her index finger. "I have lots of experience if you'd like some tips."

"You don't understand. I'm stretched so thin financially, I don't know what I'd do. I've got massive payments, student loans, bills. I actually hid my car so it won't get repossessed while I'm here. I've screwed up a lot of things and this project here in Alpine Grove is my last chance."

Mia wasn't sure what to say. "I'm surprised. You seem like such a successful over-achiever with an amazing resume. Can't you just get another job?"

"I suppose. But I wouldn't get a good recommendation, so it might be difficult. They stuck me on this residential project because it's smaller and lower profile. Or maybe it was to get me out of the office, so the competent architects can focus on the huge commercial money-makers." He shook his head. "Part of me just wants to get out of architecture entirely. I'm not kidding when I say I envy the fact you were able to just drop everything and hit the road."

"After a whole lifetime of wanting to be an architect? Are you nuts?"

"Well, I could do something else."

"But why would you if you love architecture? Do you know how lucky you are? To have found something you *want* to do? That you *like* to do? And you even have a degree to do?" Mia slumped down onto the pillows. "I would kill for that. Every time I think of something I might try, I think of seventeen reasons it won't work out. Even after years of reading every self-help and career book in the Windiberg library, I can't seem to come up with anything."

"I guess I didn't think about it like that because I've been so focused on the debt disaster I've created. I took some stupid risks." He put his palm over his eyes. "Why am I telling you all this? Revealing all your dumbest mistakes and secrets is not the way to impress a woman."

"It's okay. Maybe you needed to let it out." Mia pulled his hand down. "And you know I'm a bigger loser than you'll ever be."

His eyes widened. "That's not true!"

"Isn't it?" Mia shrugged. "I'm the bizarre mushroom girl who never went to college and up until recently worked at possibly the most boring job in America. I was so worried about losing that crappy job, I was too afraid to even ask for a raise."

"Wait a minute. You still never answered my question. If you were that afraid of losing your crummy job, how could you quit?"

Mia couldn't think of any reasonable answer other than the truth. "I, well, I came into a little money."

Chris sat up straight and looked down into her eyes. "That RAV4 is brand-new. It wasn't just a *little* money, was it?"

Mia wished she hadn't said anything. Given his financial problems, now Chris would be like everyone else and ask her for a loan. He probably already knew about the lottery—everyone else did. "Well, I'm more comfortable now. And before you ask, I'm not interested in investing in anything. No business ventures or pyramid schemes. And if you have a sick relative, I don't want to know about it. My main accomplishment since high school has been turning frugality into an art form. This money needs to last me for a long time so I can finally figure out what I'm going to do with my life."

Chris raised his palms in front of him. "Whoa, where did that come from? I'm not asking you for anything."

"It's only a matter of time. I've read a lot of books on financial management—which, by the way, are not particularly helpful if you have no money to manage. But they always warn against lending money."

"What's that supposed to mean?"

"Everyone who has found out about me…about the money…has asked for some." Mia sat up and looked into his eyes. "And you just finished telling me about how you've completely mismanaged your finances. You know, don't you?"

"Know what?" Chris threw his legs over the side of the bed. "All I know is that you're obviously feeling a lot better and it's really late. I should probably get going."

"Wait!" Mia reached out to grab his arm. "You really *don't* know, do you?"

"Know *what*? I have no idea what you're talking about."

"I'm sorry. You've been so kind to me tonight. It's just like me to make a mock of things."

"You mean mess?"

"Yes. Sorry. I'm not a particularly trusting person."

"I suppose given everything that happened with your family, that's not a surprise." Chris leaned back on the pillows and put his arm behind his head. "When we were talking, you went for a long time without mixing up words."

"I was relaxed. It happens more when I'm stressed out."

"That's why you worked at the carrot place, isn't it?"

Mia curled up next to him again and gazed at the heavy drapes covering the window. "Entering data doesn't cause much anxiety. I wore headphones and listened to music. People are less likely to talk to you if you're wearing headphones."

"That sounds kind of empty."

"I guess it was, but I got used to it."

Chris put his arm around her, but didn't say anything. Mia closed her eyes and listened to the sound of his breathing. He'd been right. It was nice not being alone, if it was only for one evening.

Mia blinked at the early morning sunlight emerging around the edges of the drapes. She sat up and looked around the room. Chris was standing up, peeking out the window. He turned and smiled at her. "I totally passed out. Are you feeling okay?"

"Yes, although I think this skirt I ironed so carefully last night has a few new wrinkles. I'm also hungry, since dinner ended up being a non-event for my digestive system."

"I should probably get back to Lulu. Even she has limits on sleep." He walked over to the bed and sat down next to her. "Are you going to be in Alpine Grove for a while? I'd like to see you again. Maybe next time we could go someplace that doesn't serve mysterious dishes that contain seafood."

Mia laughed. "That would be nice. I'll be here for a few days at least. I need to get my tire fixed and I want to do a couple other things while I'm in Alpine Grove."

"I've got to meet with the developer who is building the house, but is it okay if I call you here later?"

"Sure." She gazed at his warm brown eyes for a moment. Neither she nor Chris moved, and Mia wasn't sure what to do. They'd confided a lot of secrets last night, but what did that mean? Probably nothing, except that they were both lonely.

Chris leaned over to hug her and her tension melted away. The way he gave her a final squeeze, she could tell he was just as unsure as she was. He dropped his arms, gave her a half-smile, and stood up.

Mia crawled out of bed and followed him to the door. "Thanks for making sure I wasn't going to die. That's the nicest thing anyone has done for me in a long time."

"Make sure you stay away from any and all forms of shellfish today. I'll talk to you later."

Chapter 4

Poodle Issues

After Chris left, Mia went back to sleep for a while. When she woke up again, she slowly got out of bed and took her time going through her morning routine, enjoying puttering around without having to worry about a dog in the room. She spent some time looking at the postcards. They were typical cards with friendly messages along the lines of the time-honored phrase, "wish you were here." The first one was a classic postcard with the words "Alpine Grove" emblazoned on it with photos inset into the letters. On the back, it said, "Miss you! Everything going well so far," and was signed "Much love ~ CA." Mia flipped the card around in her hands. Who was "CA"? How did she know her father? Of course, Mia was assuming the mysterious "CA" was a she. It could be someone named Carl for all she knew, although the handwriting had a definite feminine flair.

After taking a shower, Mia walked to a little cafe near the H12, got some breakfast, and brought it back to the room. Then she called Kat, who suggested that Mia stop by around noon for the big canine excursion through the forest.

Mia went to the tire place Kat had mentioned and dropped off her tire for repair on her way out to see Gizmo. It had only been one night, but she missed her goofy dog and as she drove down the winding driveway toward the kennel, she smiled at the idea of seeing his exuberant furry face again.

She parked the car, got out, and rang the buzzer. From within the kennel building, Gizmo was barking enthusiastically, apparently going for a little competitive harmony with the baying of the beagle. Kat emerged from the house and waved as she walked down the driveway.

Mia looked up at the large trees that surrounded the clearing. She needed to ask Kat what kind of pine they were. They had to be the biggest evergreens she'd ever seen.

Kat strolled up to the RAV. "Hey, you look happier today!"

"I got kind of sick last night, but I was able to sleep in late, since I didn't have to worry about Gizmo."

"Well, he's been having fun. I know how harsh it is to deal with dogs when you're sick, so it sounds like it's a good thing he was here. I'm glad you got some rest. Shall we go get him?"

The two women went inside the noisy kennel. Kat handed her a leash and suggested that Mia collect Gizmo while she dealt with the beagle. They brought the dogs outside and Kat pointed at the brown-and-white dog. "Meet Lewis. He was adopted not too long ago and his new family is spoiling him rotten."

Mia bent to pet Lewis. "Aww, that's so sweet. He's adorable."

"Yeah, he's got quite a set of vocal cords, but he's a nice boy." Kat started up the driveway toward the log house. "We need to go fetch my dogs now."

"How many do you have?"

"Five."

"How did you end up with so many?"

Kat stopped and waited for Lewis to perform a complex sniffing routine next to a shrub. "I have no idea why this dog is so obsessed with that bush. When I moved here, I inherited four of the dogs and one was my fiancé's. When he moved in, that brought the total canine count up to five."

"I'm not sure I've heard of someone inheriting dogs before."

"I inherited the house and they were part of the deal. At first, I wasn't sure I could handle it. But then I couldn't bear to leave them. So it all worked out in the end."

"I'd love to have more than one dog. Maybe one that doesn't eat hotel rooms though."

Kat laughed. "Yes, that would be a drawing card."

They walked around to the back of the house and Kat handed Mia the leash. "Hang on to Lewis for a second. I need to get everyone ready. And when the door opens, be sure to get out of the way."

Mia nodded. Walking so many dogs seemed to be complicated. Kat went inside and a cacophony of barking arose from within. It was a miracle the woman wasn't completely deaf. Gizmo looked expectantly at the back door and uttered a bark of encouragement when the door opened and the dogs shot out.

Two dogs were wearing harnesses that were attached to each other with a leash. One of the dogs was a gigantic brown hairy thing and the dog he was leashed to was a golden retriever, who was running ahead of him. A pretty black-and-white dog charged out after them, followed by a tan collie mix. Kat came outside with a little brown-and-white dog and closed the door behind her. She took Lewis's leash from Mia and gestured toward the forest. "Follow them. The trail goes off into the woods."

Mia and Gizmo walked alongside Kat, Lewis, and the brown-and-white dog. The other dogs raced around chasing each other among the trees. It was quite a show of canine vigor and Mia couldn't help but grin at how much fun they were having. She gestured toward the pack. "What are their names?"

"Chelsey is here with me and Lewis. The big one is Linus, the black-and-white one is Lori, the collie-ish mutt is Lady, and the golden retriever is Tessa."

"I love golden retrievers. Tessa looks so much like a dog I had named Rusty."

"Rusty is a popular name for goldens. I guess people look at all that red fur and think *rust*! Kind of like Snowy for American Eskimo dogs."

Mia smiled. "I guess I wasn't particularly creative back then. But he was the best dog. I still dream about him all the time."

"Tessa is a sweetheart as long as she gets her exercise. When I first moved here, I thought she might drive me insane though."

"How long have you lived in Alpine Grove?"

"A little more than a year."

Mia stopped to wait for Gizmo. "I'm hoping to find someone who might have met my father here in the seventies."

"Well, my aunt Abigail lived here then, but unfortunately she died." Kat gestured toward the house. "I inherited the house from her. From the sounds of it, she knew everybody. I have about four hundred questions I wish I could ask her."

They started walking again, and Mia shook her head. "The idea of finding my father is probably nuts anyway. Someone mailed me a set of postcards that were from someone who lived in Alpine Grove. I'm guessing my father was the one who mailed the package to me because the postcards were addressed to him."

"You can't ask him?"

"Not easily. We lost touch a long time ago. This is the first contact I've had since I was a kid. And of course, Gizmo ate the envelope, so I don't have an address." Mia stopped again as Kat paused to wait for Lewis. "I said some horrible things to my father right before my parents got divorced. I never wanted to see him again, but it's been a long time and I'm curious if someone here might know where he is now."

"I guess no one in your family knows?"

"My mother is dead. My dad was an only child and my mother said my grandparents are dead too."

"I'm sorry. What's your father's name?"

"Dan Riggins. It just seems odd that he'd send these postcards to me after all this time. Maybe he wanted me to come here for some reason. I don't know. Maybe he's not even alive. I mean, someone else could have sent them for some reason. If I can't find anyone here who knows anything, I guess I could hire a private investigator. Or just forget about it. I can't decide. It might be better to just leave family stuff alone and let the past stay in the past."

"I understand how confusing that would be." Kat gestured toward the forest. "Moving here caused me to learn a lot of things about my family I never knew. It was stressful at the time, but I'm glad I found out."

"Really?" Mia glanced at Kat, who was gazing off into the distance. "That makes me feel a little better, I guess. Do you know anyone other than your aunt who lived here twenty years ago?"

Kat turned back to look at her. "Actually, now that you mention it, I do. Several people, in fact. You could start with the Sullivans. Tracy works at the vet clinic. She grew up at the commune and her mom, Bea, owns the gift store in town."

"There was a commune?"

Kat grinned. "Yeah, although now the land is a nature preserve, I think. Normally, Tracy hates talking about it, but if you give her wine, she'll start telling funny stories from her flower-child days. Her mom is incredibly nice too."

"Maybe I'll get up my nerve and talk to them. I guess it wouldn't hurt."

"You'll never know if you don't ask. Tracy is coming over tomorrow night with a couple of other people. We've got to talk about PR stuff for the dog-rescue group I'm involved with, but it will probably turn into a Wine and Whine. If you want to come, you're welcome to join us."

"What's a wine and…what did you say?"

"Wine and Whine. It's a girls' night in. We drink and talk randomly about whatever is going on. Work, men, critters, happenings on the mean streets of Alpine Grove. The usual stuff."

Mia giggled nervously. The idea of meeting more people was disturbing, particularly once they realized what a freak she was. But maybe it would be worth it if she got the information she wanted. She made an effort to sound enthusiastic. "Thanks, it sounds like it might be fun."

On the way back to town from the kennel, Mia picked up her tire and waited while they checked all the other tires and put the spare back on the back door of the RAV. She felt a happy sense of security, knowing that Flicka had a spare tire again, given all the miles she was going to be logging.

Back at the H12, Mia curled up on the bed to relax with her novel. She paged through, trying to remember how much she had heard Chris read before she'd fallen asleep. The phone rang and she jolted upright, dropping the book onto the bed. Maybe she should turn down the ringer.

She smiled when she heard Chris say hello. His radio voice worked nicely over the telephone too. She asked, "How was your day?"

He paused for long enough that Mia wondered for a second if they'd been disconnected. Finally, he continued, "I feel bad about saying this, but I don't think I can see you tonight."

Mia tried not to sigh audibly into the handset. He wouldn't be the first person to figure out that she had a whole lot of baggage. Chris wasn't stupid, after all. "That's okay. Did something happen with the guy building the hutch... *house?*"

"No, that was fine. This sounds like a lame excuse, but I have to wash my dog. I tried and it turns out Lulu really hates water. Mostly, I've soaked myself and the room. Now she's squeezed herself under the bed and refuses to come out."

Mia tried not to laugh. Given all of her misadventures with Gizmo, the situation was all too easy to imagine. "Do you need help? I managed to wash Gizmo in the bathroom of an Airstream. If I can do that, hosing down a little poodle in an actual bathtub should be easy."

"Would you mind? Maybe it would be better with two people. She's really spry for an older dog. Not to mention slippery."

"What did you say your room number was?"

"One fifty-six. Go around back and the door is one of the ones that faces toward the RV park. Once Lulu is clean, I'll take you to dinner as a thank you."

"Okay, I'll see you in a few minutes."

Mia smiled as she hung up the phone. This was the first time she'd looked forward to seeing another human being in ages. She'd forgotten to ask why he was so intent on washing Lulu. Hmm. One thing was certain: she didn't need to worry about dressing up to wash a dog.

Driving around Alpine Grove all day had been enjoyable and the trip north to the Enchanted Moose was no exception. Fall was bursting forth in its last few gasps of color and the sky was a crisp, brilliant blue. Although Windiberg had seasons, the changes were nowhere near as dramatic as they were here in the mountains.

Half of the Enchanted Moose appeared to be under construction and Mia drove around to the back and parked in front of the RV park. It was nicer than the Edgewood Paradise Estates, if for no other reason than that there was some degree of landscaping with grassy picnic areas and trees, rather than ugly spans of asphalt with tiny strips of dried-out weather-beaten sod between the parking spaces.

She knocked on the door of room one fifty-six and Chris opened it a crack, peeking out before he moved aside quickly to let her in. He gave her a "move it" gesture, hustling her inside and slamming the door.

Mia looked up at his face. "Are you afraid Lulu is going to make a break for it?"

"She's not happy with me." Chris wrung the bottom of his soggy t-shirt with both hands and water dripped on the floor. "I tried again, and it was a massive failure."

Mia bent to look under the bed. Two eyes reflected back at her. "How did you get her out?"

"Food. It worked before, but now she's on to me. She may never come out of there."

"What's that smell?"

"Lulu. I think she rolled in something. I let her off her leash when I was down at the shoreline talking to the developer, so she could go do her business."

"Why did you do that, after she ran up the hill yesterday?"

"That's the only time she's ever run off and I figured it was because of your dog. I didn't want her to pee on the guy's foot or something while we were standing there. And I figured she must be tired out. Running up the hill was more exercise than she's had in years." He waved his arms helplessly. "I swear, Lulu is normally the most mellow dog. She never gives my sister any trouble."

"Lulu is your sister's dog?"

"Yes. I had to fly into LA to come up here and stopped by her place to visit because she was having knee surgery. I agreed to take Lulu to Alpine Grove with me, since it's kind of hard for her to deal with a dog while she's recovering. 'It will be fun,' she said. Yeah, right."

"I guess the first thing we need to do is get her to come out from under the bed. Do you have any snacks? I mean people food, not dog food. Nothing healthy. The junkier, the better."

"I have some chips." He walked to the desk and grabbed a bag. "Ruffles have ridges."

"So I've heard." Mia took the bag and sat down with her back leaning on the foot of the bed and her legs out in front of her. She patted the floor. "Sit next to me."

Chris settled in next to her and reached into the bag for a chip. "I think I see where you're going with this idea."

Mia made extra crinkly noises as she extracted a Ruffle. "Yummy. I love these things. Fattening, salty, greasy potatoes."

A scrabbling noise came from behind them and Mia raised her eyebrows at Chris. "Gosh, I'd love to share these. Gizmo can probably feel a psychic vibe that I'm eating chips without him. If he were here, his head would be right here on my leg." Mia patted her thigh a few times. "When it comes to begging, it's amazing how effective a heavy head can be. Suddenly, I feel compelled to share whatever I'm eating."

Lulu crept out and around the side of the bed and looked up imploringly at Mia with a tentative wag. Chris started to move and Mia put her hand on his arm. "I think there might be a hungry poodle here somewhere."

Chris smiled. "Probably starving."

Mia held out a chip in Lulu's direction. "So, what are you waiting for?" The little dog launched at the chip and snuffled it down. Mia patted her leg. "Don't you want to hang out? Even though you smell like rotten dead fish, I'm not holding it against you, I promise."

Mia fed Lulu a few more chips and let the soggy poodle settle into her lap. She stroked the dog's wet fur and turned to look at Chris. "Did you put water in the tub?"

"Yes, although the dunking process did not go well, so I'm not sure how much is still in the tub."

"It's probably cold too. Let it drain out and we'll try a different approach." She looked up at the desk. "Is that an ice bucket?"

Chris got up. "I'm guessing you don't want me to put ice in it."

"No, but I was thinking Lulu might be afraid of running water. We can use the bucket to pour water on her." Mia scooped up the soggy poodle in her arms. "We're going to try to make this as easy on you as possible Lulu, but you do have to cooperate. You need to get clean because Chris has to share this room with you, and you smell really bad."

Lulu started to squirm as Mia carried her into the evil domain of watery torture. Mia kicked the door closed behind her and faced Chris. "Okay, here's the plan. It looks like you've got the shampoo ready. Once the water is done draining, lay a towel in the tub, and put warm water from the sink in the ice bucket. I'll put her on the towel, so it's not so slippery for her. Then we'll hold her and pour water on her. Then soap, then rinse."

Chris nodded and did as instructed. Mia put Lulu on the towel, holding her firmly while she tried to come up with nice things to say about the stinky dog. What a revolting smell. Good thing Mia's stomach was back to normal. Pungent fishy odors were the last thing she needed.

Chris assisted as Mia washed and rinsed the small dog while continuing to softly console her about the indignity of bath time. It took quite a while, because she had to do two shampoo–and–rinse passes to remove the smell. Thank goodness Lulu wasn't Gizmo's size or they'd have been there for hours.

At last, Mia finished, gave Lulu a final potato chip, and let go. "Okay, go for it, Lulu. Shake yourself!"

Lulu shook her body from head to toe multiple times, spraying water everywhere, and dancing around in the tub. Mia lifted her out and let her run around the tile, then toweled her off while Chris watched. He laughed, "It's like she's possessed. Watch out for the demon poodle!"

Finally, Mia opened the door and Lulu charged into the room, shaking and then stopping to lick a paw in disgust. She glared at them for a moment, ran into her sky kennel, and plopped herself down onto the bed, licking one of her front legs maniacally. Chris shut the door to the kennel behind her and turned to smile at Mia. "Mission accomplished."

Mia looked down at her sodden t-shirt, shrugged, and raised her fist in victory. "Go team!"

"Thanks for your help. I wasn't sure what to do." He gave her a mocking leer. "You look like you're ready for your wet t-shirt contest now."

"So do you."

"Yeah, but your t-shirt is a lot more interesting."

Mia attempted to wring some water out of the bottom of her shirt. It had been a long time since anyone had made a flirty comment to her. "I don't suppose you have one I can borrow, do you?"

"Okay." He grinned. "I owe you dinner and if you wear that, you might cause a commotion among all those guys in the parking lot working on the Enchanted Moose remodel project."

She gave his shoulder a playful shove. "Shut up and give me a t-shirt. I'm hungry."

He turned and handed her a navy blue t-shirt with University of California, Berkeley emblazoned across the front. "Enjoy."

She held up the t-shirt in front of her, and then headed into the bathroom to change. This t-shirt was the closest she'd ever gotten to higher education.

~

On her way out of the bathroom, Mia collected all the soggy towels. She went around the room finding places to hang them up. Chris went into the bathroom, grabbed another towel, and attempted to wipe up the water that had been sprayed around virtually every surface.

He hung his towel on a rack, peeled off his t-shirt, and yanked on another Berkeley one. "I really hope housekeeping doesn't make surprise visits. They aren't going to like what they find here."

Distracted by the glimpse of half-naked man and wondering if she should care that they were going to look like twinsie over-the-top Cal fans, Mia just nodded. Chris definitely didn't look like a turkey vulture anymore. She never would have expected that someone who was so skinny and funny-looking in high school could morph into a nice-looking guy.

Although Chris did still have the same expressive round eyes she remembered from high school, he often had such a warm, kind look that she had started to forget about the cartoon factor. She cleared her throat. "I suppose by the time you check out, the horrible smell of Lulu might be gone. Maybe."

"We can only hope." He gestured toward the door. "Ready to eat?"

"Lead the way."

They crossed the parking lot toward the restaurant. It had a classic old-fashioned diner look, and if the attire of other patrons was any indication, Mia didn't have to worry about being under-dressed for the occasion.

After they settled into a booth, a waitress came by, plunked some paper placemats and silverware rolls on the table, and handed them menus. Chris opened the plastic booklet, gave it a glance, and closed it again. "I've eaten here enough that I think I have this thing memorized."

"When did you get to Alpine Grove?"

"A couple of weeks ago, although I had to fly back once for a meeting. That was when I boarded Lulu at the kennel. I miss my kitchen more than anything. Eating out gets boring when you have to do it for every meal."

"It's more exciting when your dinner companion barfs, although that may not be the type of excitement you want."

Chris laughed. "That's very true. You seem a lot better today."

"It was a good day. I spent lots of time with dogs, which is better than data entry."

"Data entry must be pretty bad, if washing a smelly poodle mix was an improvement."

"I made my peace with it, but every day I don't have to sit in that cubicle, I feel better. Part of me still can't quite believe I don't have to go back there."

The waitress returned and after they ordered, Chris pulled a blue crayon out of a mug that was sitting next to the ketchup. He began doodling something on the paper placemat. "Have you thought about what you're going to do next?"

Mia leaned across the table. "Is that a happy carrot?"

"Well, you wouldn't want me to draw a *sad* carrot, would you?" He looked up and grinned. "Here, let's give him an Airstream to hang out in."

"Hey, that's not bad! Mine was a lot more beat-up than that though. You see the new ones and they're all pretty and shiny, but I can tell you they don't stay that way. Those people at the trailer park will be lucky if they can find someone desperate enough to rent that thing again. It's falling apart."

"Well, if I completely screw up this project on the lake, maybe I'll move in. It would be better than moving back in with my parents."

"Parents weren't an option for me, but you're right, once you're out of your twenties, people tend to think you're pathetic if you're crashing with mom and dad."

Chris stopped doodling. "I'm sorry for bringing that up *again*. I don't know what is wrong with me. It's just that you're easy to talk to, so I say what's on my mind without censoring myself. But you probably think I'm an insensitive jerk."

"It's okay. I've spent so much time avoiding ever talking or even thinking about my mother and everything that happened, it's like I'm numb to comments about family, I guess."

Chris drew a frown face, crossed it out, and leaned forward, resting his elbows on the table. "I understand why you were so eager to get out of Windiberg. For one thing, it smells really bad there. You won't realize this until you go back. After my first semester of college I went back home for Christmas break and couldn't believe how gross it was."

Mia shook her head. "Everyone always says that, but I have no intention of ever returning. I'll just take your word for it."

"I was thinking about it and I understand why you pushed people away in high school. Family stuff that bad doesn't come out of nowhere."

"My home life was completely screwed up and I felt like everyone knew. Or maybe I wanted them to know. It's like I wanted to be invisible, but for someone to notice how unhappy I was at the same time. That probably doesn't make any sense."

Chris looked down at the crayon in his hand. "No, it does. I get it. Is that why you wore, uh, what you wore back then?"

"Probably. I always felt like an outsider. Like people could tell that my mom wasn't like other moms. Everything was dictated by her mood swings. If she was happy, it was all sunshine and unicorns. But when she sank down into one of the lows, it was awful. And let's just say marrying Howard didn't help matters."

"It sounded like he was pretty messed up."

"Yeah, and it got worse over time. When Mom was in one of her moods, he'd go off to a bar and get drunk. I went to the library, then after it closed, I'd go study at that Denny's on Jefferson Street. They were nice about letting me hang out and do my homework if I bought something. I drank a lot of coffee, which probably only added to the doom-and-gloom look. Dark circles under your eyes aren't attractive.

You end up with zombie Elvira, which is even worse than regular Elvira."

He moved his hand across the table and covered hers. "I wish I'd been nicer to you in high school."

"Well, I wasn't nice to you either. I thought you were a total geek. Your brainy crowd of people did not associate with freakazoids like me."

"True. I never really thought about why the freaks might be, well, freaky, you know? Mostly I was too worried about what other people were thinking about me."

"And we freaks were worried about what you were thinking, which is really just sad in retrospect." Mia smiled. "As you know, I still am not exactly Ms. Personality and have all kinds of problems communicating with people, but nothing has ever been as bad as high school."

Chris drew a happy face on the placemat and circled it. "We can always take comfort in that fact. I'm guessing you won't be attending the next reunion, huh?"

"Not likely. Did you go to the one they had a few years ago?"

"Are you kidding? No way." He drew an elaborately decorated arrow pointed at her. "You didn't answer my question. What are you planning to do next?"

"I'm not sure."

The waitress came up with their plates of food and placed them on the table. After she left, Mia handed her plate to Chris in exchange for his. "Thanks for not ordering anything from the sea."

"After the last twenty-four hours with you and Lulu, I'm swearing off seafood for a while."

"Good idea."

He pointed his fork at her. "Speaking of plans, are you avoiding the question? You still didn't say. What's next?"

"I don't know exactly. I'm going to travel and look for a new place to live. Then figure out what I want to do with the rest of my life." Mia turned her palms toward the ceiling. "That's as far as I've gotten. How about you? How long are you in Alpine Grove?"

"Probably another week after I've hashed over all the preliminary stuff with the developer. Then I go back to the office and get to work drawing my fingers to the bone. They want to begin construction on the house in the spring."

Mia took a sip of water. "Your plans are a lot more organized than mine."

"Yours sound like a lot more fun. Being away from the daily grind of my life and meeting you has caused me to think about a lot of things I normally don't think about." He picked up the crayon again and began doodling a cartoon thought bubble.

Mia pointed at the drawing. "It's empty. Is this you emptying your mind? Cartoon meditation? Are you being Zen here?"

"Very funny." He scrawled a twisted black blob into the bubble. "Here you go. I give you a representation of complete confusion."

"What are you confused about?"

He looked up. "Everything. I hate my job, I'm broke, and I have a girlfriend I fight with constantly. I wish I could just run away and join the circus with you."

"I don't think your girlfriend would approve." Mia was not entirely surprised to hear about a girlfriend, and yet she was startlingly disappointed nonetheless. Just when she was sort of starting to like him. It figured.

She shook off her irritation and made a wry face. "You do get points for coming up with maybe the only idea I actually haven't considered. The circus, while interesting in theory, upon reflection, I don't think it will work for me. Clowns creep me out."

Chris laughed. "Good point. Maybe traveling minstrels?"

"I can't carry a tune."

Chris drew a jester on the placemat. "Can you juggle?"

"Nope. Sorry."

He crossed out the jester. "I'm starting to see what you're dealing with here."

"Don't feel bad; I have this problem with every idea. I told you—you're lucky. You are qualified for a career where you can be creative. How cool is that?"

"I guess it could be cool. But right now, it's not, for a bunch of reasons."

"Then maybe those are the things you need to change."

~

Chris ordered some coffee while Mia pondered the dessert menu. All the dog walking and washing had made her hungry. The chocolate cake was calling her name. What the heck. Why not? Presumably Chris's expense account was paying, so she may as well live it up. She handed the menu to the waitress. "Chocolate crack, please."

The waitress raised her penciled brows. "What?"

"Cake. I mean *cake*." Mia glanced at Chris, who smiled at her. As the waitress retreated, Mia silently mouthed "sorry" at him.

"No big deal." He picked up the crayon again and drew a slice of cake. "It's interesting to me how you can talk with me for so long, then someone else walks up and all of a sudden the wrong word pops out."

"Welcome to my world of weird. It's because I'm not nervous around you anymore. Maybe because you knew what I was like in high school, I figure how could you possibly think I'm any more strange than you already do."

"I never thought of it that way. Maybe that's why it's easy for me to talk to you too." He scribbled a remarkably accurate caricature of himself as he looked at sixteen, complete with the black-framed owlish glasses and huge backpack.

Mia laughed. "That's fantastic. If the whole architecture thing doesn't work out, you can do caricatures of people."

"Not everyone appreciates this form of illustration."

"Do one of me in high school. That could be frightening."

"Are you sure you won't get mad? I mean, I didn't know you then, and I only sort of remember what you looked like."

"Oh, come on. I'll be fine. Go for it."

Chris began drawing while Mia looked on. The waitress arrived with the coffee and cake and they both looked up. She put the food down without comment. Drawing on the placemats was undoubtedly a common occurrence. If they were going to put crayons on a table with paper placemats, drawing was inevitable.

Chris turned the placemat around. "Okay, here you go, but you promised not to get mad."

"I think you didn't give my hair enough gel." She took the crayon from his hand and added a few more spikes. "It was the eighties. Big hair, remember?"

He laughed. "You're taking this with remarkably good humor. I did one of my girlfriend and I thought she was going to rip my throat out."

"What's her name?"

"Donna."

"Well, at least you have a girlfriend. I haven't gone out with anyone in forever, well, except with you, and that doesn't count."

"Hey, why don't I count?"

Mia raised her eyebrows, "Hello? Remember Donna? The girlfriend you just mentioned thirty seconds ago?"

"Oh, yeah. I'm pretty sure she hates me though. She hasn't called me the whole time I've been in Alpine Grove."

"When was the last time you saw her?"

"Well, I had to fly back to go to that meeting. I tried sending an email from work, but she was busy."

"So you didn't see her?"

"I didn't, but I wasn't there long. I guess the last time we saw each other in person was sometime before I left. It's been maybe a month I guess. Six weeks?"

Mia doodled a flower on her placemat. This was getting interesting. "Have you called her from here?"

Chris took red a crayon from the cup and scrawled some lines that looked like the beginnings of a house. "I, uh, well, I was going to. Okay, no." He drew some flames coming out of the house.

Mia pointed her crayon at his placemat. "I'm guessing there's trouble in paradise?"

"The truth is I don't want to talk to her. I know it's horrible to say that, but it's true. I feel like such a failure when I'm around her. When I had to admit to all my money problems, we had the fight to end all fights."

"So you broke up?"

"Not exactly." He drew a bouquet of roses. "I apologized and begged her to forgive me. I promised to change things, and it was this whole big drama. Donna gets really emotional. I can't handle it when women cry."

"So you didn't break up?"

"No, not technically. But in a way I wish we had. I can't see any type of future with her anymore. It's not like I'm suddenly going to change and become the wealthy, successful, revered architect she wants me to be. There's not going to be a spread in *Architectural Digest* about my work anytime soon."

"Well you never know. You might design something amazing."

"Not gonna happen. I'm more likely to end up in *MAD* magazine as part of a round-up of the twenty dumbest investments ever made by struggling architects." He scrawled a tiny person jumping out a window of the house with limbs flailing. "She said I lied to her and misled her. I don't know, maybe I did."

"About being a rich architect?" Mia drew a swirly question mark. "You seemed pretty up-front about your money problems with me."

He slapped the crayon down on the table. "I know! What's that about? I have no idea why I felt compelled to dump all that personal stuff on you last night."

"I already proposed the theory that it's easy to spill your guts to the loser mushroom girl, but you didn't buy it."

"Maybe I wanted to make sure you know who I really am. With Donna, I kept thinking I'd be able to fix the debt problems, so I didn't say anything for a long time. Too long."

Mia added more tendrils to her curly question mark. "Maybe you needed someone to listen without getting mad, instead of trying to change or fix anything. Just to listen."

He leaned back in the chair and looked at her for a moment. "I think that's the least judgmental thing anyone has ever said to me about this whole mess. You're full of surprises. I'm so glad we met."

"I am too." Mia smiled. "Does that mean we can be friends? I guess technically we'd be vacation friends, since neither of us lives here and we're both leaving in a week. But like you said, it's nice to have someone to talk to for a change."

"I'd like that."

"It's been a long time since I've had a friend. Well, except Gizmo. And he isn't much of a conversationalist. Maybe I should threaten to throw up on people more often."

"I don't think you need to barf on anyone." Chris reached across the table and pulled the crayon from her fingers, so he could clasp her hand. "It's been a long time since anyone has cared enough to take the time to listen to me."

Mia grinned. "You probably figured out that I'm better at listening than talking."

"I don't agree. I like hearing what you have to say. Even when you say the wrong word, it's okay. I know what you mean. And you usually get your words out eventually."

"You must be a patient guy."

"It takes a long time to build a house, but in the end it's worth it." He squeezed her hand. "So, do you want to do something more fun than washing a stinky dog tomorrow?"

"Sure. I'm going out to Kat's place to walk Gizmo in the afternoon, and I have to meet some people there after that, but I was thinking of driving out and visiting some places around here in the morning. I have some postcards with pictures of the area and I'd like to see the real thing."

"Want company? I have some work to do, but it can wait until the afternoon."

"That would be fun."

Chapter 5

Postcard Tour

After bonding with Chris over dinner and doodles the night before, Mia woke up in a good mood, looking forward to exploring Alpine Grove with him. She picked up a postcard off the nightstand and examined it. Not all of the postcards were particularly interesting. Many were of buildings that now housed different stores downtown. There was even one with a picture of the H12 motel, which looked more or less the same in 1976 as it did in 1996.

She held up a postcard that had a beautiful view of the lake. It was taken from a rocky overhang high above the lake, but the back of the card didn't indicate a location other than Alpine Grove. Maybe if she showed it to Kat's friend who had lived here for a while, she'd recognize the spot. In the meantime, she and Chris could check out one of the places that was identified on one of the other cards.

When she'd gotten her flat tire, Mia had been headed for Garfield Beach, but ended up turning back. She was determined to get there this time. Chris had said there was a trail along the water that was nice. They'd agreed she'd pick him up and drop him off back at the Enchanted Moose, since she'd be heading north to Kat's house afterward.

She got a bagel at the cafe and then got into the RAV for the trip back north. She drove around to the back of the Enchanted Moose and parked near Chris's unit, but he was already outside with Lulu. She walked across the parking lot to the picnic area, where Chris was sitting hunched over with his back to her. Lulu jumped up and barked as Mia approached. He turned to look and hurriedly jammed a cigarette into an ashtray on the picnic table.

Mia squinted at him as he flopped his leg over the bench to extract himself. What had happened to him? He looked terrible and had dark circles under his eyes. She waved a hand in greeting. "Ready to go?"

He nodded and smiled. "It's good to see you."

"You too, although I guess I need to establish some ground rules. Dogs are fine in my brand-new car, but cigarette smoke grosses me out. There is absolutely no smoking in the car."

"I don't smoke."

"Well, you do a good imitation of it." Mia gestured toward the picnic table behind them. "The cigarette in your hand was my first clue."

"That's the only one."

"Yeah, but you've got my zombie Elvira thing going today. You're a stress smoker, aren't you? What happened?"

Chris opened the back door of the RAV, lifted Lulu into the backseat, closed the door, and got in the front. He turned to Mia as she settled into the driver's seat. "I was working this morning and kind of freaking out about it. Smoking is one of those leftover bad habits from architecture studio in college. I got very little sleep back then. There was a lot of pressure and the cigarettes helped keep me awake. The room here is nonsmoking, so I went outside."

Mia glanced at him. "Is the project going that badly? You didn't say anything yesterday."

"It's fine so far. The developer, Ben, is a nice guy. He loves Alpine Grove and has a summer place here."

"Then what happened between yesterday and today?"

"After everything we talked about, I ended up calling Donna." He looked out the passenger-side window. "That was a mistake."

"How come? I thought you wanted to talk to her. Well, okay, maybe you sort of didn't, but talking to your girlfriend is a good thing, right?"

"I suppose. She wanted to find out how the project was going, telling me how important it is and that maybe I could submit it for awards, if I can meet some deadline. After I talked to her, I looked at my preliminary sketches for Ben for today and decided they were crap. I kept thinking, these are horrible and I have no business designing this house."

Mia briefly took her eyes from the road to look at him. "Now I'm curious. What does she do for a living?"

"She's an interior designer. We met through a client."

"Interesting. So you design the house and she furnishes it. You could be a power couple."

"Sure, except she thinks my designs stink. When I talked to her, it was like the pressure to be creative and unique in my designs all came rushing back. Talking to her is as bad as being at work. It's like my brain shuts down and I can't think."

Mia tapped her finger on the top of the steering wheel. "That's really odd to me because when you told me you were an architect, you said it was exciting to see a project go from start to finish."

"It's true. I do feel that way, and I even believe it when I'm just sitting here with you, driving around Alpine Grove.

But usually I work on buildings like retail complexes, where I'm dealing with one tiny aspect of a massive project." He pointed at the road. "The turn to Garfield Beach is up there, by the way. You might want to slow down."

"When you think about the house on the lake, what are you most excited about?"

"Bringing that view into the house." He smiled. "It's going to be an interesting design challenge. You saw that property. Imagine a house built into the hillside, cantilevered so most of it is actually airborne over the water. Then windows that bring the outside in. It would feel like you're flying over the lake. Absolutely fantastic."

"Okay, I'm sold. I thought almost the same thing when I saw the lot. It sounds way better than my aged Airstream."

He tapped the back of her hand on the gear shift. "Hey, you said you came into some money."

"Don't get excited. It's not that much money. How much is this guy Ben going to sell this place for when it's done?"

"More than I can afford. Your trailer is looking pretty good for me, remember?"

"Hey, you said you wanted to travel. Technically, it's a mobile home. Well, maybe not so mobile anymore. I think it was trying to return to the earth by decomposing into its core elements."

"Nice."

"So when you're designing, maybe you need to think about the house itself. Not winning awards or all that. Just focus on what you're excited about."

"I suppose. But I think the other moral of the story is don't call Donna again until this project is over. After freaking out last night, I told myself that if I got up super early, I could fix my designs. But I think I just made everything worse."

"You're pretty hard on yourself."

"I might deserve it." He pointed toward the road ahead. "There's the trailhead up there."

Mia parked the car and they got out. Lulu had been such a perfect, polite traveler that Mia had forgotten the little dog was in the backseat. Lulu stood up, but was too short to see out the windows.

Chris unloaded the dog and put her on the ground. He crouched down and stroked her head. "Remember this place?"

Mia smiled as Lulu marched toward the trailhead. "I think she does. Follow that poodle!"

Chris took her hand. "Thanks for talking me down off the ledge. You must think I'm a basket case. Maybe I'm having an early midlife crisis or something."

"Aren't we all?" Mia pulled the postcard out of the bag and handed it to him. "Here's what we're looking for. I wanted to see the view for myself. I guess Riddell Point is along this trail somewhere."

Chris looked at the front of the card. "Pretty." He flipped it over. "So I guess your dad is Dan? It says, 'It's beautiful here today and I reflected upon the simple pleasures of a walk through the forest. Just me, trees, nature, and the babies. Love, CA.' Who is 'CA?'"

"I don't know."

"Did you ask your dad?"

"I haven't talked to him in years. He did something unforgivable, and our relationship was really bad, then nonexistent. He moved out of the house and I refused to talk to him. Then after my mom married Howard, he moved away."

Chris handed the postcard back to her. "You have no idea where he moved to? After all this time? Didn't your mom tell you?"

"Nope. I made it pretty clear I hated his guts after what he did. And my mom, well, she refused to even acknowledge the fact I *had* a father. Howard got jealous if she even mentioned his name."

"Weren't you curious?"

"Not really."

"So why are you now?"

"I think he sent the postcards to me. There are a bunch of them, and who else would have twenty-year-old postcards addressed to Dan Riggins? And they just happened to arrive on my thirtieth birthday. Who else would know that?"

"I guess that is a little strange. Maybe he's trying to make amends. What did he do that was so bad?"

"He took my dog away. My golden retriever Rusty was my best friend in the whole world."

"What do you mean he took him away? Where?"

"Well, he said Rusty was going to a good home, but every kid above the age of six knows that's just a line for dumping a dog at the animal shelter."

"That's awful. Are you sure he did that? I mean the Windiberg shelter was, well…not a place I'd ever want Lulu to end up."

"Yes, I know. That's why I refused to speak to my dad. There was nothing to say."

As they strolled along the trail, Chris was silent for a few minutes. Maybe he was busy digesting the information. Mia had already thought about it way too much. She'd spent years trying to get over the grief of losing Rusty and her father's betrayal.

The trail turned to the right and suddenly the view from the postcard was in front of them.

Chris stopped and pointed at the lake. "It's exactly like the photo. I guess some things haven't changed here in the last twenty years."

"Looking at the postcards, it's interesting to see how much is the same. The motel I'm staying at, for example."

Chris picked up Lulu, who was sitting next to him with a surly look on her face. "I'm guessing I'll be carrying her back." He stroked the fur on the dog's head thoughtfully. "So who are the babies 'CA' mentions in the post card?"

"I have no idea. Maybe my dad had a second family. I'm hoping to ask around a little and see if anyone has heard of him."

"Well, if he did have another family, maybe that's where your dog ended up. Maybe that's why he sent you the cards. As proof."

"Yeah, I thought about that possibility. It would be nice to know that was where Rusty ended up. Maybe I have stepsiblings. That would be strange."

"Maybe you do." He took her hand. "I think I finally understand why you're here now."

"I'm not really sure what I'm looking for exactly. I don't know what to think about it all and I'm half afraid of what I'll find out. I'm not even entirely sure my father is the one who sent the postcards because Gizmo ate the return address. If I had that, I'd know a lot more."

"Your dog sure is an enthusiastic eater." Chris gave her palm a squeeze. "I'll help you find—whatever it is—if I can."

~

After dropping off Chris and Lulu back at the Enchanted Moose, Mia drove north to the kennel. She was looking forward to seeing Kat again, not to mention Gizmo. It was difficult getting used to not having him around all the time. Back at the H12, she found herself expecting him to jump up with his cheerful expectant face when she turned around or walked out of the bathroom.

When she got to the kennel, Kat was already outside with Gizmo and Lewis. She waved as Mia drove up.

Mia got out of the car and gave Gizmo a big hug. "How's my goofy guy?" The dog wiggled and wagged with joy.

Kat handed her Gizmo's leash. "I think he's glad to see you."

"In some ways, I feel bad leaving him, but it is nice to be able to eat in grown-up restaurants again."

"Ready to go?"

Mia nodded and followed Kat up the driveway and around the back of the house. Kat disappeared inside and when the door opened, dogs burst forth, followed by a tall man with long sandy-colored dark blonde hair that was pulled back into a ponytail. Kat gestured toward him, "Mia, this is Joel, my fiancé."

He smiled and gestured toward the dogs running through the trees. "Welcome to the zoo."

"It's nuts to meet you...*nice. Nice* to meet you," Mia said. Joel had dark-green eyes and a short beard. The red-and-black flannel shirt completed the lumberjack-mountain-man motif he had going.

"Joel has been swearing at his computer, so I suggested he might need a break," Kat said.

He poked her in the ribs with his index finger. "I never swear."

"The dogs all ran into my office," Kat said.

"That was Tessa's fault. Everyone wanted to leave after she generated that smell, including me." He took Chelsey's leash from Kat because Lewis was yanking her toward a particularly special bush. "So speaking of swearing, how's that article going?"

Kat stopped and waited for Lewis to finish his shrubbery investigation. "I don't want to talk about it."

Mia said, "What are you writing about?"

"Nothing at the moment. Sometimes I feel like I spent more time procrastinating and avoiding writing than actually writing. Oh, and sometimes I spend time whining about it too," Kat said.

Mia glanced at Joel, who wasn't disagreeing. Perhaps he was used to the whining. "I can't imagine getting paid to write. I would never be able to think of anything to say."

"Well, I get assignments. Right now, I'm supposed to be explaining why someone would want to buy one inkjet printer versus another." Kat stopped to wait for Lewis again. "But so far, I wouldn't want to buy any of them. An article that says they are all garbage doesn't tend to go over well with the editor."

Joel chuckled. "And your office looks like the corrugated cardboard fairy exploded in there."

"The dogs are all annoyed because all the packing and unpacking of printers is affecting their sleep time," Kat said.

"Not to mention all the swearing," Joel said.

"I haven't been swearing. That was you. Well, maybe a little. Half the time some hairy dog is under my office chair and I end up rolling on tail fur." Kat started walking again. "Then there's a whole yelping incident, and everyone else runs into my office to see what awful thing I did. They glare at me, and then decide everything is okay and leave."

Mia laughed. "That is so easy to imagine. Back at home, there wasn't much space and I was always stepping on Gizmo. He always forgave me though."

"Dogs are like that," Kat said.

They continued to chat as they walked along the trail that looped through the forest. Gizmo was panting happily, thoroughly enjoying his walk. After making the circuit through the forest and dropping off Lewis and Gizmo at the kennel, they returned to the back door of the house, and Kat invited Mia inside.

The entrance led into a long hallway. At the other end, a gate blocked access to the bottom of the staircase that led upstairs. Two rooms went off to the right and left. Joel disappeared into one of the rooms while Kat unhooked Chelsey and undid the harnesses Linus and Tessa were wearing.

Kat hung the harness-and-leash contraption on a hook next to the door. "Sorry the place is kind of a mess. Don't look in my office. Upstairs is better. Well a little. At least there are fewer boxes. But there's an equal amount of dog hair."

The dogs milled around for a few minutes, then Chelsey curled up on a dog bed under a table in the hallway, and the rest of the dogs vanished into the two rooms for afternoon naptime. Kat opened the gate and indicated that Mia should follow her upstairs.

At the top of the stairs, Mia turned to look at the house. The kitchen led to an open dining room and living area that had a high cathedral ceiling. The walls were log and the ceiling was tongue-and-groove. The scent of aged wood filled the space.

Kat leaned back against the counter. "I'm going to chop up some veggies and make some hummus for people to eat. I'm not much of a hostess. Fortunately, Brigid is bringing munchies, because she knows this about me."

Mia tried not to panic. How many people were showing up? The thought of a huge social event requiring elaborate hors d'oeuvres made her want to crawl under a rock. "I don't think you mentioned Brigid."

"She started the rescue group. We tend to refer to it as 'Brigid's Dogs,' but technically the name is Alpine Grove Animal Adoptions or AGAA. I think I told you that Lewis is an alumnus."

"That's nice." It was good that the dogs were getting new homes. It was bad that Mia now had to meet all these new people. "So, uh, how many people are coming over?"

Kat paused in her food-gathering activities and looked at Mia. "You have the same deer-in-the-headlights look I get when I have to go to a party."

"I'm not good with groups. Or people I don't know."

"Don't worry. It's just three people. Brigid runs the dog rescue, Tracy works at the vet clinic, and Maria works at the ad agency in town. They're all really nice. You'll see."

Mia wasn't sure about this, but it would be incredibly rude if she left. And Kat had been really nice about letting her come by and go on walks with Gizmo. She turned at the sound of the gate closing downstairs. Joel walked into the kitchen and smiled at them. "Going for the default veggie dip, huh?"

Kat said, "It's my cooking speed. Are you heading out?"

"Give the ladies my regards. I'll be at the Shack if you need anything." He turned toward Mia. "It was nice meeting you."

Mia wondered where he was going. Was the Shack a bar? "You too."

Kat followed him to the front door and stood on tiptoes to give him a hug. It looked like she whispered something in his ear before kissing him goodbye because he grinned.

After Joel left, Kat walked back into the kitchen. "Okay then, want to chop some carrots? Tracy is like a bunny. You'd think the woman never eats."

Mia nodded and took a few carrots from the bag on the counter. Maybe they had passed through Round House Distributing. "You said Tracy is the woman who grew up here, right?"

"Yes, and I don't think I mentioned it, but Brigid is living with a guy who grew up here too. Except she won't say she's living with Clay. She's renting his guest house." Kat held up the knife she had been using and tilted it for emphasis. "But it's just semantics. She spends all her time at the ranch.

Anyway, Clay is a second-generation Alpine Grove native, I think."

"Okay." Mia looked down at the carrots "I hope I don't say something wrong."

"You won't. But don't be surprised when Maria razzes Brigid about the fact that she's living with Indiana Jones. She does it all the time."

"Indiana Jones?"

"Clay kind of looks like Harrison Ford a little. He has the same hat anyway."

"I see." Mia didn't see, but she wasn't going to worry about it. Right now, she had larger worries, most notably the possibility of making a fool of herself in front of Kat's friends.

~

Kat put down her knife at the sound of a knock on the door and the resulting clamor and ferocious barking from the pack of dogs downstairs. She smiled at Mia as she went to answer the door. "I don't have to worry about burglars."

A woman yelled, "Girlfriend!" from the entryway.

Mia put down her knife and turned to look. A woman with lots of brunette hair piled up on her head was hugging Kat. They released one another and Kat said, "Mia, this is my friend Maria."

Maria was wearing clothes that seemed to be several sizes too small. Her ample curves were seriously taxing the power of the magenta spandex top.

Mia tried not to look nervous and waved the knife in greeting. "Hello. I'm, um, my dog is straying...*staying* here."

Maria dropped a small duffel bag onto the floor and walked into the kitchen with Kat. "Lucky you. That means you should be meeting a man in approximately fifteen minutes."

Mia raised her eyebrows. How did she know? "Did Kat tell you Chris gave me her phone number so I could board my dog?"

Maria turned and glared at Kat. "Chris? I'm guessing this is a Christopher and not a Christine. Is she kidding me here?"

Kat turned her palms toward the ceiling. "I boarded his poodle, Lulu."

Maria strolled toward the pantry, shaking her head. She pulled a bottle of wine out of the cabinet and pointed the top at Kat. "This is unbelievable. Are you ready to drink wine? Because I am. Today, I am having a bad hair day, I broke up with Fred, and you still won't board cats. I swear I'm doomed to be the last single woman in this wretched town."

Mia was confused. What did cats have to do with anything? "It doesn't look like the kernels...*kennels* are set up for cats. Is there a separate area?"

Kat shook her head. "They're not, and I don't board cats. Maria is convinced that every time I board a dog for a woman, she meets a man and falls in love."

Maria stomped her foot. "It's true! I'm developing a serious complex about this. I'm gonna need to talk to a shrink or something."

"Chris is just a friend. We went to the same high school," Mia said.

Maria poured wine into a glass. "That's just like Beth and Drew, and they got married...what...last summer? I think I have a cat-lady curse or something."

"You do not. They wrote their own vows for the ceremony and it turns out they were high school sweethearts," Kat said.

"I didn't know that, and I swear everyone was just bawling their eyes out at the story. Drew is a really good writer. He writes mysteries, but maybe he should try romance instead."

"Chris and I didn't even know each other in school. And he has a girlfriend," Mia volunteered. "I'm sure you're not cussed...I mean *cursed*."

"I might want to cuss. In fact, I'm feeling an urge to do a lot of cussing. Loudly and vigorously." Maria poured wine into two more glasses and handed them to Kat and Mia. "To women who use bad words. Say them loud and say them proud. Let those nasty words run wild and be free!"

Mia laughed as Maria launched into a fair recitation of George Carlin's seven dirty words with a number of creative embellishments.

Kat said, "I don't think that one is physically possible."

"You have no imagination, girlfriend," Maria tilted back her glass and sucked down the last droplets of wine. "Where are these women? Brigid's never late."

"They're carpooling. Tracy had to bring a rescue dog out to the ranch that was neutered at the vet clinic today, so she's picking Brigid up there," Kat said. She pointed at Maria's head. "So I hate to ask, but what's with your hair?"

"I told you I'm having a coiffure situation. I need to sit down. It was a long day in the ad game and I'm spent." Maria poured herself some more wine and settled into a chair at the dining room table.

Kat collected Mia's carrots from the cutting board and put them on a tray, along with the celery she'd chopped up, and a bowl of hummus. She walked to the table and set the tray down in front of Maria. "So I'm guessing hair-gel failure."

"I don't want to talk about it," Maria said.

Mia sat down next to Kat. "In my hair-gel days, I found out that the really cheap stuff can dry out your hair. Mine started to get stiffy...I mean *stiff and icky!*" Mia could tell her face was turning red and she hurriedly took a gulp of wine.

With a grin, Maria tilted her wine glass at Mia. "Sadly, I haven't heard the word *stiffy* in far too long, but returning to the subject at hand, you're right. My hair was experiencing some stress." Maria said, "So I decided to take action. I read in one of those magazines that natural hair care is the way to go. So I tried to get all healthy and do a homemade hot-oil treatment. The problem is I may have overdone it. My hair is naturally curly and I think I killed it dead. Now it's the opposite of a stiffy."

"It does look remarkably limp," Kat said.

"This turn in the conversation is distressing me. Let's not be using words like limp in my presence. I have enough problems right now," Maria said. "The recipe was an olive oil-mayonnaise mixture, but I didn't really have that, so I improvised."

Kat set down her glass. "Uh-oh."

"I figured that ranch dressing was pretty close," Maria took a sip. "And it's from some hidden valley, so I thought that might help too, since it has those secret family recipe ingredients and stuff."

Mia wasn't sure what to say, but her ruminations on secret ingredients were interrupted by a knock at the door and subsequent frantic dog barking. Kat leaped up to answer it and quiet the dogs.

Maria had her palm on her chest and yanked on the edge of the magenta spandex top, pulling it back into place. "I don't know how Kat stands that. Every time someone comes to this place, those animals go nuts and I practically jump out of my skin. At least the girls are still under wraps. I hate having a wardrobe situation every time people come to the door."

Kat walked back into the kitchen followed by two women. The first was as short as Kat, with flaming red hair. She was carrying a grocery bag that she set on the kitchen counter. The other, taller, woman had bone-straight blonde hair and made a beeline for the food on the table. Kat pointed to the redhead and said, "Mia, this is Brigid."

Mia smiled and glanced at the other woman, who was gobbling down a carrot. "I guess you must be Tracy."

With a nod, Tracy said, "Sorry, I'm starving. Brigid made a bunch of food and it smelled so good on the way over here, so now I'm dying. That's probably the best that evil hunk-of-junk car has smelled since at least 1980."

Kat was busily removing items from the bag and ferrying them to the table. She set down a tray full of phyllo triangles and turned to Brigid. "You made them! I love these things."

Mia handed Tracy the wine bottle just as Kat returned to the kitchen with glasses. Tracy shook her head. "I'm having water. Driving, remember?"

Brigid took a glass and held it up while Tracy poured. "I'm not. All right ladies, let's talk about homeless dogs." She pulled out a sheet of paper and listed her agenda items.

Mia felt like a third or fifth or some type of outsider wheel that had fallen off the rim. She didn't know the dogs they were talking about, so she mostly sat quietly and ate the munchies piled up on the plates.

Kat was right about the triangular phyllo things. They were filled with spinach and you couldn't eat just one. She tried to look casual as she grabbed another one. Right as she took a huge bite, Kat turned to her and said, "Mia, you wanted to ask about someone who was here in the seventies, right?"

Mia choked down her food, "Mmmph, yes. Um, my feather."

"Your father," Kat said.

"Yes, right. Dan Riggins. He might have been here in the seventies sometime and someone from here wrote to him. I have postcards."

Brigid, Tracy, and Maria all stared at her, suddenly silent. Mia's cheeks were aflame. This was so mortifying. She was babbling and no one knew what she was talking about. Finally she stammered, "I...I haven't heard from my father in a long time. My parents divorced."

Brigid said, "So are you trying to find him or someone else?"

"Both. Someone sent me the postcards and I think it must mean blushing...I mean *something*. They're signed 'CA,' but I don't know who that is," Mia said.

"Clay lived here then. He might know. Or his sister TJ. What's your father's name again?" Brigid said.

"Dan Riggins."

Tracy waved a carrot. "I was really little and splashing around in creeks at the commune, so unless he was a hippie, I'm no help. But I can ask my mom."

Kat said, "That's a good idea. Bea knows everyone."

Maria took a sip of wine. "I'm thinking about adopting a dog."

Tracy, Brigid, and Kat all made incredulous exclamations at once and Maria waved them off. She put down her glass. "Drastic measures are required here, ladies. Earlier this evening, it came to my attention that our new friend Mia has been in Alpine Grove for approximately forty-eight hours, boarded her dog, and has *already* managed to meet a man. Kat continues to discriminate against felines, so I'm being forced to make a concession."

"That's not a good reason to adopt a dog and you know it," Brigid said.

"You don't even *like* dogs," Tracy said.

Kat sucked down the last of her wine. "Oh for heaven's sake. Bring Scarlett, the wild-and-crazy destruct-o cat, for a weekend. I'll let her stay in my office or something."

"The engineer isn't gonna like that," Maria said.

"I know. Joel is going to kill me, but I'm going to make a special exception just for you, so you'll stop harping on the idea that my dog-boarding kennel is some type of bizarre matchmaking service." Kat waved her empty glass at Maria. "You are going to owe me big time."

Tracy giggled, "Whoa, you really got her all riled up."

"Hey, don't get on my case. You're one of the matches made." Maria pointed her glass at Tracy, then tipped it at Brigid. "And so are you!"

Kat poured more wine into her glass. "Y'all are giving me a headache."

"I think that's the wine," Maria said. "Speaking of drinking, I've been thinking about party planning. Do you know where you're getting married yet? Picked a dress? How about the reception? I want to talk bachelorette party too."

"No." Kat had the type of sulky look on her face that Mia had seen many times in the mirror. Perhaps the wedding was a touchy subject.

"You are going to have to think about this sometime, girlfriend," Maria said.

Kat set down her glass. "Can we please change the subject? Doesn't anyone *else* have anything interesting going on?"

"I think I might be pregnant." Tracy covered her mouth with her hand, and then let it fall to her lap. "Oops. I just said that out loud, didn't I?"

Brigid and Kat sat motionless with their mouths hanging open, and Maria clapped her hands together, "Yessiree! You sure did. Does Rob know about this?"

"No, and I'm not really sure either. I might be just, you know, late," Tracy said.

Maria said, "When that happened…"

"Shut up!" Kat said.

"As I was *going* to say, you might want to go to the drug store and get a test," Maria said.

"I know." Tracy put her elbows on the table and her forehead on her palms. "It's just not…I'm a little freaked out. Right now, Rob is so busy. Ben wants him to set up a fancy web site for some house he's building and showcase it on the real estate section of the Alpine Grove site."

Brigid put her arm around Tracy. "That must mean his boss likes his work. It sounds like a good thing to me, assuming Rob is getting paid well. Babies are expensive."

Tracy looked up. "He's working lots of hours though, and I miss him. And I'd have to quit my job at the vet clinic."

Kat said, "Get the test. You don't know anything for sure yet."

Tracy looked at her. "I'm just so jealous. I want to travel so bad. Do you know what I'd give to get out of Alpine Grove and go to Hawaii in March like you are? Now it might never happen."

Brigid squeezed her shoulders. "You don't know that. I didn't think I'd be here now, much less running a rescue for homeless dogs. A lot can change in a short time."

The other three women nodded at Brigid's comment. Mia had a feeling there was a whole lot of stories she didn't know, but she couldn't disagree about things changing quickly.

If someone had told her a month ago that she'd win the lottery and be sitting in a tiny mountain town talking with a room full of women about everything from pregnancy to ranch dressing, she would have just laughed.

～

After everyone left, Kat called Joel and told him the coast was clear. He'd wisely left the house while the PR committee meeting of the Alpine Grove Animal Adoptions group was in session. She fed the dogs, let them out, and flopped onto the bed, exhausted.

At a bright light, Kat opened her eyes. Joel was standing next to the bed, looking down into her face. "Rough meeting?"

"Kind of. Welcome home."

He bent to give her a kiss. "I didn't realize you were lying in here in the dark. I can't believe the dogs didn't wake you up when I came in."

"I just incorporated dogs into my dream, which was one of those wine-induced 'a little too close to real life' type dreams where you wonder what the point was. Yuck. I need to brush my teeth. Sorry about that." Kat sat up, threw her legs over the side of the bed, got up, and walked across the hall to the bathroom.

Joel followed her and leaned on the door frame, watching her in the mirror while she scrubbed her pearly whites. He raised an eyebrow. "So what happened? You look annoyed. Or disturbed. Or something."

Kat spat out the toothpaste and rinsed her mouth. "I am." She walked out of the bathroom and gestured for him to follow her. Closing the bedroom door behind them, she whispered. "Maria is downstairs snoring away on the bed in my office, hopefully sleeping off the pinot grigio."

"Are you annoyed at her?"

"Yes. No. More annoyed with myself. I agreed to board her cat."

"You're kidding, right?"

"I wish I were." Kat crawled back onto the bed and rolled over with her arms outstretched.

"So where do you plan to keep Scarlett? I don't think she'd appreciate a dog kennel and would stage a speedy exit, never to be seen again."

Kat moved her arm listlessly. "I guess I'll put her in my office."

Joel shoved her aside and sprawled out on the bed next to her. "I want absolutely nothing to do with this."

"I know." She rolled over to look at him. "We also are going to have to deal with the whole wedding thing. If we ever figure out what we're going to do and where, we'll have to make reservations and what not, so we need to fork over money for deposits. I'm not sure how you want to handle that."

"I suppose I've been avoiding it too. I'm looking forward to the day *after* the wedding. March twenty-first is going to be a happy day."

"The whole wedding problem is not going to go away. We talked about paying for everything ourselves, since my family...well...I don't even want to go there. Anyway, you mentioned merging finances. Maybe we should do that sooner, rather than later."

"That might make sense. I guess." He put his arm around her and kissed her forehead. "I guess we should talk about this."

Kat snuggled into his embrace with her cheek on his chest. "I don't really know much about your money situation other than that you're cheap. But I don't know if you have seven bank accounts, organized by interest rate, or something."

"I prefer the word frugal. And no, I don't."

"This isn't particularly romantic thing to say, but maybe we should call one of those finance people at the bank and set up an appointment. Because of my inheritance, things could be complicated and it's a well-known fact that I do not play well with numbers."

"We? You mean me, don't you?"

"No, I mean we. I didn't say *you*. I said *we*. That means you or me."

"It does. So are you going to call the bank?"

Kat paused for a moment. "No."

"Then you mean *me*, don't you?"

"I hate it when you get all logical like this."

He squeezed her shoulders. "I'm just looking at the facts objectively."

"I suppose. So you'll set up an appointment?"

"All right. Where are we going to get married?"

"I'm not sure. Thoughts?"

"I was lobbying for elopement, remember?" Joel grinned. "Otherwise known as running away."

"I want to be married, but not the wedding so much. Every time I look at those bridal magazines Maria keeps throwing at me, the whole thing stresses me out. And you can spend a fortune on a wedding. I don't want to go into debt for one day."

"I can't argue with that. I'm the frugal one, remember?"

Kat tickled his ribs. "I know, and that has been extremely helpful during the kennel construction process. So here's an idea: what if we do the courthouse deal for the actual legal part, and then have a separate reception? That way we completely sidestep the whole religion issue. Because I'm absolutely not going there, no matter what my mother thinks."

"You're willing to go without all the flowers and pomp-and-circumstance stuff?"

"That involves a lot of traditions and Emily Post garbage that I'll get wrong, which will leave someone mortally offended. The reception is just a party, so expectations are lower."

"Where do you want to do that?"

"Given that we're getting married in March, it has to be somewhere inside."

"Definitely. The big party the dog rescue did at the lodge was nice."

"True. If we held it at the North Fork Lodge, out-of-town folks can get a room. Then everyone can drink and pass out. Meanwhile, we can sneak away. Robin would probably give me a decent deal, since it's off season."

"Way off season." Joel pushed some hair back behind her shoulder and kissed her ear. "It works for me, if it works for you."

"I'll talk to Robin and see what she says. Relatives booking rooms at the lodge in March would make her happy. If there's a party for Maria to plan, she'll be happy too."

"Speaking of the woman sleeping downstairs, how was the big PR committee meeting? Did you get anything done?"

"A little, but then Tracy said she thought she might be pregnant and that pretty much trumped everything."

"Uh, yeah, that would do it."

"I know. And poor Mia looked so confused. I probably shouldn't have subjected her to that much wine and whining."

"Did she drink too much? Is she down there sleeping in your office too?"

"She was fine and went home. I think she was too busy being shy and embarrassed to drink much. It's no fun being an odd duck, particularly when everyone else knows each other. I've had that experience."

"Are you having some gray-sheep-of-the-family flashbacks?"

"Yes, you know me so well. The expression on her face reminded me of me at family dinners with my sisters and mother. Maria was in fine form and then Tracy dropped her little bombshell."

Joel sat up straighter. "Does Rob know Tracy is pregnant? I hope she's going to be a little more forthcoming than you were with me."

"She hasn't told him yet, since she's not sure. But yeah, I know, talk about flashbacks. All in all, it was a rather disturbing evening. It's like every insecurity and problem that has ever set up residence in my brain made an appearance at tonight's big déjà vu fiesta."

"I can imagine."

"The only thing that would have been worse is if my mother had called to round out the evening. So let us be thankful for small blessings. I assume chopping up firewood and hanging out with Jack was more peaceful."

"It was. Their wood is all stacked and Jack will be by sometime this week to help with ours."

Kat gave him a hug. "I'm looking forward to snuggling in front of the fire with you this winter."

"Me too."

Chapter 6

At the Ranch

After Mia returned to her motel room, she collapsed on the bed for a while and read her novel. It had been a day filled with far too much human interaction, which was way out of her comfort zone. She needed to decompress.

Before everyone left Kat's house, Brigid had invited Mia to come out to the ranch in the morning to talk to her boyfriend, landlord—or whatever she thought he was—before he started work training horses. Clay, the guy Maria said looked like Indiana Jones, had grown up in Alpine Grove, so presumably he might have heard of her father or the mysterious "CA" person who wrote the postcards.

After her exhausted, introverted soul had recovered somewhat, she called Chris at the Enchanted Moose and suggested they meet later in the day for the next installment of the Alpine Grove postcard tour. Mia was completely talked out and he sounded terrible, so the conversation was brief, but she agreed to pick him up the next day after she walked Gizmo.

Maybe she was just cranky from all the intense people time, but as she lay on the ugly plaid bedspread at the H12 staring at the ceiling, Mia couldn't help thinking about her uncharacteristic curiosity about these old postcards. What on earth was she was doing? The whole thing was insane. Why did she even care that her father sent the postcards and lottery tickets, anyway? Assuming it was even Dad who sent them. Mia had vowed never to speak to the man again, so why did she suddenly want to look him up?

Truth be told, she undoubtedly was using this whole postcard mystery as a complicated avoidance tactic. After several days loitering around Alpine Grove, she was no closer to figuring out what to do with her life. While she was busy looking into her past, she could avoid dealing with the ugly reality of her future. Although she had some money now, it wasn't like she could spend the rest of her life aimlessly driving around the country forever.

Even if her stay here was all about avoiding other issues, every time she looked through the postcards, her curiosity was reignited. She couldn't help wondering about them. Who was "CA"? Apparently she had kids who were just babies in 1975 or 1976, so that made those people roughly ten years younger than she was. What if Mia had younger brothers or sisters living here somewhere? How could she leave without at least trying to look them up? She had lots of lottery money to live on in the short term. Although the money wouldn't last forever and she did need to find a job, for a while she had the flexibility and time to get a few questions answered. If she found out her father had sent the package, she also could say "thanks for the lottery tickets." A tiny part of her wanted him to know she'd won.

It was amusing that now that Chris had seen the postcards, he seemed to be as curious as she was. He'd been disappointed that she wasn't able to meet him in the morning, but perked up when she'd suggested that they meet later in the day. Chris said he wanted a full report on her meeting with Clay out at the ranch.

Talking to Chris again would be fun. The evening at Kat's reminded her how much she preferred conversing with just one person at a time. Being in a room full of women she didn't know was just way too much information to process all at once. Kat had seemed sympathetic and given her a hug when she left, so that was nice anyway.

Tired of her thoughts, Mia rolled over onto her side and resumed her novel. It would be great to be someone like the woman in the story. Clarissa the Fabulous was never at a loss for words. Never embarrassed and always able to come up with the perfect witty comeback in any situation. And always ready for smoking-hot sex at the drop of a hat with men swooning at her feet. Yeah, right. Mia would have to have a complete brain transplant for that to ever happen.

Although Mia was grateful for the money and the changes it had made possible, it couldn't change the fundamental aspects of who she was. Once the odd mushroom girl, always the odd mushroom girl.

The next morning, Mia got ready to go out to the ranch, which was north of town. The fact that Brigid was so direct and organized during the meeting had been a little intimidating and Mia was anxious about meeting Clay. What if he was even more uptight than his girlfriend?

Mia tried not to let her imagination get the best of her, but she had visions of using the wrong word with Indiana Jones. He'd probably roll his eyes, lasso her, and throw her over a cliff to put her out of her misery. In the movies, Indy didn't waste time with pleasantries.

By the time Mia turned on V Bar H Ranch Road, she had worked herself into a state of considerable agitation. What was she doing coming out here, subjecting herself to even more people she didn't know? Why was she willingly entering situations that would just lead to humiliation? It couldn't possibly end well. She took a deep breath as the road crossed through expansive pastures. The drive was beautiful, with the last of the fall aspen leaves quaking and putting on a pretty show.

The road entered a heavily wooded area and then opened out into a clearing that had a cedar-sided house with a wrap-around porch in the center of it. In front of the house, a few horses were grazing in the pasture, which was bordered by white wooden fencing.

A number of outbuildings surrounded the house, and two red barns sat along the driveway. One had white lettering that said V - H on the front, above the sliding doors.

A man, presumably Clay, given that he was wearing a cowboy hat, was leaning on the fence. If Mia didn't know better, she'd think he was giving the horse a lecture. The horse even looked a little bit chastised, shaking his head a few times before he turned and trotted off into the pasture to graze.

At the sound of the car turning into the driveway, Clay turned and began strolling toward the barns while Mia parked and got out of the car. He took off his battered leather hat and ran his fingers through his light brown wavy hair before replacing the hat on his head.

Mia smiled politely and tried to think of something to say. "I'm Mia. Last night Brigid said I could come out here to tank."

His brown eyes widened slightly, but he didn't say anything.

"Talk. I mean *talk*. Just for a minute. I know you must be bleary. *Busy!*" The way he looked at her so calmly was unnerving. "I'm sorry."

"Nothing to be sorry about." He held out his hand. "Welcome to the V Bar H Ranch."

She shook his hand, which was somewhat rough and chapped. "Thank you."

Clay started walking toward the smaller barn. "I'm not real busy right now, but I do have some horses that could stand some brushing. Maybe we can talk while I do that."

"I guess." Mia followed him, unsure what else to do.

In the barn, he grabbed some halters from a hook and turned to her. "Brigid tells me you're looking for someone."

"I am, but I'm not sure who it is." Yeesh, could she be any less eloquent? This guy was going to think she was some sort of nitwit. "I got some old postcards. They might be from my father."

Five horses strolled over to the fence as Clay walked up. He went inside the gate and put a halter on one horse that was a pretty light tan color and another smaller horse that had big brown-and-white patches. He pointed at the gate. "Could you get that?"

Mia opened it for him and he strolled through with the horses in tow. Never in her life had she been so close to a horse. They were absolutely beautiful.

After she closed the gate behind them, Clay handed her a lead rope for the brown-and-white horse. "This is Willy. He's been rolling in the dirt and he's going out on a trail ride later, so he needs a good brushing. The buckskin is Hank."

"I've never brushed a horse before."

"It's kinda relaxing, particularly for the horse. Don't be surprised if Willy looks like he's falling asleep. He's just enjoying it."

"Kind of like when people get a massage?"

"Yeah. Horses are more sensitive than a lot of people realize. They can feel a little tiny fly sitting on their butt."

They led the horses toward the barn and Clay went through some safety information while he tied up the horses. He was obviously used to dealing with people with zero experience around horses, which was a relief to Mia.

She stroked Willy's warm neck and took the curry comb Clay handed her. "Willy seems nice."

"He's an old cow-horse enjoying his retirement." Clay peered around Willy's neck at Mia. "Now tell me about this person you're wanting to find."

While she brushed Willy, Mia explained about her father and the mysterious "CA," attempting to give Clay as much detail as she knew. Somehow having Willy standing there in between her and Clay made it much easier to discuss this whole thing without feeling like a fool.

Clay patted Hank's neck and walked around Willy. He gave the horse's withers a pass with the brush. "I can't remember ever meeting anyone named Dan Riggins, offhand. But I also left Alpine Grove around that time, so we coulda missed each other."

"He may not have been here long. It might have been a visit. I have no idea. But the postcards were addressed to him before he moved out of the house where I grew up. Can you think of someone with the initials CA who lived here in Alpine Grove then?"

Clay scratched a scar on his chin with his index finger. "Well. I'm not sure. Clara, uh, somebody or other used to own the diner, but I'm pretty sure she's dead now. And there's a girl named Colleen who was in my sister's class. She woulda been maybe twenty or twenty-one then. Her maiden name was Abbott. She married a guy named Brandon Fisher right after high school. He drives a truck, so he's never around, but she works at the DMV. Sometimes I see her when I renew my driver's license or deal with car registrations and stuff like that."

"Does she have kids? The postcards mention babies."

"I think so. To be honest, she's kind of a grouch, so I usually just do whatever car business I have to do and run away."

Mia laughed. "I guess working at the DMV could make people cranky. Going to official offices like that makes me really nervous. I always say something wrong, and then I worry that they won't give me my license or something."

"Maybe you're worrying more than you need to."

Mia suddenly felt self-conscious. Why were people here so nice? Instead of looking at her like she was insane, they seemed to accept her speech problems without question. Chris, Kat, the women at the meeting, and now Clay. It was strange. "I should let you get to work. I really appreciate your time and thoughts on this...situation. I know it's a little odd to be asking you about stuff from twenty years ago."

"There's nothing wrong with wanting to know about your family, I don't think."

"I guess that's true." Mia stroked Willy's neck. Clay had a low, soft way of speaking that was oddly comforting. Like the older brother she never had. "Most of my family stuff has been worth forgetting, so this is new for me."

"Everyone has stuff they want to forget, but it sounds like you're moving forward."

"For a change, I think I actually might be."

~

After thanking Clay again, Mia left him to his newly brushed horses and drove north to Kat's place to walk Gizmo. When she arrived, Kat looked sort of wrung out. It was possible she was hung over, given the amount of wine that had been flowing the night before.

Whatever was wrong with her, she certainly wasn't chatty. But it was okay. Mia was used to people not wanting to talk to her. The weather was still nice and the walk through the forest was beautiful. Gizmo was thriving in the environment and Mia felt a little bad that soon she was going to subject him to countless hours cooped up in the RAV4 and tiny Motel 6 rooms again.

She bent to hug him goodbye and gave the leash back to Kat. "I hope you feel better."

Kat nodded. "I'm okay. After the last person quit, I still haven't found a dog walker, and today I have to go to the bank to talk about money. I'm really bad with numbers, so it will be stressful. But it will be over soon and then I can return to words again."

Mia paused and stretched out her arms. "You look like you could use a hug."

Kat hugged her. "Thanks."

After they said their goodbyes, Mia drove to the Enchanted Moose to meet Chris. She couldn't wait to tell him what she'd learned. When she was parking the car, her stomach growled loudly. Before they did anything else, she wanted lunch. She walked to room one fifty-six and knocked on the door. Small-dog yapping came from within, voicing the alarm.

Chris opened the door with Lulu cradled in his arms. "Come on in."

Although the room was less of a soggy disaster than it had been during the Great Poodle Washing Event, Chris was definitely not a neatnik. Papers were strewn everywhere and a laptop sat on the desk. Mia shoved some papers away from the edge of the bed and sat down. "Are you ready to go? I'm starving."

"Do you want to grab some food at the diner here before we head out?" He nodded at the dog in his arms. "If so, I need to put her in her bed for a lunchtime snooze. Then she'll be ready for the afternoon's activities."

"While we eat I can tell you what I learned at the ranch." She rummaged around in her bag and pulled out a postcard.

After stowing Lulu, Chris turned around and took the card Mia held out to him. "That's a pretty waterfall."

"I was thinking of going there later today. But then I thought maybe I should save it for another day. Gizmo would really love that kind of hike. I think Kat would be okay with me taking him for the afternoon, but today she didn't seem to be in a good mood, so I didn't ask."

"Maybe some other time then?"

"We'll see." She took his hand, dragging him toward the door. "Right now, the first thing I need is food."

They walked across the parking lot to the diner and settled into the same booth where they'd eaten before.

The same surly waitress was also there, but Mia ordered without mixing up any words, so she felt less uncomfortable this time.

Chris leaned toward her, across the table. "So what did you learn from the guy who supposedly looks like Indiana Jones? Does he really look like Harrison Ford? I'm not sure I'm buying it."

"Kind of, I guess. He's definitely got the same hat. Actually, Clay was really nice to me and let me brush one of his horses, which I've never done before. It might be fun to learn to ride someday."

"Did he know your dad?" Chris plucked a green crayon out of the mug and began drawing a horse with a flowing mane and tail.

"No. But he did know someone named Colleen Abbott. She works at the DMV. I guess she's married now, so her last name is Fisher, but back then she was CA."

"Does she have kids?"

"Clay seemed to think so. But assuming she had kids after she got married, wouldn't her initials be CF?"

"Maybe she has more than one kid." Chris paused in his sketching and pointed the crayon at her. "You were thinking they might be your dad's kids."

"I guess so. The only way to find out would be to ask. I hate that idea. I mean, walking up to someone at the DMV? Even Clay said she was grouchy, and he's pretty mellow."

"You sound like you're into this guy." Chris grabbed a red crayon and drew an elaborate heart on the placemat.

"He's Brigid's boyfriend, remember? Speaking of which, how's Donna?"

"Actually, I decided to call her again." Chris made a slash through the heart. "*That* was an even bigger mistake than the first call. But I do know we broke up for sure now."

"What happened? Yesterday you were talking about design."

"Well, I kept thinking about the fact that I told you I didn't even want to talk to my own girlfriend. That seemed unfair to her."

Mia held up her thumb and index finger an inch apart. "And maybe an indicator of an itty-bitty problem."

"Yeah, that too. But I thought maybe because I was so ashamed of being an idiot, I wasn't as truthful as I could have been. I didn't give her the chance to listen or offer suggestions like I did with you. So I decided to call her and see what she said when I laid everything out and was totally honest and up-front about everything. She's an incredibly smart woman, after all."

"No doubt. But I'm guessing that if you say you broke up, it didn't go well." Mia took a crayon and drew a skull and crossbones. "What on earth did you say to her?"

"Pretty much the same stuff I told you. I've got a credit card problem that's out of control to the point that I'm dodging calls from the Visa and MasterCard people."

"What did she say?"

"I guess she knew I was having financial problems because I wouldn't...or really couldn't...pay for our dinners out or much of anything else for a long time. But when I laid out the whole story, she started calling me a bunch of names. It all boiled down to the fact that I am even more of a loser than she thought I was and she never wants to see me again."

"Wow." Mia drew a bomb exploding into fiery oblivion. "That's rough."

"At least she didn't cry this time."

"Still, that must have been hard to deal with. You seem remarkably okay, considering what happened. Better than yesterday, that's for sure. You don't smell like an ashtray, either."

"Okay, while I'm being all honest, get ready, because this will sound really awful." Chris added a rider to his horse drawing. "I'm so *incredibly* relieved! It's like this great weight has been lifted off my shoulders. I don't have to feel guilty for never calling her again."

"I guess when she was calling you names, she didn't have any suggestions for getting out of debt, huh?"

"She was way too busy being mad. I don't suppose you have any ideas, do you?"

Mia grabbed the green crayon from him. "Actually yes, I do. Last night, meeting all those people made me anxious. It was too many humans for me to handle at once. After I got back to the H12, I had trouble winding down. While I was trying to sleep I thought about your debt situation."

He wiggled his eyebrows. "So you were lying in bed thinking about me?"

"Give me a break. You're on the rebound." Mia rolled her eyes melodramatically. "Returning to the point, the big problem with credit card debt is getting out from under all the interest. If you don't pay down the principal, you end up paying interest to the credit card companies until you die."

"That's true. I've been paying minimums for a long time."

"Sometimes credit cards offer zero-percent balance transfers to get you on board. Once they hook you, then they jack up the rates."

"That's the last thing I need."

"Before your credit rating goes completely into the toilet, find a card with a promo offering that lasts a really long time at zero percent. Go for one that gives you zero percent for more than a year or something." Mia drew a dollar sign and an arrow. "Then transfer your debt balances to it. Once you've done that, lower your overhead as much as possible, so you can pay off the balance during the zero-percent period."

"How would I lower overhead?"

"Ditch the car, move to a cheaper place, stop eating out, don't buy anything other than basic necessities like food, and dump anything that has a monthly fee like cable TV. Put every cent you make into paying off the debt."

"Ouch."

"Hey, you're the one who wanted to know." Mia raised her palms toward the ceiling. "I told you, I'm the Queen of Spartan Living over here."

"My life would be completely dreary. I would have no fun at all. That's way too bleak." Chris drew a frowning person with shoulders slumped.

The waitress brought their sandwiches and Mia dug in. People hated ideas that involved any type of personal austerity. To her, it was obvious that paying off debt wasn't as much fun as accruing debt. She'd done it many times herself, even with a meager income.

Chris was obviously annoyed now. Mia finally had a friend and she'd managed to piss him off after only a couple of days. Apparently, she was way out of practice on the whole friendship thing. Why hadn't she just kept her mouth shut?

He looked up from his sandwich. "So do you want to talk to the grumpy lady at the DMV today?"

"Are you crazy? For one thing, it's the DMV. Have you ever been to any department of motor vehicles that did not have a line out the door? And assuming I actually ever get to the front of the line, she'll think I'm a moron."

"Why? You're just asking if she knows your dad. Or knew him way back when."

"I'll probably say it in some bizarre way and she'll bite my head off. I don't need that."

"You worry way too much about that." He shook his head. "Honestly, I keep telling you, it's no big deal."

Mia frowned. "That's almost exactly what Clay said."

"Listen to Indiana Jones then. Maybe he's right."

∽

Mia parked the RAV in front of a brick building that had Department of Motor Vehicles emblazoned in gold letters across the large plate-glass window. There was no one else around, although she could see an older man was standing and waving his arms at the woman on the other side of the counter.

Mia turned to Chris, "I'm not sure I want to do this."

"Oh come on, there's hardly anyone here. All your worries about lines out the door were for nothing."

"I suppose."

"The last time I had to go to the DMV I waited for three hours. At least you know that won't happen here. Score one for small-town living. I'll hang out here with Lulu."

"All right. I'm going." Mia got out of the RAV and went inside. The man was clutching a grubby baseball hat in his hands. The hat had probably been blaze orange once, but it had obviously spent too much time on his bald head in between cleanings, so it was mostly brown.

He made a slurping noise and said, "Listen here Miz Fisher, I need to get my truck registered."

The woman had short brown hair that had been pulled back severely from her face with two barrettes, one on either side of her head. The hairstyle looked painful. She leaned forward across the counter. "Bud, if you spit that on my floor, I'm going to get my forty-five out from under this counter and blow your sorry head off."

"I know you're lying."

"But you can't be sure now, can you?"

Mia slunk over to the row of chairs in front of the window and looked over her shoulder at Chris, who gave her an encouraging smile and held up Lulu's paw as a show of support. She silently mouthed, "Help me!" He waved both his hands in a sweeping gesture to indicate she should go up to the counter.

With a sigh, she stood up and stood behind the man. Might as well get in line. His beat-up denim overalls were almost as filthy as his hat and the scent of diesel surrounded him like a cloud. Maybe he was a mechanic.

Bud said, "Colleen, you know who I am. What is your problem?"

Mia clasped her hands in front of her. If nothing else, she had found Colleen Fisher. Given the low population of Alpine Grove, maybe the DMV only *had* one employee.

Colleen leaned over and stretched an arm across the counter to point at Mia. "You! Take a number and sit down."

Mia turned her head to look around the room. Where were you supposed to get a number? "I, uh, just have a little depression."

"What? Listen, I don't have time to discuss your mental health. Just take a number," Colleen said.

"*Question*, I mean I have a question," Mia said. Now Bud was staring at her too.

"So if I have some type of medical situation, can I git my goddam registration?" Bud said.

"I don't have a medical problem. I have a question!" Mia said.

Colleen shook her finger at Mia. "I told you. Take a number and sit down. Don't make me throw you out of here."

"Where are the cucumbers? *Numbers*! I mean numbers." Mia's shoulders slumped. This was getting her nowhere.

Colleen pointed toward the back of the room. "On the wall."

Mia looked and finally spotted the red number dispenser hiding behind a brochure stand.

"Now go sit down." Colleen turned back to Bud. "Bud, I need you to bring me the old registration. And proof you own the vehicle."

"Well, that might be a challenging proposition." He slurped to emphasize the point. "See my truck, well, I went hunting and there was a little accident and then I had to fix it."

Colleen put up both palms in front of herself. "Bud, I don't want to hear this again. You're repeating yourself and the story was boring the first time."

"But the cop pulled me over because I don't have my license plate. I need to fix this. I gotta dee-spoze of some, uh, something at the dump." He slapped his hat on the counter. "What am I a-sposed to do?"

"I told you, you have to pay the penalty for late registration, pay all your parking tickets, the maintenance fines, and then we'll talk," Colleen said.

"It's just a little electrical problem with my taillight. I can't track that bugger down," Bud said.

"You told me that, but I need the paperwork. Go find it and get out," Colleen said.

Mia sat up straighter. The Bud drama might be winding down. She looked at the number in her hand. Two forty-seven. The display said Colleen was happily serving number one fifty. What? Were ninety-seven people hiding somewhere she didn't know about?

Bud grabbed his hat from the counter and stomped toward the door. If he spit his chaw on her car on his way out, Mia was going to be so grossed out. With any luck, the fact that Chris was sitting in the car would keep him from spewing too close to the RAV. Yuck.

She looked at Colleen, who was hunched over, busily writing something at the counter. No one else was here. Mia raised her hand, "Excuse me?"

Colleen looked up. "Yes."

"My number is two forty-seven."

Colleen looked over her shoulder at the number display. "Oh jeez." She walked over and fiddled with some buttons until the display showed two forty-eight.

Mia stood up and held out her number. "I'm two forty-seven."

"Close enough. I'm not pressing that button two hundred forty-seven times to get it to go around again. But make it fast before someone comes in and pulls two forty-eight." Colleen rested her elbows on the table and glared at Mia. "What's your question?"

"I, uh, was wondering if you knew someone named Dan Riggins."

"No."

"Are you sure? He might have been in Alpine Grove around 1975."

"Why are you asking about someone who was here twenty years ago?"

"Well, um, he's my father and I've lost touch." At the woman's intense gaze, Mia wanted to slither under the counter and curl up into a fetal position.

"How is this my problem? You're sitting here wasting my time with some little personal genealogy project? Can't you see I'm working? It's against policy to be talking about personal business during working hours."

"I just thought...well, I got postcards that were signed with the initials C.A. and...um, someone told me your last name used to be Abbott."

"It was. Who is gossiping with you about me? They have a lot of nerve."

Mia shook her head. "No, it wasn't gossip. I'm just trying to find my father and this "CA" person."

"Well, it's not me." Colleen made a shooing motion with both hands. "Get out. I have work to do."

"Okay. Thank you." Mia practically ran out the door. Why did she thank that woman? She couldn't possibly have been any less helpful.

She got into the driver side of the RAV and looked at Chris. "That was horrible."

"What happened?" He stroked Lulu's head. "Did she know your dad?"

"Not at all. This is all completely ridiculous. I have no idea what I'm looking for. I'm wasting time and money on something I don't even understand." She put the car in neutral and turned the key in the ignition.

Chris put his hand over hers on the gear shift. "Let's go see that waterfall. That might make you feel better."

"All right. I should enjoy one last day here. Then I've got to move on. It's way past time for me to get out of Alpine Grove."

Chris pointed at the street. "The map says that to get to the trailhead for Lilly Falls we need to go that way. Turn left."

"Thanks. Let's get out of here."

～

Chris was quiet on the drive to the waterfall trail. Maybe he knew that Mia was annoyed and didn't feel like talking. That was considerate of him, since she did have a strong urge to sulk for a while. She turned on the radio, which had been tuned to the one local station that came in with any reliability. The Eagles began crooning about the Hotel California. Even if you could never leave, it was still probably nicer than the H12.

She parked the car in a small lot and they got out. No one else was around and the only sounds were squirrels scurrying about and the occasional bird calling to avian friends. Chris put Lulu on the ground and she snuffled some fallen leaves, obviously enjoying the earthy scents of fall.

A wooden sign next to the trail said "Lilly Falls" with an arrow pointing up the hill, so they were in the right place. They began walking up the well-trodden path, and after a few minutes of wandering through the pine forest, Lulu stopped abruptly and sat down. Mia looked at Chris. "Is she okay?"

"This is her way of letting me know she's done, and it's time to carry her." He bent to pick up the dog.

"It's an effective technique."

"Yeah, it works for her." He readjusted the dog in his arms. "Are you done being mad?"

"I'm not mad."

"Yes you are. I bet you're beating yourself up for messing up words when you talked to the DMV lady, aren't you?"

"No I'm not." Yes, she was, but she wasn't telling Chris that.

"So what if she didn't know your dad? I bet someone does. You said Kat knew a bunch of people who have lived in this area for ages."

"I suppose." She turned her head to look at him. "Why are you even interested in this foolish pursuit of my past anyway?"

"I don't know. It's interesting. Hold on for a sec." He stopped and put Lulu back on the ground next to a patch of yellowing bracken fern. "This dog sure gets heavy after a while."

Above them, a gray squirrel noisily scolded, encouraging the intruders to get out of the way so he could resume his fall foraging project.

Chris looked up. "I think Mr. Squirrel is almost as grumpy as you are."

Mia took a deep breath. "I'm not as grumpy as I was before. It smells so good here. Like leaves and pine needles. I'm glad you convinced me to go for this hike, although I wish I'd brought Gizmo. I've never been on a trail like this before and he'd love it. Windiberg isn't exactly known for its scenic beauty."

"No kidding."

They hiked quietly for a while until they reached the overlook for the falls. Chris picked up Lulu again and they stood by the railing gazing down at the stone canyon. A stream of water plunged over the cliff down into the pool below. A light mist floated through the chilly air and the sound of the cascading water echoed throughout the rocky crevasse.

Mia leaned on the railing. "This is amazing. And look, there's a little rainbow down there over near those rocks at the bottom."

"I wish I had a camera."

"We'll just have to remember it." She looked up at the sky. "A picture couldn't capture the sound of the water, the birds singing, and that whispering sound the breeze makes in the pine trees."

Chris bent to put down Lulu again. "I think Lulu needs a little break. And I need to rest my arms for a while. Let's go over there."

They walked away from the overlook to a cleared area that was surrounded by trees. Below the pines, the ground was covered with a blanket of moss. Mia sat down and ran her hand back and forth across the green carpet.

Chris sat down next to her. "I can't believe we're the only people here. Doesn't anyone go hiking anymore?"

"Well, they might be at work."

"Oh yeah. I guess I'm kind of skipping out on that." He leaned back on his elbows. "I could get used to this. Being here seems so far away from my life in San Francisco; it's like a different world."

"I know what you mean. Just a couple of weeks ago, I was living in my trailer doing the same thing that I'd been doing every day for years." Mia rolled onto her side and stroked Lulu's fur. "I fantasized about taking a vacation like this for so long."

"Why didn't you?"

"Are you kidding? I had no money. When you are operating in basic survival mode like I was, it's really hard to dream. Vacations were just fantasies—not something that could really happen."

Chris rolled over to face her. "I didn't realize it was that bad."

"My Spartan Queen title was hard-won." She smiled at him. "I never could get ahead, and pinching pennies only takes you so far."

"I suppose that's true."

"It sounds silly, but I spent so long worrying about all the things I needed to do just to keep a roof over my head, I have no idea what I actually like or want anymore. That's what this trip is about."

"So you came to Alpine Grove to find yourself?"

"Well, not Alpine Grove specifically. Now that I've been on the road for a while, I'm discovering that figuring out the rest of my life might take longer than I thought." She sat up and put her hands around her knees. "I can't float like this forever though."

Chris sat up. "Floating sounds good. I'd like to float for a while."

"Aren't you?"

"Hey, I'm working! Okay, maybe not right this second. But I'm supposed to be here for work."

"What happens after that? When you're done with this project, are you going to go back to your job and what you were doing?"

He shrugged. "I don't really have much choice. I've been doing the site visits and working with the developer on the preliminary designs. But I need to go back to the office to do the final design development and construction documents. I'll have to return to my regular life again."

"I'm sorry I suggested you make your life dreary before to pay off your debt. I didn't mean to upset you."

"It's okay. I think I was just annoyed that you were right. Transferring balances and lowering overhead makes sense."

"Getting out of debt is no fun. I had a long-standing payment plan with my veterinarian, thanks to Gizmo." Mia sighed. "After the last episode, I ended up in the hole with the emergency clinic too."

"But then you got money." He turned to look at her. "How?"

"It's a long story." Mia pulled her feet under her and moved to get up. "Maybe we should get going. I need to get back to the H12, pack up my stuff, and call Kat."

Chris stood up and Lulu stretched deeply. She walked a few steps and looked up at the humans expectantly.

Mia walked back to the railing and gazed down at the waterfall. It was so beautiful, she hated to leave. Chris walked up next to her, trailed by Lulu. "Are you really leaving tomorrow?"

She turned to face him. "I need to go to the post office and pick up my mail, but after that, there's no reason to stay. The whole thing with the postcards was a little crazy. I never do stuff like that, and I should get back to figuring out where I'm going to live and what I'm going to do."

Chris slid his hand up the side of her neck and cupped her chin with his palm. "Please don't leave yet."

Trying to ignore the shimmery thrill from his soft fingertips on her cheek, she looked up into his eyes. "Why?"

"I don't want to say goodbye to you." He met her gaze, leaned forward, and kissed her slowly and deliberately, focusing all of his attention on her.

It was so startling to discover he wanted her, for a moment it was as if time stopped. And then every one of Mia's nerve endings woke up after an extremely long slumber and she was bombarded with sensation. She threw her arms around Chris's neck and returned the kiss with frenzied abandon.

Chris wrapped his arms around her, the fist holding Lulu's leash digging into her back. Mia's blood roared in her ears and finally she let go of him. With a great exhale of breath, she said, "Okay, what just happened there? What are we *doing*?"

"I'm not sure, but it was fantastic." He grinned. "I think you vaporized a few of my brain cells."

Mia giggled, pulled him back to her, and kissed his neck. "No kidding. But this is really stupid. I'm homeless and you're leaving in a few days."

"We could have a *very good* few days though." He pushed a tousled lock of auburn hair behind her ear. "I meant what I said. Please don't leave yet."

"I have to pick up my mail tomorrow, but maybe I could stay a little longer. It's not like I'm on some type of rigid schedule."

"I've heard that the people who work at the Alpine Grove post office aren't very speedy. It might take some time to get your mail." He bent to whisper in her ear as he ran a fingertip down her neck and traced her collarbone. "Agonizingly slow, like warm honey oozing ever so slowly over your body."

Attempting to ignore the heat coursing through various parts of her anatomy, she leaned back to look at him. "I thought we were friends."

"We are." He moved put his arm around her again. "But you never know. Maybe we could be more than friends. I could be the friend you fall hopelessly in love with. The person you finally let in and share all your secrets with. I'd like to be that kind of friend."

"I've never had a friend like that."

"I guess I haven't either. But I'd like to, and I think it could happen with you. I like how I feel when we're together. It's like I've known you forever. And even though I've told you about my worst mistakes, instead of just writing me off as a loser, you give me ideas for fixing them."

Mia smiled. "Well, we mushroom girls are a rare breed, you know."

"So it seems."

Chapter 7

Fans and Mail

Mia was quiet on the drive back to Alpine Grove. She shouldn't make a big deal out of just one kiss, but Chris obviously had far more feelings for her than she'd expected. And her response to him was unprecedented. She'd practically jumped on top of the guy. What was wrong with her? It had been a long time, but still.

Chris had just broken up with the infamous Donna and had said more than once that he was lonely. To a guy, even the weird mushroom woman probably looks good when you haven't gotten any action for a while. Men were sort of predictable that way.

Mia's history with the male of the species hadn't been particularly satisfying, so there was no reason to believe that anything with Chris would work out well. The death of her mother and Howard had happened the day she graduated from high school, and led to what Mia thought of now as her slutty phase.

On graduation day, before she found out what had happened, she had been furious. It was just like her mother to flake out. Her high school graduation should be a big deal, and yet her undependable mother missed it. Just like she always missed everything else. After getting her diploma, Mia had returned home, ready to read her mother the riot act for not showing *again*. But when she arrived at the house, flashing lights and police tape had been everywhere. All Mia remembered was being hustled off to the station to make a statement.

After that, it was like Mia's brain checked out for a while. She didn't know what to do once she was completely, utterly alone. Her life had turned into some horrible country song and maybe to continue the theme, she began looking for love in all the wrong places. If you wanted to pick up a random guy in Windiberg, it wasn't difficult. Certain bars were known to serve minors, and in the dim light no one seemed to care that the creepy mushroom girl who talked funny was mooching free drinks from the guys at the pool tables.

In the seedy ambiance of the bars, Mia sought out any human touch to fill the void left in her life. She didn't worry about mixing up words because usually she was too drunk to care. A string of sloppy one-night stands mostly left her depressed, and even worse, reality began to intrude. Because of her mother's mental-health issues and Howard's slacker, freeloading nature, they were behind on the rent on the house. Way behind. Everything they'd had was sold or taken away to pay off their debts and burial expenses.

Mia had been left with nothing. Absolute ground zero. Although she'd accomplished her mission of finally losing her virginity, she'd also amply proven to herself that sex didn't fix much of anything. She'd had to get over everything that had happened and start being an adult. That was when the revolving door of employment failures began.

Chris put his hand on her thigh, startling her from her grim recollections. He gave her a half-smile. "Are you okay?"

"I'm fine. Why do you ask?"

"You have an odd look on your face, that's all."

"I was thinking that you don't know me very well." She gestured toward the road ahead. "I mean, there are *so* many things you don't know."

"I'd like to know."

"But why?" Mia pulled into the Enchanted Moose and drove around back. "Honestly, I don't understand why you're interested."

After she shut off the car, he took her hand. "Why wouldn't I be interested? You're funny and smart and beautiful."

"Oh please, I have looked in the mirror, you know."

"Maybe you don't see yourself that way, but I'm serious."

"I don't know what to say."

"How about saying you'll have dinner with me again? After that hike, I'm hungry. And I've still got today's perdiem meal allowance to burn."

Mia grinned at his hopeful expression. "Well, we can't let those lovely expense-account funds go to waste, can we?"

"No way."

Mia spent much of dinner laughing and commenting on caricatures Chris created of their classmates from high school. By the time they were having dessert, the placemats looked like an eighties rogues' gallery.

She took a bite of ice cream. "Except for the nasty woman at the DMV, this has been a great day. Thanks for feeding me again."

"I'm sure the number crunchers at Gilbert, Tingler, Halberstam, and Associates Architecture will get over it."

"That's a mouthful. I'm glad I don't have to answer the phone there."

"We usually call it GTH, which helps."

"Goth? Good thing they didn't hire me in my Elvira days. People would talk."

Chris laughed. "So do you want me to go with you to talk to the gift-store lady tomorrow?"

"That would be great. After the mean DMV woman, I'm traumatized."

Chris paid the check and they walked across the parking lot toward her car and his room. He gestured toward the door. "Do you want to come in for a minute? Lulu probably wants out."

Mia shook her head. "I should go."

"I wanted to show you the drawings of the house. I've been staring at it so long, I'm losing perspective on it, and I'm curious what you think."

"I don't know anything about architecture."

"That doesn't matter." He walked toward room one fifty-six holding the key toward the door. "Please? It won't take long. I have a meeting bright and early tomorrow with the developer and I'm worried it might be terrible."

"All right. But I don't know how much help I'll be. I've been living in a tin can for years. All you have to do is include normal-sized windows and I'll think it's great."

"Cool. You can bolster my confidence then." He opened the door and held it open for her. Lulu barked a few times in welcome.

Chris crouched next to the crate and opened the door. Lulu charged out into the room and stopped in front of Mia, who bent to pet her. "Don't look at me. He's the one who feeds you."

"The drawings are over there on the desk." He went to the tiny kitchenette area, dispensed some dog food for Lulu, and placed the bowl on the floor.

Mia stood in front of the desk. It was covered with sheets of vellum, rolls of tracing paper, a calculator, tape measures, white rulers, and what appeared to be thousands of pens, pencils, and notes. She wasn't sure what she was supposed to be looking at exactly. "I'm afraid I might cause an avalanche."

"Sorry about that. My work junk gets out of control." He held up two of the triangular white rulers. "I think the architectural and engineering scales I brought are starting to reproduce in here."

"At least I know you weren't fibbing about having a job."

"No one would cart around this much stuff if they didn't have to." He pulled out a few sheets of vellum from the stack and laid them on one of the beds. "These are the preliminaries of the exterior and the floor plan."

Mia bent to look. "Wow, this is going to be a big house, isn't it?"

"As I may have mentioned, the guy is loaded."

"You were right about the windows looking out at the lake. That's going to be beautiful. I think you could fit my entire Airstream in that living room."

"It's going to be huge. If it were my lot, I would make the house smaller, but it's not my decision."

"I think this will be gorgeous." Mia sat on the corner of the bed. "But I'm curious what you would do instead, if it were your house?"

He turned and grabbed a sketchpad off the desk and handed it to her. "I have a thousand ideas. When I'm stuck creatively, I goof around with ideas for imaginary houses."

Mia flipped through the pages and looked up at him. "I want to live in one of these. They're more like a real home, where you could have a dog. The lake house is beautiful, but I can't imagine actually living there."

He sat down next to her. "I know. It's nice to know I'm not the only one who feels that way. If you think the lake house is pretty, Ben will probably like it. He wants it to make a *statement*, which translated from developer-speak means he wants it to look expensive, so he can sell it for boatloads of money."

"It works for that." She pointed at the paper. "But if I had that kind of money, I'd want a bigger kitchen. Maybe move it over and ditch that part of the dining room so you could see out to the lake. While I was living in the trailer, when I wasn't fantasizing about vacations, I fantasized about kitchens. The idea of a full-size refrigerator makes me swoon."

He chuckled. "An interior designer would cringe at the idea of removing part of the formal dining room. Where would you put the long mahogany table that seats sixteen?"

"I don't know, but since I can't think of sixteen people I would want to eat with, that's not a problem." She pointed at a house in the sketchpad. "I think this one is my favorite. I could live there."

"I like it too. I went on a mountain-cabin jag after I got here, as you can probably tell."

"The wood and stone is beautiful, and the circular room with the windows is so cool. I'd love to sit and read up there." She pointed at the page. "You're incredibly talented. I hope you're not still thinking of giving up architecture?"

"Not today anyway." He took her hand and leaned over to give her a quick kiss. "Thanks. No one has said anything nice about my work in a long time."

"You must have been hanging out with the wrong crowd. I mean, I'm not an expert, but maybe all you need is a few more fans cheering you on."

"I never thought of it that way, but you're probably right. Everybody could use more fans." He gave her hand a slight squeeze. "Someday you might actually believe the potential I see in you too."

"Maybe." Mia stood up and looked down at their interlaced fingers. "Gizmo has been my only fan for a while. And I suspect he might be thinking about food, not me. In any case, I think I should get back to the H12."

He stood up and put his arms around her. "Do you really have to go?"

"I think staying would be a bad idea. When is your meeting tomorrow?"

"In the morning. Can we meet after that? What's next on the postcard tour?"

"I'll bring a selection and let you pick this time. After we stop by the gift store, we can explore another fabulous scenic location in the greater Alpine Grove area."

"Sounds great." He pulled her closer. "Can I have a goodbye kiss before you go? Because that's all I've been able to think about."

Mia flashed a grin. "I'm glad it's not just me." She put her arms around his neck, pulling him to her, and pressed her lips to his. He responded eagerly, sending thrilling shock waves of pleasure ricocheting throughout her body.

Mia pulled away and put her hand on his chest. This was getting complicated. They were six inches away from two large and inviting beds. "Okay, wow, um, I gotta go. I'm really going now."

Chris put his palm on the back of her neck and bent to give her a final kiss. "I'll see you tomorrow."

Mia put her hand on his and gave it a pat before leaving. "Tomorrow."

~

The next day, Mia enjoyed a relaxing morning of doing absolutely nothing. She was relieved to have some time alone to think before dealing with humanity again. Chris had convinced her to take one last shot at finding her father by talking to the woman at the gift store, since Kat had said that Tracy's mom Bea Sullivan knew "everyone."

If that didn't work, Mia would pick up her mail and give up on the whole finding Dad program. Maybe it just wasn't meant to be. Who really cared if he never found out that she won the lottery anyway? Maybe he hadn't even sent the tickets to her.

All the lethargic reading time she'd had meant she was now officially out of books. While she was in town, she also might check out the used-book store. For the first time in years, Mia didn't have a stack of library books, so she didn't have a ready supply of free reading material. Since she wasn't staying in Alpine Grove, they wouldn't give her a library card, assuming there even was a library lurking in town somewhere.

Fortunately, she'd found a way to get her mail while she was in transition. One advantage of living in a trailer park was that she was exposed to a lot of ads directed to full-time

RVers. By using a mail-forwarding service based in South Dakota, she had a forwarding address to put on the forms when she left Windiberg. Then all she had to do was let the mail-forwarding company know when she was going to be in one place for a little while. They would then send her accumulated mail general delivery to the local post office for her to pick up.

When she gathered her mail at the Alpine Grove post office, she'd undoubtedly find a few final bills for lab work related to her doctor's appointment when she'd gotten her physical. She also was supposed to get a check refunding her security and pet deposits, but it was entirely possible the Edgewood Paradise Estates would think up some way to screw her out of the money. She was also likely to receive countless offers to help her spend her lottery winnings. Being repeatedly hit up for money by everyone she met was something she hadn't missed one little bit.

After getting breakfast at the cafe, Mia walked down the main street to the bookstore. It was a cute little shop called Twice Told Tales, which had a display of books and crafts in the window. As she walked in, the bells on the door jingled. A woman with short, graying curly hair was sitting at an antique desk reading a hardback book. She put down the book and smiled. "Hello. May I help you?"

Mia shook her head. "Just booking. *Looking*. I mean, I'm just *browsing*."

"I like booking. That's appropriate here. My name is Margaret. If you need help finding anything, just let me know."

Mia nodded and settled into perusing the covers of novels by her favorite authors. It was a well-stocked store with books crammed into just about every possible nook and cranny. Margaret mercifully left her alone to her selections, which was wonderful. Mia hated being hounded by people when she was shopping.

She brought a stack of books up to the desk. Margaret smiled as she picked up a novel off the stack. "Oh, you're going to love this. And the best thing is that there are five more in the series."

"It looks grape...*great*."

"He's a local author, and I promised him I'd put the covers face out. He'll be so pleased; it seems to be working." Margaret carefully moved a sheet of carbon paper and wrote up the receipt on a little pad. "Now that he's my son-in-law, I need to keep him happy."

Mia picked up the book and turned it over. "A.J. Emerson is your son-in-law? He's very handsome."

"Oh, that's not Drew. It's a model. But yes, my daughter married him last summer. It was a lovely wedding."

"Congratulations."

Margaret handed her the receipt. "They were high school sweethearts. I'm not much of a romantic anymore, but I think everybody cried at that wedding."

"Oh wait, I heard about this! Your daughter is Beth, right? Kat said everybody cried when they read their vows."

Margaret counted out change and handed it to Mia. "They certainly did. You know Kat?"

"My dog Gizmo is staying at her kennel. That's where I'm going now, actually. She lets me go on their midday walks. I miss Gizmo so much, but the place I'm staying doesn't allow dogs."

"It's beautiful out there and Kat became one of my favorite people when she agreed to board Beth and Drew's puppy while they were on their honeymoon. Thank heavens. I'm too old to deal with a puppy." She handed Mia the bag of books. "Enjoy!"

Mia thanked her and was about to leave. "I have a sort of odd question. Have you lived here for a while?"

"Yes, I raised my daughter here."

"I don't suppose you ever met anyone named Dan Riggins, did you? He might have been through around 1975."

"The name doesn't sound familiar, but I was going through some issues of my own at the time."

Mia moved her hand dismissively. "I'm sorry to bother you—never mind."

"If you're looking for someone, keep asking, dear. This is Alpine Grove. Eventually you will find someone who knows him."

"I hope you're right. Thank you again."

Mia walked back to the H12 to drop off her books before driving out to Kat's to walk Gizmo. She riffled through the stack of postcards and pulled out a few of the more scenic ones for Chris to consider later.

She smiled at the idea of seeing him later. A little twinge of excitement skittered in her chest at the thought of kissing him again. No one had ever made her feel like that—all those little butterflies of anticipation twirling around her insides indicated they really had some serious chemistry going.

Intellectually, she knew that he was on the rebound from being dumped. But it was only a matter of time before she wouldn't be able to restrain the impulse to kiss those thrilling lips and then leap into bed with him afterward. She gazed down at the dingy plaid bedspread in her room. So many available motel rooms and so little control. But they were two consenting adults now, not the geeky, awkward teenagers they were in high school. Maybe she'd stop by the drug store on her way out of town. Just in case.

When Mia got to the kennel, Kat seemed to be in a better mood than she had been the day before. Gizmo was all leashed up and ready to roll. Mia took the leash from Kat. "So I was wondering if it would be okay if I took Gizmo for a hike…I mean a hike somewhere else. And then brought him back here."

Kat smiled. "Of course. He's your dog."

"I mean, I'm not going to steal him and run out on my boarding fee or anything."

"I didn't think you would."

"Okay, so I can just take him?"

"Sure." She pointed at the sign next to the door. "If you could bring him back during the pick-up and drop-off hours, it would make my life easier."

"I will. Thanks!" She bent down to cuddle Gizmo. "You ready to go for a hike with me and Chris?"

Gizmo wagged happily and circled around, reveling in the attention.

Kat said, "So it sounds like Chris is still in town. How's Lulu doing?"

Mia stood up again. "They're both fine. We went for a hike yesterday and I wished I'd thought to bring Gizmo. He would have loved it."

"I see. Well, I'm sure you'll have a great time today." Kat gestured toward the road. "They're saying the weather is supposed to turn, so you should take advantage of the sun before it goes away. Sometimes when it leaves, it stays gone for a while."

Mia loaded Gizmo into the RAV and waved goodbye to Kat, who was walking back to the house. Gizmo was wandering back and forth across the backseats, eagerly anticipating whatever was next. It was a good thing he was such an enthusiastic traveler. Mia smiled at his reflection in the rearview mirror.

At the Enchanted Moose, she parked in front of room one fifty-six and told Gizmo to behave himself while she went to collect Chris and Lulu.

Mia knocked and when Chris opened the door, they just stared at each other for a moment. Then she reached up, moved her hands behind his head, and pulled him toward her. Her lips moved against his and it became obvious he'd spent as much time thinking about kissing her as she had about kissing him. He walked backward, pulling her into the room with him toward the bed, and flopped down so that she landed on top of him.

A few moments later, Lulu yipped from her crate, and Mia raised her head. "Gizmo is in the car. We need to stop before he eats his way through the interior."

Chris gave her one last kiss before releasing his hold on her and letting her roll off him. He sat up and looked around the room. "We didn't even close the door. Just give me a second to compose myself and think about something not sexy."

"Work, cubicles, your boss, deadlines."

"Okay, you can stop. That's plenty. I have to say, you sure know how to make an entrance."

"I guess I'm glad to see you."

"Me too." He pressed his palm lightly against the side of her face and traced a fingertip across her jaw. "Really glad."

~

Mia drove toward town while Chris looked through the postcards. He held one up. "This one with the massive rock jutting out over the water is amazing, but it doesn't say where it is."

"I know. Obviously, it's on the lake somewhere, but I don't know where. I was hoping maybe you'd seen it."

"Nope. I'd remember that. If you find out where it is, I want to go there."

Mia glanced at him. "What's your second choice?"

"This one says it's a park, so we should be able to find it." He pulled out the map. "It's off Farm-to-Market Road."

"Okay, after we talk to the gift-store lady, we'll go there." Mia looked in the rearview mirror. Gizmo was standing at the window with a contemplative expression, watching the scenery go by. She couldn't see Lulu because she was so small, but she was undoubtedly back there somewhere.

Chris reached over toward the driver's seat and Mia moved her head. "Don't distract the driver."

"I'm not, although I'd like to." He rubbed the upholstery. "I think your dog may have taken a nibble here. Sorry about that."

"It might not have been today. I've had to leave him while I ran inside to check into motels. There are a few little tooth marks. I'm trying not to think about it. I should buy some seat covers to slow him down."

Chris laughed. "Better get those extra-thick sheepskin ones. Or better yet, if they make Kevlar ones, that would work."

"Maybe being bulletproof would make them Gizmo-proof."

"Couldn't hurt."

Mia went through some side streets to turn around, so she could nab a parking spot right in front of the gift store. She parallel-parked and turned to Chris. "I didn't plan this out very well. With two dogs in the car, I guess you can't go in with me."

"Someone has to guard the RAV from destruction. If you like your car, you're on your own."

"Oh well. If this person is like everyone else, it won't take long. I mention Dad, they look at me like I'm some kind of crackpot, and I move on."

Chris put his hand on her thigh. "Don't be nervous. It will be fine. You're just asking a question."

"Yeah, yeah. Wish me luck."

He leaned over and gave her a kiss. "Good luck."

Mia got out of the car and walked across the sidewalk to Bea Haven Gifts. The window display was full of cute knickknacks and shiny baubles. People who lived in spaces larger than motel rooms or travel trailers probably loved buying stuff at this place.

An older woman with streaked blonde and gray hair was standing behind the counter laughing with a tall thin man wearing glasses. He took them off and rubbed the bridge of his nose. They both turned as Mia walked up.

The woman said, "May I help you?"

"I'm looking for Bea," Mia said.

"Well, you've found her." Bea gestured toward the man. "And this is Rob. He lives upstairs with my daughter."

Mia was relieved she'd found the right person. "Yes, Tracy! I met her the other night. You're the baby…father… boyfriend. I mean *boyfriend.*"

Both Bea and Rob stared at her in silence. Bea looked confused and Rob looked concerned.

Mia closed her eyes for a second and took a deep breath. No one in their right mind should ever tell her secrets they didn't want revealed. "I'm sorry. It's just I have a problem with mixing up words."

"That's fine. What can I help you with?" Bea said.

"I saw Tracy and Kat the other night and they mentioned that you've lived in Alpine Grove for a long time."

Bea smiled. "A very long time. Why do you ask?"

"I'm hoping you might have met someone around 1975. Or earlier. I'm not really sure. His name is Dan Riggins."

Bea leaned forward and rested her elbows on the counter. "Hmm, I'm not sure. Do you know if he was at the commune?"

"Tracy said something about being at a commune. Where is it?" Mia glanced at Rob, who smiled but didn't add anything.

"Well, the land is still there, but the commune disbanded a long time ago," Bea said. "Many people came and went during the late sixties and seventies. It's hard to remember their names. But I think Domingo's name might have been Dan."

"Domingo?"

"Sunday in Spanish. That's when he arrived. Gardenia used to call him *Domingo soleado* because it was a sunny Sunday when he helped her move." Bea stood up straight. "Good heavens, that was a long time ago. I feel old."

"Have you seen Domingo recently?" Mia said. This was the closest she'd gotten to anyone actually having heard of her father.

"Oh no, not for years. If anyone would know, it would be Gardenia. Although her name is Gwen now. She lives out near Abigail Goodman's place."

"She changed her name to Gwen?" Mia was getting thoroughly lost. "Who is Abigail Goodman?"

Rob said, "It helps to know that at the commune, people had different names."

Bea nodded. "I'm sorry; this must all be terribly confusing. Abigail died more than a year ago. It sounds like you already know Kat, who owns the boarding kennel. Abigail was her aunt and Kat inherited the house. Gwen lives next door, although I hear she wants to leave before winter, to move closer to her daughter. I don't know if she was successful in selling the place or not."

"Do you have her number?"

"I'm sure she's in the book. Her last name is Davis."

"Thank you! This is so helpful." Mia said.

"Why are you trying to find this person?" Rob asked.

"Dan Riggins is my father. I think he sent me some postcards. I haven't seen him for years and well..." Mia paused at their mystified looks. "It's a long story. Anyway, I appreciate your help."

"My pleasure. If you find him, tell him to stop by the store and say hello. It's fun seeing people from the old days again." Bea said.

Mia left the store, walked around the RAV, and got in. Chris looked up from the postcard he was studying. "I'm still curious about the babies "CA" keeps talking about."

"Me too, but I have news." Mia snatched the postcard from his hands, leaned over, and gave him a kiss. "I actually made progress. Bea may have met my dad."

"Really? That's great! What did you learn?"

Mia explained what she'd learned about Domingo and Gardenia while she drove to the Alpine Grove post office. She parked in the lot and turned to Chris. "Sorry you have to watch dogs again."

He pointed at the line that had threaded outside the lobby and into the area where the post office boxes were located. "This might take a while."

"Ugh." Mia leaned over and reached for the glove compartment. "I don't have anything to read other than the RAV manual, but here's a pad of paper and a pencil. Sorry about the Gizmo tooth marks, but I bet you can amuse yourself."

He grinned as he took the items from her. "It's so cool that you get that about me."

Mia went inside and took her place at the end of the line. She gazed at the posters advertising pretty collectors' stamps and tried not be too obvious about eavesdropping on the many conversations taking place around her. There was a lot of chatter. Apparently, if you wanted to find out what was going on in Alpine Grove, the post office was the place to be.

A tall woman with sandy blonde hair was chatting with another woman. She had a somewhat loud voice and Mia caught the name Joel. Maybe that was the same person Kat was living with she'd met the other day.

The woman proclaimed, "Joel drives me nuts. I mean he's marrying that woman. You'd think they'd have some type of plan by now. He never tells me anything."

Mia couldn't hear what the other woman said, but the blonde bore a striking resemblance to Joel. Maybe it was his sister. From what she was saying, it sounded like she was angry with him.

As the woman continued to rant, Mia was even more pleased than usual that she was an only child. Adding a sibling into her already hugely screwed-up family situation would have not helped matters.

While she waited in line, Mia learned that the sole employee of the Alpine Grove post office was named Ethel and her rheumatism was starting to act up. That was slowing down progress even more than usual because the cold of fall was hard on her joints.

By the time Mia made it to the front of the line, she knew far more about Ethel's health than she wanted to know.

Ethel shouted, "Next!" and Mia scuttled up to the counter.

"May I help you?"

"I need to pick up General Delivery mail for Amelia Riggins."

Ethel turned and disappeared behind a wall that divided the lobby from the sorting area. A collective sigh ran through the line. Whenever Ethel went into the back, it could take a while for her to resurface. Mia turned to look at the many eyes glaring at her. "Sorry."

Ethel finally hobbled back to the counter with a stack of mail in her arms. She plopped the pile on the counter. "Here you go."

Mia collected her mail and left, amid grumblings. The consensus in the line was that she should take care of things like that earlier in the day. Sheesh, how was she supposed to know?

She returned to the car and deposited the pile of mail in Chris's lap. "I'm so sorry that took forever. The lady who works there moves like a turtle on Quaaludes."

Chris held up ten sheets of paper in his hands, fanned out like playing cards. "I'm creating an Alpine Grove montage."

Mia pointed at one of the drawings. "I think that one is Joel's sister. She doesn't like him much, but she likes Kat even less."

"Wow, you really got the local gossip."

"I didn't have much choice." She started the car. "Let's go find that park."

～

While Mia drove out to Farm-to-Market road, Chris thumbed through the stack of mail. "You got a lot of junk."

"Probably bills too. I'm expecting some final bills from Windiberg. Oh, and maybe my security deposit, assuming they really give it to me."

"Mostly, it's stuff from financial people. Tax people." He flipped through envelopes and cards. "Estate planning. Insurance. A lot of people want to help you with money stuff."

"Yeah, that's not a surprise."

He paused in his perusal. "Lottery annuities? The *lottery*? Oh my God, you won the lottery, didn't you? You actually won the lottery? Is *that* how you have money all of a sudden?"

"You got it." Mia sighed. It was pointless to try to keep it a secret anymore. "Please don't tell anyone. Every sleazy person comes out of the woodwork when they hear about it. Given the gossip parade at the post office, I can't imagine what would happen if anyone in Alpine Grove found out. The entire town would know within a half an hour."

"I'm floored. I can't believe this. *No one* wins the lottery. You've got a better chance at being struck by lightning."

"Believe me, no one was more surprised than I was. Let's face it, my life hasn't been chock full of a whole lot of good luck. The lottery tickets came with the postcards."

"No wonder you want to find out more about them." Chris resumed riffling through the mail. "Hey, this is a regular letter. I think it's from your dad. The return address says Dan Riggins."

Mia quickly took her eyes off the road to glance at the envelope. "Whatever you do, keep it away from Gizmo. He ate the return address last time."

Chris looked over the seat at the dogs in the back. "The Great Paper Eater is busy sniffing the air, so I think the letter is safe. When we get to the trail, could you open it? I'm dying of curiosity over here."

Mia grinned. "You better believe it. After talking to all these people, I want some answers. Maybe Dad will give me some clue about what's going on. I think we're getting pretty close to the park. It should be up ahead a little ways."

They turned off into a parking lot for Cedar County War Memorial Park. A bronze statue on a stone pedestal with a plaque below it sat in the middle of a large grassy area.

Chris handed her the letter. "It's pretty here. The map says this park is dedicated to the soldiers from this area who fought in World War I."

The dogs were milling around in the back seat. Mia turned to look at them. "Just a minute, you guys. I need to read this letter. Then we'll go for a walk. I promise."

Mia looked at the return address, which was a post office box in Santa Barbara. She'd just been right near there. If Gizmo hadn't eaten that envelope, she could have avoided a whole lot of time running around Alpine Grove. Not to mention the trip to the emergency vet. But then she never would have met Chris. She glanced at him and he responded by raising his eyebrows.

He gave her the classic charades speed-it-up motion, spinning his index finger. "What are you waiting for?"

"Sorry." She ripped open the envelope and pulled out a piece of paper. Even after all these years, she still recognized her father's handwriting. She read the letter aloud. "Since I haven't heard from you or Gwen, I assume you decided not to talk to her. I was hoping the postcards would prove to you that it wasn't my fault. I was trying to do what's best. I promise I'll leave you alone now, but know that I'll always love you, no matter what. I wanted to see you before I go, but I guess that's not meant to be. At least I know I tried."

Chris frowned. "What does that mean?"

"I'm not sure. Now I know about Gwen, but what does he mean 'go'? Go where? Or is he *dying*? Maybe he's already dead. It almost sounds like there was another letter."

"I thought you just got the postcards."

"Well, I got the lottery tickets too. The manila envelope was kind of mangled. Maybe Gizmo ate a letter. If the tickets hadn't been in a separate envelope, he would have chewed those up too. It's all kind of a blur, since I was in the middle of dealing with cleanup and running Giz off to the emergency vet."

At the sound of his name, Gizmo put his head over the seat next to Mia's face. She put her hand on his muzzle. "Okay, okay, I know. We're going. But you know this is all your fault, right?"

Gizmo wagged happily, having accomplished his mission of mobilizing the human.

Mia and Chris leashed the dogs and they walked into the park. They stopped at the statue and stood in silence reading the names on the plaque for a few moments.

Chris took her hand and waved their clasped fingers toward the forest. "I think that's the trail over there."

They began walking and Mia gazed at the tree canopy above them. "This is really pretty here. Even though most of the leaves are gone, with all the evergreens it's still green. I love that about this area."

Chris stopped and turned to face her. "Are you okay? That letter was…well…I don't know what it was. *Odd,* for lack of a better word."

"My father never was much for talking I guess. For ages, he was the steady one. My mom was all over the place. She could be fun and hilarious one minute, then morose the next. I never knew what to expect. But Dad was solid, dependable." She looked into Chris's brown eyes and found sympathy there.

Clearing her throat, she tried to figure out how to articulate her tangled emotions. "I guess that's why I felt so betrayed when he took my dog Rusty away. Rusty was my best friend. My *only* friend. And Dad had been the only reliable person in my life. It was like everything fell apart."

"What do you think he means about saying 'it's not my fault'?"

"I'm not sure. I guess I need to talk to this Gwen person and find out. Maybe it has to do with Rusty. I mean, I told my dad I'd never, ever forgive him for that and that I would hate him forever. Even for an angry, bratty kid, what I said was terrible. Not too long after that, Dad moved out and my parents divorced."

Chris put his arm around her and Mia rested her cheek on his shoulder. He rubbed her back. "I'm sorry. It sounds like your mom had some serious problems. Maybe he had good reasons to leave."

Mia lifted her head. "For a long time, I blamed myself for the divorce. I thought that if I hadn't gotten so mad, maybe my father wouldn't have left."

"I'm sure that isn't true. That's a lot for a little kid to take on."

"My mom never disagreed with me though. Then because of Howard, we never talked about my father again. If my dad ever tried to contact us, I didn't hear about it. You pretty much know the rest."

Chris nodded. "Howard Peterson shot your mom and then himself."

"Yes. On graduation day. But I believe my mother killed herself."

"That's not what it said in the newspaper."

"You've heard about people who commit crimes so the police will shoot them, right? I have often wondered if my mother did something similar. Suicide by Howard."

"You think she would do that?"

"I can't be sure, but she was depressed and had tried to kill herself before. When I was little, she tried overdosing on pain medication. I thought she was just taking a nap, and I shook her and couldn't wake her up. I screamed for my dad, who called 9-1-1. At the time, he tried to downplay it, but as I got older I realized what had happened."

"I guess I understand better why you want to find your father now."

"I do and I don't." Mia wiped a tear from the corner of her eye. "When it comes to family, I'm so incredibly screwed up. Part of me hates him and the other part of me still loves him. Maybe it's because he's the only family I have left."

"I think you'll feel better once you get some answers."

"Will you come with me to talk to Gwen?"

"Absolutely."

"Supposedly she lives near Kat. I'll leave Gizmo at the kennel this time."

"That would be nice. I didn't want to interrupt what you were saying, but I think he chewed up one of my shoelaces while we've been standing here."

Mia jerked on the leash. "Gizmo, no!"

The dog wagged and belched proudly. Apparently, shoelaces were quite tasty.

Chapter 8

Getting Answers

After walking around the nature trail at the park, Mia and Chris loaded the dogs back into the RAV for the drive back to the kennel. Mia's emotions were still tied in knots. Fortunately, Chris seemed to understand her need for quiet and was just watching the scenery go by as they drove. Finally, he picked up the pad of paper and pencil and began doodling something. The fact that he was so easily entertained and didn't need to talk all the time was helpful because Mia needed to think.

Mia kept rewinding the text of her father's letter in her mind. It had taken ages for her to come up with the existence of Gwen, and in all likelihood, her father probably had provided contact information in the letter Gizmo must have eaten. Whatever he'd said before, now he was obviously disappointed that she hadn't followed up.

Little did Dad know that she'd driven hundreds of miles and talked to countless people in her efforts to follow up. She'd gone way out of her comfort zone, faced hugely mortifying situations with a whole lot of people, and she still had no idea where he was. The letter indicated he was leaving Santa Barbara. And it almost sounded like he was sick or dying. At this point, she had no idea.

She gripped the steering wheel more tightly. Gwen had better have some answers. Maybe she could ask Kat if she could look up Gwen's number in her phone book. It was time to resolve this whole thing once and for all.

She parked the car in front of the kennel, got out, and rang the buzzer. Kat opened the door of the house and walked down the driveway toward them.

Chris got out of the car while Mia was unloading Gizmo. He stood next to the RAV with his hands in his pockets, looking up at the trees.

Kat walked up to them. "Hey Chris, it's nice to see you again."

"Lulu would give you her regards, but she's too short to see out the window." He pointed at the car. "And she's too lazy to get up on her hind legs."

Kat peered into the window. "Hi Lulu."

Mia handed Kat Gizmo's leash. "I was wondering if you either have the phone number for Gwen Davis or have a phone book. I need to get in touch with her."

"Sure. She lives next door, over that way." Kat pointed toward a copse of massive cedars. "Joel plows her driveway in the winter sometimes, so her number is on the refrigerator. Let's put Gizmo away, and then we can go up to the house and I'll give it to you,"

"This is such a beautiful home site," Chris said. "The trees in this area are huge."

"A lot of them are cedars. We have a friend who is a forester and he claims it's an unusual habitat type," Kat said.

After Gizmo was settled into his kennel, they walked up to the house. Mia could tell that Chris was studying the log home. He probably knew every nuance of how they were actually put together. All Mia knew was that it was probably significantly more complicated than stacking a bunch of

Lincoln Logs. How did you run the wiring or plumbing in a log house?

They went inside and Chris and Mia stood in the entryway listening while the dogs launched into a frenzy of barking from the downstairs hallway. Kat glared down the stairs, announced her presence, and they dispersed.

Joel waved from the kitchen. "What's up?"

Kat reached into a drawer and pulled out a pad of paper and pencil. "I'm getting Gwen's number for Mia. The house is still for sale, right? But I think she's still there, isn't she?"

"I think so." Joel leaned on the counter. "I talked to her a couple weeks ago and she was really upset that the real estate season is ending and she might be stuck here for another winter."

"Well maybe she'll find someone who loves shoveling snow to rent the place." Kat handed a piece of paper to Mia. "Here you go."

Mia thanked Kat and then turned to look at Joel. "I don't suppose you have a sister, do you?"

"Cindy," Joel said. "Did you see her walking dogs in town?"

"I was at the post office. She looks a lot like you."

Kat closed the drawer with a thump. "I bet she said something nasty about us, didn't she?"

Mia looked at Chris, who shrugged. "Well, I don't know..."

"It's okay, we're used to it," Kat said. "Are you coming by tomorrow?"

"I think so. I'll let you know if I can't make it," Mia said.

"Okay, see you then." Kat followed Chris and Mia to the door and closed it behind them.

Chris took Mia's hand as they strolled down the driveway back to the RAV. "It's probably not cool for an architect to like log houses, since half of them are made from kits. But I love the warmth of the wood, and how it smells inside."

"It did smell a little like trees in there. Well, trees mixed with dog. I know you didn't see the whole place, but even though it's old, the house has that same type of well-loved, homey feel that I got from your sketches."

"The house I grew up in was like that. When I'm goofing around, I think about families raising their kids and spending holidays together in the houses I'm designing."

"Why do you work for a firm that designs office buildings and shopping malls?"

"There's more money in commercial architecture."

"I think I'm starting to see why you don't like your job." Mia gestured toward the forest. "You should be designing houses, not retail complexes."

"Usually, it's more like I design the storage closet on the second floor of a retail complex."

Mia opened the door of the RAV and looked over the roof at him. "I bet it's a great storage closet though."

He laughed as he got into the car. "I don't know about that. You're being pretty generous."

"Speaking of generous, is Gilbert, Tingler, Halberstam, and Associates Architecture taking us to dinner again?"

"You'd better believe it. I've been skipping breakfast and heating up canned soup on the hot plate for lunch, so we can go wild on fine Enchanted Moose diner fare."

"I think my cheapskate ways might be rubbing off on you."

"Well, it's about time. I also made a bunch of calls related to my student loans, trying to figure out if I can lower the payment. It's confusing."

Mia glanced at him. "I'm impressed. Are you really going to work on the whole debt problem?"

"Ignoring it and hoping it will go away hasn't been working out too well." He reached over and took her hand. "I'm glad you said something, even if it didn't seem like I appreciated it at the time."

"Friends are supposed to be honest with one another."

"I think our friendship is evolving. I don't usually spend most of the day thinking about ripping all the clothes off my friends."

"I hope not." Mia released his hand to change gears, and slowed the car as she pulled into the Enchanted Moose parking lot. "That's got to be distracting."

"It is."

~

Mia moved papers off a chair, sat down at the desk, and looked through an array of sketches while Chris fed Lulu and settled her in for a nap.

When he was done, she followed him to the door. He suddenly turned and wrapped his arms around her, pulling her toward him into a fierce embrace. Nuzzling her neck, he whispered, "How hungry are you?"

As she attempted to catch her breath, Mia's stomach growled loudly. "Pretty hungry I think."

He released her. "You're not going to eat and run away again, are you? Because I'm hoping I can convince you to stay here tonight. I'm not sure my persuasive skills are up to the task, but I'm warning you that I'm going to give it my best shot."

"You don't have much to worry about." Mia reached into her bag, yanked out a box of condoms, showed him the front, and dropped it on the desk. "I was planning on it."

He grinned. "This is going to be the longest meal ever, isn't it?"

"Maybe. But dessert could be pretty fantastic." She took his hand. "Let's go eat. You might need your stamina. If that kiss earlier was any indication, we're not going to get much sleep tonight."

They walked hand in hand to the diner and settled into what Mia now thought of as "their" booth. Chris pulled out a crayon and began doodling on the placemat while they waited for the server to show up.

Mia leaned on her elbows, peering across the table. "What are you drawing over there?"

"Lines."

"Those are some suggestive lines. I think our waitress might raise her eyebrows if she sees that."

"Sees what? It's just lines." He turned the placemat around so she could see. "Look. It's three lines. No big deal."

"You're saying those curves don't remind you of anything? Nothing at all?"

"Maybe. Sometimes what you're thinking about comes out in art." A corner of his mouth turned up as he added more lines. "Maybe I'm still thinking about dessert."

Mia reached over and traded placemats, flipping his over in the process. "She's coming. Draw a chocolate cake or something."

"You're no fun."

Mia stared at him intently and licked her lips slowly. "Mmm, chocolate. Melted chocolate. Oozing chocolate. Sweet, luscious, creamy chocolate."

Chris dropped his hands into his lap as the waitress walked up to the table. The woman stared at them impassively and pulled her order pad out of her apron pocket. "May I take your order?"

Mia ordered a big salad, vegetable soup, and a sandwich, since it felt like she hadn't had many vegetables lately. Being on the road was turning her into a junk-food junkie. Chris got a hamburger and fries, apparently not worried about nutrition for the time being. He seemed to have other things on his mind.

After the waitress left, he resumed drawing on the placemat. The chocolate cake had some rather interesting embellishments. Maybe no one would notice.

Mia had been taking the placemats with her when they left the restaurant because she loved Chris's the doodles and sketches and couldn't bear the idea that they'd be thrown away.

It had been fun to look at the drawings and reflect on the conversations later when she was back in her room at the H12. Remembering to grab these placemats before they left this evening would be particularly important. If the next occupants of the table sat their children in front of X-rated placemats, they might not be quite as amused by them as Mia was.

Mia reached across the table and pulled the crayon from Chris's hand. "Do you have any meetings tomorrow?"

"No, although I should work. I'm kind of behind on my drawings. Not having a real drafting table slows things down. There's not really enough space on the desk."

"Not to mention that you've covered every flat surface with stuff."

He took the crayon back from her and sketched a teetering stack of papers. "Tomorrow, you call Gwen. Then what?"

"I'm not sure. I guess it depends on what she says."

The waitress returned with their food and Mia dug into her salad. Chris pointed a French fry at her. "Okay, I guess you were really were hungry, and not just putting me off."

She lazily ran her tongue along the tines of the fork. "Why would I do that?"

He stared at her for a long moment. "Uh, I um...I was thinking you might be worried about the whole rebound thing again."

Sucking on the fork languidly for a few seconds, Mia finally put it down. "I thought about that and decided I don't care."

"What do you mean you don't care?"

"You're going to leave in a few days, and I'm going to go find my father. Well, assuming he's not dead, that is. It's quite possible we'll never see each other again. But so what? If I were about to die would I want to miss out on spending the night with you?" She licked the fork suggestively again and pointed it at him. "No, I definitely would not. In fact, I think we're going to have an extremely good time tonight."

"I think so too." Chris leaned forward and his eyes widened. "The death part is a little worrisome though. You're not sick or something are you?"

"I'm fine. I went to the doctor for a physical before I hit the road. I've just decided I need to take more of a *carpe diem* approach to life."

"*Carpe diem*? You mean, seize the day?"

"That's all the Latin I know, but it's the best way to describe what I'm feeling. I have spent a lot of time being afraid, and I'm tired of it. Years in a cubicle, protecting myself from anything scary, and just existing. Worrying about talking to everyone all the time."

"I keep telling you, it's not a big deal."

"I decided you might be right. I've probably spent more time talking to strangers in the last three days than I have in the last three years. Yes, it was embarrassing, and some people were mean, but some were nice too. Talking to them wasn't the end of the world. It didn't kill me, and I survived."

He shook a fry, flapping it in front of her. "See! I knew you would."

"It's not like I'm going to run out and get a job in customer service. I still hate talking to people I don't know. It's stressful, and half the time I make a fool of myself. But winning that money—it's like the universe is giving me a second chance to live my life. *Really* live it. So at least for today, I'm not going to worry about your ex-girlfriend or what happens tomorrow."

Chris picked up another French fry and held it up to his mouth, encircling it with his tongue before taking a bite. He gave her a small half smile. "I'm glad you feel that way."

Mia held up her fork and skimmed her tongue across a leaf of lettuce, licking off the dressing provocatively. "Oh, I definitely do."

They spent the rest of the meal watching each other eat. It was by far the sexiest dinner Mia had ever had, and by the time Chris paid the check, she was achingly desperate to get back to his room.

Chris took her hand and they ran across the parking lot to room one fifty-six, laughing. He opened the door and they were greeted by a yip from Lulu in her crate. He bent down to peer inside. "Sorry Lulu, you know it's bedtime."

Mia closed the door behind her and turned to face the room. "This time, we are not going to jump each other in front of the entire parking lot."

In two steps, Chris was in front of her. He put his palms on either side of her head on the door and pressed his lips to hers. Mia reacted instantly, pulling him closer and then pushing her hands under his shirt, wanting to feel the warmth of his skin.

The next few minutes were a flurry of laughter, flying clothing, and papers. Chris threw his glasses on the nightstand and shoved sheets of vellum off the bed onto the floor. They leapt under the sheets together, unwilling to stop touching one another, even for a second. Mia closed her eyes and gave in to the sensations, letting all her worries evaporate in the heat.

Later, she was curled up next to Chris, her legs trapped in a complex tangle of sheets. "Help. I think I'm knotted in place."

He stroked her hair and kissed her forehead. "That's good. It means you can't leave."

"I should get back to the H12."

"Why?"

"You said you have to work."

"It's the middle of the night. Why would you leave *now*?" He slowly ran the tip of his index finger behind her ear, down her neck, and rubbed the hollow at the base of her throat. "I'm not thinking about work at all right now."

Mia struggled to disentangle herself from the sheets enough to roll over and look into his face. "Then what are you thinking about?"

"That this is the best evolution of a friendship I've ever experienced." He smiled. "Ripping off your clothes was even better than I thought it would be. I think you should consider being naked more often."

"*Carpe* nudity?"

He laughed, gave her a hug, and kissed her earlobe. "That's it exactly. *Carpe* nudity."

~

Mia jerked awake, her heart pounding in her chest. When she opened her eyes, she was disoriented for a moment until she saw Chris looking down at her.

He gently placed his fingertips on her temple and pushed her hair back from her face. "Are you okay?"

"I had one of those falling dreams. You know when you step off a curb or trip and there's that moment of panic when you realize you're falling?"

"I hate that feeling."

"Sometimes I have that sensation in a dream, but there's no context. It's just the falling part. Maybe I fell out of bed when I was little." She put her palm on his cheek. "Usually there's no one around though, so I just lie there and wait for my mini heart attack to subside. It was a little startling to wake up and see you there."

"Where would I go?" He grinned. "This is my room, remember?"

"I know. Usually, I'd have left by now."

"What do you mean usually?" Chris readjusted himself so he was lying alongside her with his head resting on his arm. "You said something about that last night. There's no way I wouldn't want to wake up next to you."

"I've never spent the entire night with someone before."

Chris propped himself up on his elbow. "Really? That's, uh, I don't know...unusual, I guess."

"*Unusual* being code for 'wow, what's wrong with you,' right? It's okay. I'm sure it won't come as a surprise that the mushroom girl didn't have a lot of boyfriends in the traditional sense."

"Okay, well, maybe not. It probably won't come as a surprise to you that the geeky nerd didn't get much attention from the opposite sex either. I didn't have a girlfriend until, well, I was so old it was turning into a joke among everyone I knew."

"College?"

"Yes—and remember I was in college for an extra-long time. A few guys in my dorm tried to fix me up. They had become completely obsessed with me losing my virginity. It was pretty humiliating."

"I took on that problem myself. Remember the Eagle's Nest Tavern? It was over off Fourth Avenue."

"That dive? I hope you didn't go alone."

"I'm not proud of some of the things I did. But at that age, all you hear about and think about is sex. I wanted to just get it over with."

"That's not very romantic. Not to mention potentially dangerous."

"I went through a self-destructive phase, probably because I was so unhappy and messed up, I guess."

"Yeah, I suppose you weren't dancing for joy back then."

"I also was worried there was something really wrong with me. That maybe I might have inherited my mother's mental health problems. Looking back, it might have been better if I'd just avoided those medical books at the library."

"You seem fine now." He smiled. "At the moment, your mental health seems better than mine, in fact."

"Bipolar disorder does run in families, but over time I determined I was just angry and sad, not clinically depressed or manic."

"Given what happened, who *wouldn't* be sad?"

"I suppose." Mia curled up closer. "I don't know why I'm telling you all this, but that's my sordid past in a nutshell. Basically, I was a mess for a long time. I thought you should know."

Chris stroked her hair. "I think you're pretty great now."

"You're pretty great too, you know." She inclined her head in the direction of Lulu's crate. "But I think your dog wants to go outside."

"I know." He gave her a kiss. "Don't leave."

"I'm not going anywhere."

Chris got up, located his clothes, and got dressed. While Mia observed from within her warm cocoon of blankets, he wandered around picking up the many papers and notes that had been thrown onto the floor.

He went outside with Lulu and Mia rolled over on her stomach. Had she ever been this relaxed before? If she had, she couldn't remember when. Reveling in the moment, she snuggled her head deeper into the pillow.

With a whoosh, Chris came back inside and put Lulu on the floor. The small dog ran around in a frenetic circle, stopping only to shake a few times.

Mia sat up. "I see the rain arrived."

"I need to dig out my umbrella. It's here somewhere." He grabbed a bag of dog food from the closet and filled the dog bowl while Lulu capered around his feet.

After giving Lulu her breakfast, Chris sat down on the edge of the bed next to Mia. She reached up and pushed a sodden clump of brown hair back off his forehead. "You look sad all of a sudden. What happened?"

"Nothing tragic. But I have to work today and I don't want to because I'd rather spend the day with you. My last meeting with Ben about the house is tomorrow and I'm really behind. I've got to finish these preliminary drawings before I talk to him."

Mia took his hand and interlaced her fingers with his. "I have to see if I can track down the mysterious Gwen and go walk Gizmo today. I'll let you know if I can meet with her. If you're working later, maybe I could bring you dinner here."

"I'd like that." He looked into her eyes. "Last night was... well...I can't even think of the right word. Incredible?"

"I know. For me too."

"So when you stop by later does that mean you'd be willing to stay overnight again?"

Mia grinned. "I'm counting on it."

The phone on the nightstand rang and Mia lurched in surprise. Chris scrambled over her and sprawled across the bed to grab it. Mia moved over so he could sit up.

The expression on his face turned serious. "Yes, I know. But I do have the meeting with Ben tomorrow. I also have to drop off my sister's dog at her house."

Mia raised her eyebrows in silent query.

Chris put his hand over his eyes. "All right, make the reservations. Fine. Wednesday morning will work. I can be there for the meeting at four."

After he slowly hung up the phone, Mia said, "I'm guessing you leave Wednesday."

"There's some major all-company announcement Wednesday afternoon and they want me back there for it. After my meeting with Ben tomorrow, I need to get in the car, drive to my sister's house, and drop off Lulu. Then get on a plane early the next morning."

"I knew you had to leave sometime."

"The thought of going back makes my stomach hurt. I hate to think why they want me at this meeting so badly." He leaned back on the headboard and put his arm over his eyes. "It can't be good news."

Mia pulled his arm away and peered down into his face. "Why do you say that? Is there something you haven't told me?"

"I have a bad feeling they're going to do a big layoff and I'll lose my job."

"You said you were afraid of getting fired before, but I don't believe it. I've seen your work. I know I'm not an expert, but you seem really good at what you do. Are you sure there's not something else going on?"

"No, there's nothing I haven't told you. I was comfortable with you from the moment we met and I have no idea why. It's like I don't have to pretend with you. I'm just me." He smiled. "Geeky warts and all."

"I know what you mean." Mia snuggled up against him, resting her cheek on his chest. "My mushroomy warts get along with your geeky warts."

"All this time, I didn't know what I was missing until I met you." He smoothed her hair. "Are we ever going to see each other after tomorrow?"

"I'm not sure, but I hope so."

"Me too."

Chapter 9

Potty Mouth

Mia gave Chris a final hug goodbye and drove back to her room at the H12 in town. After eating and showering, she couldn't think of any more excuses to put off calling Gwen. What was she supposed to say to this woman? It was like the little kid's book with the baby bluebird who went around asking everyone, "Are you my mother?" Mia wasn't the only one with missing-parent issues.

She stared at the phone and fiddled with the piece of paper with the phone number in her fingertips, but it didn't help her figure out what she was going to say. Oh well, she was just going to have to improvise.

Finally, Mia dialed the number and waited while the phone rang. Maybe Gwen wasn't home. After fifteen rings, Mia was moving the handset away from her head to hang up when she heard a voice. She jerked the receiver back to her ear quickly. "Hello? Is this Gwen?"

"Yes. What? Who is this? I can't talk now."

"I'm, um, my name is Mia, Amelia Riggins."

There was a clattering noise and finally the woman said, "Mia? Oh wait, yes, I've been expecting your call. What took you so long?"

"It's a long study…uh…*story*."

"I can't talk right now." Another crash came from the other end of the line.

Mia looked around the room as if it might reveal some answers. "Is this a bad time? Are you okay?"

"I have a squirrel situation." She squeaked and said, "Shoo! Get out of there!"

"Do you need hurt? I mean *help*?"

"I have to go."

Mia wasn't sure what to do. Gwen was the only person who seemed to have any answers, and she needed to talk to her. "Maybe I could stop by and help you. Kat said you live next door to her, right?"

"Yes, I do. Come by if you want. I've got to go. Hey! I said, *shoo...scoot*, no, get out!"

"Okay, I'll be there in a half hour. Is that okay?"

"Fine! See you later."

Mia held the handset away from her head and looked at it as the dial tone buzzed. For once, she wasn't the bizarre one in the conversation. What did Gwen mean by a squirrel situation? After hanging up the phone, Mia gathered her things, went out into the pouring rain, and got into the RAV. Whatever the situation was, she was about to find out.

As she worked her way through the back roads toward the kennel, the rain grew heavier. Kat had indicated that Gwen's house was before hers along the road, so presumably Mia had driven by it quite a few times now. Most of the houses were set so far back off the road that spotting the driveway might be tricky.

Mia squinted through the windshield at the downpour, which wasn't doing much to help visibility. Gwen's house had to be along here somewhere. She slowed the car and crawled along, hoping no other cars would come zooming up behind her. A battered steel mailbox with faded press-on letters spelled DAV S. Although the letter *I* was lost to the elements, it was close enough. This must be the place.

The driveway went back into the trees, much like the serpentine path to the boarding kennel, but the route to Gwen's place didn't go as far into the forest before it opened up into a clearing. An old battered single-wide mobile home sat in the middle of the area looking oddly out of place. The two-tone brown-and-tan siding was dirty and a huge black tarp covered half of the roof.

Although the mobile home was run-down, a lot of work had gone into landscaping the garden areas around it. Everything was looking a little drenched and battered by the rain, but the bed full of black-eyed Susans and other flowers must have put on quite a pretty late-summer show when the blooms had been in their prime. The flower beds were demarcated by countless rocks and a large fenced-in area appeared to contain what had undoubtedly been a productive vegetable garden that was now mostly done for the season.

Mia got out, walked up to the door, and knocked. A commotion came from within, and as the tall skinny woman opened the door, a cat zipped by her, past Mia, and out into the rain. Mia smiled weakly. "Gwen? I'm Mia. We talked earlier."

"Yes, come in." She stepped aside and gestured toward the interior. "In about five minutes, that foolish cat will be crying at the window wanting to come back inside."

Mia walked inside the house and glanced at Gwen and then the compact space. Every wall was covered with paneling that was a distant echo of the worst of early seventies decor.

It had been painted white and the interior was filled with homey little knickknacks. Although the exterior was ugly, it was obvious Gwen had put a lot of effort into rehabilitating and remodeling the interior space.

The trailer was wider than Mia's old Airstream, but similarly configured with a long hallway that undoubtedly led to the other rooms. It also had the same feeling of being off the ground, so the thump of her footsteps caused a vibration on the floor. It made her feel like an elephant stomping around. Attempting to tiptoe, she followed Gwen into the small kitchen area.

Something skittered across the floor next to her and Mia shrieked and swirled around. "What was that?"

Gwen scowled and ran her fingers through her dark hair. She had a short pixie haircut that made her brown eyes seem unusually large. "It's a squirrel. He showed up this morning and I can't get him to leave. I'm naming him Potty Mouth."

Mia tried not to giggle, but couldn't suppress a smile. "Potty Mouth? Um, that's interesting. I guess this is the squirrel situation you mentioned."

"If you can help me get rid of him, I'll be forever grateful. I'm really late for work."

"How did he get inside?"

Gwen gestured toward the hallway. "I think he got in through a hole in the bathroom wall somewhere. After I ate breakfast, I went to the bathroom. There aren't any windows in there and I never bother turning on the light. It's not like I can't figure out where the toilet is in such a small space."

Mia nodded, not sure how to respond. She didn't like where the story was headed.

"Anyway I sit down and get ready to, well, you know. But then something splashed my butt from down below."

Mia's eyes widened. "I hate to ask, but…"

"Well, isn't it obvious?" Gwen waved her arms. "There was a whole chattering, splashy commotion and I jumped up off that toilet seat like it was on fire, screaming bloody murder. I'm tripping on my pants, but I slapped the light switch on the wall. When the light comes on, that squirrel shoots himself out of the toilet and launches out of the bathroom."

Mia looked around. "So it's the same squirrel I just saw?"

Gwen put her hands on her hips. "How many squirrels do you think I have in my potty?"

Mia shook her head. "Maybe we should open the door or the windows so he can get back outside."

"I tried that already. He's not having anything to do with the great outdoors because it's pouring out there. Squirrels are smarter than you might think. I'm lucky he didn't decide to bite me. Can you imagine explaining that to your doctor? 'Well, doctor, it was like this: nature called and then it bit me in the butt.'"

Mia bit down on her lip to keep from bursting into laughter, which, given her current mood, Gwen probably would not appreciate. Mia said evenly, "Maybe I can help you look for him. He must be here somewhere. We could try shooing him outside."

"That's what I was trying to do when you called. Potty Mouth doesn't shoo easily."

"Do you have a broom?"

"Hey, that's a good idea!" Gwen went to a narrow closet, pulled out a broom, and shoved an ironing board back inside before she slammed the door closed. "Maybe we can sweep him out of here."

The two women got down on their hands and knees and began peering under the furniture for the telltale glow of eyes. Gwen swished the broom under the sofa and the small mammal scurried out. She jumped up after him. "Potty Mouth! Get out, you nasty varmint. I have to go to work."

Mia ran to the front door and opened it. "Over here! Sweep him over here."

After several fits of frantic sweeping, Gwen finally managed to encourage Potty Mouth to vacate the mobile home. Mia slammed the door behind the squirrel and took a deep breath. That was way more excitement than she had expected on this visit.

Gwen put the broom back in the closet, again shoving back the ironing board that was trying to jump out. She turned around and smiled. "Thank heavens that's over. Let's hope Potty Mouth stays in the forest from now on. I need to check the paneling in the bathroom for holes. I have to get going soon, but can I get you something to drink? I need some tea."

"That would be nice. I'm hoping you have a minute to chomp...I mean *chat*."

"Yeah, I figured you'd get around to that sooner or later."

～

Mia sat down at the old Formica table, which sported a speckled green table top with metal edges. It was somewhat reminiscent of the decor at the Enchanted Moose diner. Maybe the green vinyl-covered chairs were cast-offs from some long-ago Alpine Grove eating establishment.

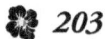

Gwen handed her a mug with steaming hot water and a tea bag. "Here you go. I'm always cold, so I drink a lot of tea."

"Thank you very much." Mia clasped the warm mug with her palms and swished the tea bag around. "I guess my father told you I might contact you."

"Yes, although I was wondering what happened. I talked to him months ago. He said he was sending you a letter for your birthday."

"I think my dog ate it."

A corner of Gwen's mouth twitched. "I suppose he ate your homework too."

"I didn't realize there must have been a letter in the package he sent until I got another letter from him the other day. It implied he'd already written to me. I just thought he sent me a bunch of postcards before. And I wasn't sure they were even from him because Gizmo—that's my dog—he ate the return address on the envelope too."

"That's quite a dog you've got there."

Mia sighed. "I know. He's a great dog, but he eats *everything*. I still miss him, anyway. Right now Gizmo is at Kat's boarding kennel."

"You mentioned that. How's Kat doing? I haven't seen her in a while."

"Fine, I think."

"She seems nice enough, but I miss Abigail. We were neighbors for so long, and I couldn't believe it when she died. Nothing has been the same since then. She was like family to me. We used to joke that we must be cousins—we just couldn't figure out how we were related."

"It sounds like Kat misses her too. She said you're thinking of moving."

"I want to be closer to my daughter. And I never want to shovel snow again. Heather lives in a condo complex where the rent is reasonable. I'll miss my garden, but I can't handle another winter like last year."

Mia cleared her throat. It was time to get to the point. "So I guess you know my father. Why did he want me to contact you?"

"Well, he tried to reach Abigail, but she'd already died. So he tracked me down instead and talked me into it."

"Into what?"

"Letting him give you my phone number so I could convince you that he really brought that dog here to Alpine Grove. He said you never forgave him for taking away that golden retriever you had."

"Rusty?" Mia's eyes widened and she turned her head to look around the small kitchen. "Was *this* his new home? My dad said he found him a home in the country, but I was convinced he was lying."

"No, he didn't bring the dog here. The dog lived at Abigail's house."

"Rusty lived there? I can't believe it." Mia clasped her hands together in her lap. "That's wonderful. Gizmo loves Kat's place. So Rusty really *did* get a wonderful home in the country. I was absolutely positive it was just a stupid story to make me stop crying."

"Dan didn't think you'd believed him. That's why he sent the postcards."

"But they don't make any sense. I didn't understand the messages." Mia hurriedly wiped a tear from the corner of her eye. "Who is 'CA'?"

"Cousin Abigail." Gwen smiled. "Dan called her that too. They got along from the second they met each other, and he thought the whole cousins–who-weren't-related thing was cute."

"Abigail wrote the cards? She kept talking about babies. Did she have a lot of kids?"

"No, but she had a lot of dogs and cats. Rusty wasn't the only homeless animal she took in. She referred to her critters as her 'babies' all the time."

"Well, that explains a lot." Mia was momentarily at a loss for words. She really needed to talk to her father. "Did you see my dad? Do you know where he is? The last letter was mailed from Santa Barbara, but it's a post office box."

"No, I haven't seen him, but I talked to him on the phone. He tracked me down after he found out Abigail was dead." With a small sigh, Gwen glanced out the window. "We have a complicated past, so the conversation was a little strained."

"How do you know him? I didn't know he'd ever been to Alpine Grove."

"Well, he brought Rusty. But we met before that too. I was a freshman in college in New York City, and we met during the blackout. The one in 1965, not 1977."

"There was a blackout?" Mia shook her head. "My dad worked in New York a long time ago, before I was born. You met him way back then?"

"It was an unusual experience. Nothing like that had ever happened in the city and people weren't sure what to do about the lights suddenly going out. Half of them thought it was the end of the world, that the bomb had been dropped, stuff like that."

"I guess it was during the Cold War, so that makes sense."

"Yeah, rumors were flying. I had been eating dinner with another student at a Schraft's Restaurant. The lights dimmed, came back on for a second, then went out completely. At first, we thought it was just the restaurant, but we looked out the window and everything on the street was dark. The waiters brought candles and we finished our food and went outside. It was strange, because there were no street lights. My friend was supposed to take a train to Long Island, but we couldn't find a bus and the traffic lights were off. So we walked to Grand Central Station. On the way, we stopped by a hotel and people were just hanging out in the lobby talking to each other. If you've ever been to New York, you know how odd that is."

Mia shook her head. "I've never been there."

"In the city, people walk around like they're wearing blinders. Everyone completely ignores the crowds around them. That's just how it is there. But that night people stopped and talked to each other. I could see the stars for the first time and everyone was joking about how Con Ed hadn't paid its bills and that's why the power was out. In a place like Alpine Grove, you lose power all the time in the winter, so the darkness didn't scare me. Everyone else's reaction to the blackout was what was so unusual."

"So you met my dad in the dark?"

"At Grand Central Station. After we got there, my friend went to look into the train situation to see if she could get home. She left me sitting on a bench to wait for her, and Dan sat down next to me. Then we started talking."

Mia gestured toward the window. "But that was ten years before he came here with Rusty, right?"

"Yes, but I saw him around that time too. He was on a business trip and stopped here. We met and he helped me move from the commune to this place. That's when he met Abigail."

"I heard about the commune from Tracy Sullivan and her mom."

"Yes, I knew Tracy. She's a few years younger than my daughter. And of course Bea. I think everyone in Alpine Grove knows Bea. When the commune disbanded, it was a big problem for me. I was a single mom who was about to lose her home and a whole lot of live-in babysitters. Abigail leased me some of her land and helped me find an old trailer to put on it."

"That was nice of her."

"It was. She was the best friend I ever had. We worked out a lease-to-own thing, so this is all mine." She held out her arms. "It's not much, but it's paid for."

Mia smiled. "That's a big deal in my book. I'm glad my dad helped you too. That must have been a difficult time."

"It was, but it was for the best. My daughter was getting to the age where I wasn't sure living out at the commune was really the best thing for her anyway."

"How old was she?"

"She was in fourth grade, and it all worked out fine. We moved here, I ended up getting a job, got married, and later got divorced. Even with her slightly odd early schooling, Heather did really well and went to college. At this point, I'm ready to retire. Unfortunately, I can't realistically do that, but I'd like to at least do something else."

"I think you've earned it. Where does your daughter live?"

"In San Diego. Where it's sunny! No snow anywhere and I won't be living in a place that has squirrels in the toilets."

Mia laughed. "Well, I hope not."

～

Gwen repeated that she had to get to work, but Mia managed to get her father's contact information before Gwen left. Given what he'd said in the letter, it was unlikely the address was good anymore, but he might be having his mail forwarded.

First, she was going to give him a call, no matter how uncomfortable it might be. The last conversation she'd had with her father replayed like a looping video in her mind. She couldn't take back what she'd said years ago, but she could apologize and acknowledge the olive branch he'd extended.

After thanking Gwen and wishing her a squirrel-free afternoon, Mia went back out into the rain, got in the RAV, and drove next door to the kennel. Kat was splashing her way down the driveway toward the kennel buildings when Mia drove up.

She got out of the car and waved to Kat. "I know I'm a little early, but I was next door, so I thought I'd take Gizmo out, if it's okay."

Kat nodded. "No problem. I was just coming out to check on the boys before the walk. Do you want to get Gizmo and Lewis and meet me around back?"

"Sure."

Kat readjusted the beat-up oilskin hat on her head and turned back toward the house. Mia went inside and Gizmo started barking and leaping around in his kennel. In the next kennel, Lewis started to bay and segued into a series of long mournful howls, punctuated with a few barks for emphasis. Mia encouraged them to be quiet and busied herself putting leashes on them. Finally, she had both dogs ready and they went out into the rain. Although Lewis seemed dismayed by the unfortunate deterioration in the weather, Gizmo was raring to go.

Kat and her dogs were waiting at the back of the house. The dogs that had off-leash privileges were chasing each other through the trees. Chelsey, Kat's little Aussie-shepherd mix, stood next to her looking worried.

Mia pointed at the dog, "Is Chelsey okay?"

"She's not a big fan of the rain."

They began walking down the trail and Mia described the squirrel incident next door.

Kat laughed. "That sounds like something that would happen to me. Except the squirrel would be trapped somewhere and unable to leave, so Joel would have to use a saw to tear another hole in the house to let him escape."

At the sound of something in a bush, Gizmo launched ahead and splashed into a huge puddle, followed by Lewis, who play-bowed and jumped on Gizmo's back. Mia pulled back on the leashes, but it was too late. Both dogs had managed to completely coat themselves in mud.

Mia turned to Kat. "I'm sorry. I wasn't really paying attention. When is Lewis being picked up?"

"Later today. I'll give him a bath. It's moments like these when I'm glad we added the grooming area."

"I'll do it. Now that I've talked to Gwen, I don't have anything else I need to do this afternoon. I told Chris I'd meet him this evening. He's supposed to be working on some drawings, so I don't want to disturb him."

Kat raised her eyebrows. "Interesting. I guess you've been spending more time together."

Mia could feel the heat on her cheeks rising against the chilly damp air. "Yes. I really like him."

"He seems nice. I have an article deadline, so if you could wash Lewis, that would make my life a lot easier. I'll show you where everything is when we get back."

"Could I wash Gizmo too? He's turned himself into a muddy mess."

"Sure. Feel free to wash any of *my* dogs too, if you get inspired." At the dog's worried glance, Kat stroked the brown fur on Chelsey's head. "Don't worry Chels, I'm kidding."

Mia spent the rest of the afternoon washing and drying Lewis and Gizmo. Kat's grooming set-up had a waist-high bathtub, shampoos, brushes, a grooming dryer, and other doggie accoutrements. It was a far cry from washing Gizmo in the infinitesimal Airstream bathroom or even de-stinking Lulu at the Enchanted Moose.

Gizmo was resting in his kennel and Lewis was in Mia's lap reveling in some extra brushing when the door opened. The beagle leaped up and launched toward a woman standing next to Kat.

Kat closed the door behind her as Mia stood up and tried to get a leash on Lewis, who was excited to see his human again. She glanced up at the clock. "I guess I lost track of time. He loves being brushed."

The woman took the leash from Mia. "I'm Jennifer. Thank you for taking care of him."

Mia crouched down to pet the beagle. "Lewis is really sweet."

Kat gestured toward the door. "Jennifer, I know you're in a hurry. Let's go get his stuff."

Jennifer pulled Lewis's leash toward her. "You're right. I'm really late. Thanks again."

Mia gave Lewis a final goodbye pat. "You be good."

A few minutes later, Kat came back inside and smiled. "You sure have a fan now."

"All I did was give him a bath and brush him. That dryer is incredible. I got so much loose fur off Gizmo, it was remarkable." She gestured toward the cage where Gizmo was lying down looking sleek. "I mean, he *never* looks this good."

"I haven't had much time to try it out. I think I've only washed two dogs." Kat shrugged. "I'm not a professional groomer and I really need to find one. Adding grooming services could help with the ole bottom line."

"How do you become a groomer?"

"As I understand it, most people start out working in grooming shops as apprentices or interns, more or less. I think there might be grooming schools too."

"There are schools for that? Really?"

"Probably, although not in Alpine Grove. There's one groomer in town. Her name is Betty. Mostly she sticks to small dogs though. I talked to her about the possibility of coming out here, but she isn't interested. She said she likes working from her house and she's too old to deal with gigantic Akitas anymore. I couldn't argue with that. I'm half her age and I think I'm too old to deal with gigantic Akitas."

Mia laughed. "I think it depends on the Akita."

"True. I know you're not planning to stay in Alpine Grove, but if you change your mind, I'd hire you to walk dogs. You're great with them. And if you can figure out a way to learn more about it, you could do grooming too."

Mia just looked at Kat for a moment. A job? No one had ever offered her any form of employment before. Jobs were something she begged for and worried about losing. "I...I don't know what to say. I've enjoyed spending time here. It's one of the only places I've ever felt comfortable."

"It's all the dog hair. Fur is very comforting." Kat gestured toward the door. "I'm having a terrible time finding another dog walker. No one is willing to drive all the way out here from town every day. Please just think about it. Because of impending book deadlines and winter, I'm starting to freak out about being able to manage everything."

"You'd really pay me to hang out with the dogs?"

"Yes, I really would. We're heading into the busy season with people traveling for the holidays. If you're interested, maybe you could talk to Betty too. You could offer to volunteer to help her in exchange for instruction."

"Do you think she'd agree to that?"

"It wouldn't hurt to ask. You'd be free labor. If you help, she can book more dogs and make more money. Have you ever seen how much groomers charge? It can be pretty lucrative."

"I've never taken a dog to a groomer, but I guess that makes sense. All that washing and brushing takes a while."

Kat put her hand on Mia's shoulder. "I'd love to hire you. Even if you just worked through the winter, it would help a lot. By spring, my book will be done and my life will be a lot less stressful. Like I said, just think about it."

Mia agreed to consider the idea. Kat gave her a goodbye hug and left to go work on her article.

As she put Gizmo back in his kennel and got ready to go, Mia's thoughts were racing. Spending all day with dogs like she had today would be so much fun. The time had flown by. It would be hard work, but so much better than data entry.

Maybe her bizarre road trip to find out about the postcards was meant to lead her here. Life was full of unexpected twists and turns, after all. She couldn't wait to talk to Chris about it. The idea of seeing him made her smile as she got into the RAV for the trip back to the Enchanted Moose.

~

Mia parked, got out, and rushed to knock on the door of room one fifty-six. She couldn't wait to see Chris. A Lulu yip came from within and he opened the door with a grin. "I'm so glad you're here."

Mia launched into his arms and kissed him. "Me too! I have lots of things to tell you."

"I fed Lulu and she's already crashed out in her crate, working on her after-dinner nap. Do you want to get something to eat? It's your last chance to freeload off the expense account."

"You bet." She took his hand. "Let's go."

They strolled across the parking lot to the diner and settled into their favorite booth. Mia tried not to think about the fact that this would be the last dinner they'd share for quite a while. She squeezed his hand. "Did you get everything done for your meeting tomorrow?"

"Yes. I was on fire and got in the zone for the first time in I can't even remember how long. So I'm absolutely ready to talk to Ben. I'll show you all the drawings after dinner."

Mia handed him a crayon, since the squirrel story would undoubtedly benefit from illustration. Chris laughed as he scribbled his way through the retelling. His caricature of Potty Mouth was particularly amusing.

While they were eating, Mia explained how Gwen and her father had met during the 1965 blackout in New York City.

He put down his fork. "So how old is Gwen's daughter?"

"I don't know exactly. She didn't say." Mia paused. "Well, wait, she said that Heather was in fourth grade in 1975 when they moved from the commune."

"How old are kids in fourth grade?"

"Nine or ten I think."

"So if the blackout was in 1965, do you think you were right and your dad has another kid?"

Mia set down her water glass. "I didn't think of that."

"Well, she said she was a single mom at the commune. Do you suppose that's how they know each other? Maybe he's been paying child support for ages."

"I doubt it." Mia shook her head. "Maybe. I don't know. Wouldn't my parents say something?"

"They might not. Or he doesn't know."

"You think Gwen never told him?"

He shrugged and added a light bulb to the placemat. "If it was a one-night stand type thing, maybe she didn't want him to know. Or she didn't ever get his contact information."

"But she saw him again in 1975. Presumably he saw Heather, right?"

"Maybe not, if she didn't want him to know about her for some reason."

"I suppose that's possible. If it's true, it would be yet another family secret. Wow." Mia put her elbow on the table and rested her chin in her palm. "I really need to talk to Dad."

"Or Gwen. Do you know when in 1965 the blackout was?"

"No, do you?"

"I have no idea. Maybe we can look it up on the Internet. I have to check my email anyway to make sure they don't have more bad news at work."

"What do you mean *more* bad news?"

"The big kahunas at Gilbert, Tingler, Halberstam, and Associates Architecture have been working on a bid to transform the old main library building into an Asian art museum."

"That sounds like a prestigious job."

Chris did a quick sketch of a trophy on the placemat. "Very much so. It's all anyone has been talking about for months. Apparently, even though we're a local San Francisco firm, after all the work everyone put into the bid, some Italian architect got the job."

"Uh-oh. Is that what the big meeting is about?"

"Probably. It hasn't been announced publicly yet, but the selection committee notified the bidders. GTH probably had the gloating press release already written crowing about how the firm is beyond compare. Easy come, easy go."

Mia took his hand so he'd stop scribbling. "You don't seem particularly upset."

"It's probably wrong for me to be happy the firm didn't get the job, but I am. I'm thrilled I won't have to redesign some obscure museum storage closet. That probably makes me a bad person or at least not a loyal employee."

"I think you might just be working for the wrong firm."

"You're probably right about that." He sketched an elaborate stone edifice. "The library is a beautiful old building. I hope the guy who did get selected doesn't ruin it."

"It won't be your problem if he does." Mia sat up straight and tapped her fingertips on the table. "With all the stuff that happened with Gwen, I forgot to tell you the best thing—I got a job offer!"

Chris looked at her in surprise. "That's great! Doing what? Who offered it to you?"

"Kat wants me to walk dogs. And maybe groom them."

"Well, you'd get Lulu's vote. Is that something you want to do?"

"Maybe. Unlike every other job option I've thought about, I can't find a downside. Well, except that it probably doesn't pay well. Kat would deal with the humans and the business for the most part, and I'd just work with the dogs. It would be fun to do, at least for a while. I washed Lewis today and his owner was so happy. It was great. Way better than typing carrot-location information."

He interlaced his fingers with hers. "So you'd stay here? Is that what you want?"

"Alpine Grove is nice. The area is pretty and I've met quite a few people that I like. It's way better than Windiberg, that's for sure."

"I guess I was sort of secretly hoping that I could convince you to move to San Francisco."

"Move? I know I have some money now, but I can't afford to live there. What would I do?"

"Well, there are probably grooming shops there too."

"I suppose. That seems like a big step. But I could visit."

He pulled his hand away and began sketching the Golden Gate Bridge. "I guess I'll have to settle for that."

"Don't you think you're rushing into this?" Mia pulled her hands into her lap. "I mean, we've only known each other for a few days."

He looked up into her eyes. "But they've been a really good few days. At least for me, anyway. The best days I can remember in a long, long time."

"I know what you mean."

"Do you think that happens every day? Meeting someone who actually *gets* you?" He waved the crayon toward the window. "Okay, maybe that type of thing does happen to other people. But certainly not to me. Most people I meet write me off as a geeky introvert."

Mia took his hand again. "I know. It's not like people tend to warm up to the bizarre mushroom girl either."

"I just don't want to lose this. Spending all this time with you, even just talking to you, has been incredible. You can't just disappear on me with a vague promise to visit."

"I won't. We'll keep in touch and we won't lose track of each other. You're still working on the house here, too." Mia gave his hand a squeeze. "It will work out."

Chris nodded, but didn't look convinced. "We'll see. At least we still have one more night together. Do you want anything for dessert? It's your last chance for free chocolate cake."

"I think I'll skip dessert. Let's go back to your room and you can show me your drawings."

"You do realize that's the architect's version of the classic line 'Would you like to come up and see my etchings?' right?"

Mia grinned. "Yeah, I kinda figured that out the other day."

~

Given how often he complained about what he did for a living, Mia was shocked at how much work Chris had managed to do on the house designs while she was off walking and washing dogs. It looked like the place would be gorgeous.

The last night with Chris was bittersweet, since neither of them had a good answer to the question of when they might see each other again. Although they discussed various options, nothing really worked.

Mia knew nothing about San Francisco other than it was one of the most expensive places to live in the United States. That was not a big selling point. Without a job, it felt way too risky. And there was no way she was blowing all her lottery money to move there either, given how little time she'd known Chris.

For Chris, the interlude in Alpine Grove had been a reprieve, but his architectural work was likely to return to normal upon his return to San Francisco. Or he'd get laid off. Neither option was particularly appealing, and job options in Alpine Grove were nonexistent.

Mia didn't sleep very well. She tossed and turned, wrestling with the idea of staying in Alpine Grove. Or even going to San Francisco. It wasn't like she could keep traveling forever and living in motels like the H12. Before she left Alpine Grove, she needed to talk to her father.

Early the next morning, she helped Chris pack up his things and load them into the car. He planned to meet the developer at the house site, then drive back to his sister's house in LA from there. The last item left to put in the car was Lulu's sky kennel. Mia walked Lulu on a leash, while Chris placed the kennel in the back seat.

He turned to face Mia. "Well, I guess that's it. I need to get going. Traffic is going to be horrible once I get near LA."

"It always is, isn't it?"

"Yeah, I suppose that's true." He put his arms around her and gave her a bear hug. "I'm going to miss you."

Mia returned the hug and added an extra squeeze for emphasis. "Call me when you get there and we'll figure out a good time for me to visit. I promise we'll work something out. Maybe you can find a swanky San Francisco groomer looking for a trainee or something. I haven't promised Kat anything, so I don't have a job here yet. And I'm basically homeless, except for my car. Let's face it, I have an extremely flexible schedule right now."

He chuckled and gave her a kiss. "I'll call you when I get there."

"I'll let you know what happens when I talk to my father."

"You'd better. I'm still dying of curiosity. You might even have a sister!"

Mia waved him off. "Yeah, I know, I know. My life is a gigantic soap opera. Drive safely."

"I will." He gave her one last kiss before getting into the car.

Mia waved as he drove away and then got into her car to return to town and her room at the H12. Now that the major distraction of being around Chris was gone, it was time to figure out what the heck she was going to do with her life. She'd delayed her exit from Alpine Grove, but now it was time to finally make some decisions and get on with whatever was next.

After showering and getting some breakfast, Mia relaxed for a while, sprawled out on the bed reading a novel. She didn't want to try calling her father too early, since he'd always been a night owl. By mid-morning she had finished the book and run out of excuses. Time to get this conversation over with.

She picked up the phone and dialed the number Gwen had given her. Obnoxious tones blared in her ear and a mechanical voice told her that the number had been disconnected. Now what was she supposed to do?

Mia rolled her legs off the bed, sat up, and stared at the ugly drapes. Part of her had known she wouldn't be able to reach him, but it was still surprising how disappointed she was at not being able to talk to Dad after all this running around. What a huge let down.

She spent some time piddling around cleaning up the room. The piles of dirty clothes were starting to become an issue, so she went to the front desk and got some change and the key to the laundry room. By the time she was finished doing laundry, she'd completed another novel, and it was time to go out to the kennel, walk Gizmo, and get her nice clean clothes muddy again.

After a reprieve earlier in the morning, the rains had returned. The windshield wipers on the RAV whapped back and forth, splashing the rain off. Mist swirled up from the roadway as she squished her way down the driveway toward the kennel. It was going to be another soggy walk.

Mia met Kat at the kennel and they walked to the back of the house with Gizmo. It was a cold rain and Kat was wearing an ugly winter coat that seemed to be several sizes too large. She pulled a glove out of her pocket and put it on. "Now that it's November, I guess I need to accept that winter is really coming."

Because she'd lived in Windiberg her entire life, Mia had virtually no winter clothes. The raincoat she was wearing was keeping her dry, but it wasn't keeping her warm. "I need to either head south or get some new clothes. I'm freezing."

"Did you think about the job at all?"

"I'm not sure what I should do yet. I still want to find my father. Gwen had a number for him and I was hoping to talk to him today, but the number is disconnected."

"So she *did* know him! That's great. Did you find out everything you wanted to know?"

Mia shrugged. "I might have found out more than I expected. Did your aunt ever have a dog named Rusty?"

"She did a long time ago. I saw him one of the last times I came up to visit Abigail when I was a little girl. She said he was a friend's dog." Kat stopped and turned to her. "Wait! Was that *your* Rusty?"

Mia nodded. "My dad brought him here. The postcards were from your aunt. She called her pets her 'babies,' I guess. And Rusty was one of them."

Kat started walking again with a laugh. "She absolutely did call them that—all the time. The furries are probably upset that I haven't carried on the tradition, but I'm not particularly maternal. I remember that Rusty was an awesome dog. Although Tessa is a golden retriever, she is a complete nutball. Rusty wasn't like that at all. He was so mellow. One time, I fell asleep on the floor with him as a pillow."

"That sounds like him. If you met Rusty, did you meet Gwen's daughter Heather? I think she's about my age."

"Maybe. When I came up here, Abigail was always doing something. We walked the dogs, did crafts, and hung out with neighbors. I don't remember meeting Gwen before I moved here, but who knows? I was just a little kid."

Mia debated revealing more, but a question was bothering her. "Gwen didn't say it, but I think Heather might be my half-sister."

"What?" Kat pulled Chelsey's leash to stop her again. "Really? What makes you think that?"

"Gwen said she met my father during the New York City blackout of 1965. I looked up the date and it was November ninth. She said she was a single mom and her daughter was in fourth grade in 1975. Add nine months and Heather would have been born in August 1966, so the ages match up. It's just a suspicion though."

"I can tell you from personal experience, this town is full of secrets. And I think Abigail knew most of them."

"I was hoping to talk to my Dad and see if he is willing to tell me more about meeting Gwen. If they didn't...well... get together, then there's no way Heather is my half-sister. I can't decide if I should ask Gwen. Maybe she never told my father she was pregnant. Maybe she didn't tell him for a good reason. I have so many questions and I'm afraid she may tell me to get lost and mind my own business."

"She might, I guess." Kat gazed toward the trees for a moment, and then looked back at Mia. "Hey, I have an idea. There are boxes of Abigail's old photos in my office closet.

Most of them are of people I don't know. Or didn't know the last time I looked. Maybe we can find Gwen among them and see what her daughter looks like."

Mia smiled. "That might help me decide what to do. If she looks nothing like my father, I'll just pretend the whole half-sister idea never happened."

"Looking at old photos is fun. And as a writer, I love any excuse to procrastinate."

Chapter 10

Old Photos

After settling Gizmo back into his kennel, Mia went back to the house. Kat let her in the downstairs door, which led to the daylight basement where her office was located. The hallway was filled with rain-drenched canines and the pungent odor of wet dog pervaded the area.

Kat led Mia into her office and shooed the dogs away, blocking them out with a baby gate. The small bedroom had a bed along one wall. A desk with a computer and large monitor faced the window. The far wall had a bookshelf and a long table with multiple stacks of books and papers strewn across it.

Kat smiled and gestured toward the table. "Sorry about the mess. I wish I could say this is unusual, but it's always a disaster in here."

"You must be busy. Are you sure this is a good time?"

"It's fine. I'm stuck on my article and I can't stand the idea of trying to write any more today anyway." Kat opened the sliding door to the closet. "The photos are in here."

Kat dragged a large cardboard box from the floor of the closet and out into the room. "Like I said, these aren't mine, so I have no idea who most of the people are. They're Abigail's photographs, and I don't have the heart to throw them out.

It's possible other people in my family might want to look at them too. Or maybe not."

A canine commotion arose from the hallway and Joel appeared in the doorway. "What's up?"

"We're looking at old pictures," Kat said as she walked over to him. "Want to join us?"

"I'll pass. Becca called, and I need to go check on something at the Shack."

"Did something else fall apart?"

"Not yet. I'll be back in a little while."

Kat stood on tiptoes and gave him a kiss across the baby gate. "See ya."

Mia bent to examine the box of photographs. It was jammed full of hundreds of envelopes. "This could take a while."

"Most of them have dates on the outside. Since you're looking for everything after 1965, that helps a little. Abigail was a pack rat. This place might be a mess now, but believe me, it was worse when I moved in."

Mia picked up an envelope and sat down cross-legged on the floor in front of the box. "This one has a note that says it's from a vacation with Paula."

"I have no idea who Paula is." Kat sat down next to her. "Notes are surprising, considering Abigail never labeled any of her canned goods. We can probably skip the ones she took while she was on vacations."

Mia riffled through a few more envelopes and began stacking them. "I guess we can organize them while we're at it. I'm starting a pile for the pre-1965 photos over here."

"I'll start the 'vacations' and 'people we don't know' piles over here." Kat held up an old photo of two girls in pink-polka-dot clown outfits and held it out to Mia. "I don't know who these twins are, but I'm sure they'd be embarrassed to find out this photograph exists."

"Seventies fashion was not kind to anyone. Even tap-dancing clowns."

"No kidding." Kat threw a few envelopes into a pile. "Hey, here's one that just has pictures around the house. Do you think that's Rusty?"

Mia took the photograph. "Yes! He had the softest brown eyes. Aww, this makes me want to cry. I loved that dog so much."

Kat handed her another photo. "This could be Gwen. She looks really different with long hair. It looks like it's her birthday, but I'm guessing by the expression on her face that a Kiss album wasn't what she really wanted."

"Maybe she was more of a Barry Manilow fan."

"That's a cute birthday hat though."

They continued riffling through photos, and occasionally commenting on them. Mia picked up an envelope that said it was from Easter 1976. In one photograph, Gwen was standing next to a little girl who was holding her hand. They were in front of a pretty bed of tulips and daffodils and wearing matching yellow flowered skirts. "Hey, I think I found one of Heather!"

Kat looked up. "What does she look like?"

"A little girl with long brown hair." Mia handed the photograph over. "Do you think she looks like me at all?"

Kat looked at the photo and looked at Mia. "I guess you could be related, but I don't know what your dad looks like."

Mia held the photo up closer to her eyes. "This picture is taken from so far away, I can't tell. Maybe there are some where you can see her face better."

Kat hurriedly stuffed a pile of photographs back into their envelope and flipped it onto a pile. "That was disturbing. I found a photo of me that needs to remain hidden from Joel forever."

"I'm sure it wasn't that bad."

"I look like I'm the plaid purple people-eater demon. With bell-bottoms thrown in for an even more peculiar seventies flashback. It's absolutely horrifying."

Mia giggled as she riffled through another stack. "Wait! Here's one where Heather is a little older and she's petting Rusty. Aww."

"What's the verdict? Are you related?"

"I think so. Her eyes look just like my father's." She looked up from the photograph at Kat. "I think I'm officially freaked out now."

"Don't feel bad. You aren't the only one with long-held family secrets. Abigail isn't really my aunt."

"What? Then who is she?"

"It's a long story, but the little-known fact is she's actually my grandmother. I usually don't bother explaining because it's too complicated." Kat put her arm around Mia's shoulder. "Don't worry. I'm sure it will be fine. You'll see."

"What am I going to do? I have no idea if my father knows about Heather. It's driving me nuts that I can't reach him. I have so many questions."

"How do you feel about the idea of having a sister? Do you want to meet her?"

Mia set down the photo. "I'm not sure. I have lived my whole life believing I was an only child. I don't have a lot of family. Okay, at this point, I pretty much have no family, since I can't reach my dad. It would mean a lot to meet her someday, just to see what's she's like. I wonder if she knows about *me*."

"Well, you'll find out when you talk to Gwen." Kat paused for a moment. "When I found out about my family heritage, it was confusing, but one thing stood out to me. Nothing really changed. No matter what happened in the past, I'm still me. Even though I found out I was adopted, nothing was particularly different, except that I finally understood why my sisters don't look much like me."

Mia leaned her head against Kat's. "Thanks. You've been so nice to me."

"That could be because I have a sinister ulterior motive. Have I mentioned lately that I *really* need a dog walker?"

With a laugh, Mia moved to get up. "Okay, okay, I know. I'm still thinking about it. First, I think I have to have another awkward conversation with Gwen."

"Yeah, I guess you do. Watch out for Potty Mouth."

"I'm hoping Gwen might be easier to talk to when there's not a squirrel in her house."

Mia helped Kat put away the pile of photos and Kat offered to let her take the one of Heather to show Gwen. After thanking her again, Mia left the kennel, drove back to Alpine Grove, picked up some dinner at the cafe, and collapsed in her room. It had been an extremely long and emotionally draining day.

The message light on the phone was flashing. She listened to the message and smiled at the sound of Chris's voice. He said, "Hi Mia, sorry I missed you, but I made it to LA finally. Now my sister wants me to drive her to do about a hundred errands and then we're going out to dinner. Hey Lulu, what are you doing? Oh okay, you want to sit in my lap, don't you? Here you go. Watch it with those paws! Good girl. Um, sorry about that. So hey, I wanted to talk to you about the meeting with Ben. It was great, and he loved the drawings. It was probably the best meeting ever. Okay, well, my sister is giving me the stink eye, so I have to go. I miss you. I'll call you when I get home. Bye."

Mia giggled, thinking about Lulu making a pest of herself while Chris was trying to leave the message. It was so easy to imagine. She was sorry to have missed the call too. Everything seemed a little less bright and cheerful as the reality of not having Chris around started to sink in.

Mia had been on her own and alone for years, so it was ridiculous that she'd miss him like this already. They'd only been apart for half a day. Maybe it was just the gloomy rainy weather that was affecting her mood.

～

Kat was sitting on the sofa reading in the living room when Joel returned. At the sound of the door opening, all five dogs leaped up and charged through the room toward the entryway. He shooed them away as he walked into the kitchen.

Kat tossed her book aside and went to greet him. "So how is the Shack? Did you fix what was falling apart?"

"I think so."

"What happened?"

"Well, it turns out Frank likes to try to catch flies."

Kat leaned against the counter, watching as Joel pulled items out of the refrigerator. "So given the expression on your face, I'm guessing the Great Bernese Fly Hunter did something bad."

"He missed. And when a hundred and twenty pounds of furry dog lands on a cabinet door, the door loses."

"I see."

"Fortunately, I have extra hinges and a lot of wood glue, so it should be fine." He leaned over and gave her a kiss. "So did you have fun playing with old photos?"

"It was kind of surprising in a way. I think Mia has a half-sister."

"That must have been…interesting."

"I told her we all have secrets."

"That's certainly true."

"In other news, it turns out Tracy is not having a baby."

"Did she ever tell Rob she thought she was?"

"Yes, but she took the test and it was negative. She was probably late because of a recent bout with the flu and stress related to stuff at the vet clinic and Rob working so much. Then telling him increased everyone's stress level."

Joel took a bite out of a cracker. "You look sad."

"I think they're going to break up." Kat reached over and grabbed a cracker. "They had a huge fight and when I talked to Tracy, she started to cry. Then I started to cry. It was awful."

"There's nothing you can do other than be her friend."

"I know. It's just sad because I like both Tracy and Rob. They seem so happy and have been living together for quite a while now. It makes me worry that we'll break up."

"We're not breaking up." Joel raised an eyebrow. "Unless there's something I don't know."

Kat put her hand on his forearm. "Not at all. It's just I know I've been a pain to be around because of the book deadlines and trying to find a new dog walker. I was really hoping Mia would agree, but it's a hard sell. It's not like I can pay much. But in a few weeks, we're going to have a lot of dogs here."

"How many is a lot?"

"After the latest booking, I can report that the kennels will be completely full. Every last one of them. Even your fly-obsessed buddy Frank, the klutzy mountain dog will be here with his roommate Mona because Jack and Becca are planning to spend Thanksgiving in Colorado."

"Filling all the kennels is the idea, isn't it?"

"I know, and it's sort of startling that suddenly, the business is going to be in the black for a change. But my first book deadline is right after Thanksgiving. When am I going to have time to write if I'm walking dogs all day? I was *supposed* to have a dog walker by now. I wrote a business plan!"

Joel broke off a corner of a cracker and handed it to Linus, who was sitting at his feet. "Well, we knew this was a possibility. I can help some, but I've got my own deadlines to deal with."

Kat wrapped her arms around his waist and gave him a hug. "I know. When Mia comes by tomorrow, I think I'll resort to begging. She'd be perfect. The dogs love her."

"Except she doesn't live here. You're boarding her dog."

Kat leaned back to look up into his face. "Correction: she doesn't live here *yet*. She might have a half-sister whose mom lives right next door. That might keep her here."

"You said she's traveling. Do you know where she's going?"

"Not really. But I think she should stay here. At least until my book is done."

Joel chuckled. "You have this all figured out."

"Why not? I moved to Alpine Grove and so did you." Kat spread her arms wide. "Hey, even Maria moved here, and no one would have *ever* predicted that."

"Speaking of which, when are you boarding her cat?"

"I'm not sure. I'm hoping she forgets about it."

"You know she won't."

Kat shook her head. "She's talking about spending Thanksgiving with her grandmother in New Jersey. I'm trying to discourage that idea. The last thing I need is a cat terrorizing my office while I'm trying to write."

"I'm sure you'll figure it out. Did you talk to Robin about renting the lodge for the wedding reception?"

"Yes, and she's up for it. She and Alec are going on a trip in February, so they want to board Leroy and Emma. We might be able to pay for some of the reception in trade."

"Now that our finances are so intertwined, I'm extra pleased to hear that."

"Your frugality is showing again." Kat waved her hand dismissively. "But that's okay. I want to save our money for the honeymoon. That's where I want to splurge."

"On what?"

"Everything. I want to go out to eat, do fun stuff, and not worry about money the whole time we're in Hawaii."

"We'll see."

"Oh come on—it's our honeymoon! When are we ever going to have the opportunity to just relax and celebrate our marriage? It's a once-in-a-lifetime thing."

"Well, there are wedding anniversaries. They celebrate marriage too."

Kat narrowed her eyes. "Wait a minute. Are you saying we get to go to Hawaii on our anniversary too?"

"Well, we could. Maybe not every year. But sometimes. Maybe every five years?"

"That's a great idea!" Kat grinned. "I didn't think it was possible, but I think I love you more now."

"Good, because I love you back."

∼

The next morning, Mia called Gwen and got her answering machine. Instead of leaving a message, Mia wimped out and hung up. She hadn't considered that Gwen might be at work. Had she mentioned where she worked? With a sigh, Mia ran through the many questions she hadn't asked. Because of the quest to remove Potty Mouth, they'd both been distracted and it hadn't been a particularly relaxing conversation.

It was raining again, so after breakfast Mia curled up with a novel. Going on an excursion to see one of the places on the postcards was less appealing in a downpour. Once she turned the last page on the book, she put it with the others on her nightstand.

In addition to having a completely worthless ending, the book was the last one she had left. Maybe she could give them back to the bookstore for Margaret to resell. It was time to venture forth and get more reading material. Mia was going to have to settle somewhere and get a library card; otherwise, she'd end up spending all her lottery money on books.

At lunchtime, Mia ventured out into the rain for yet another muddy midday walk with Gizmo. Kat joined them with her pack of dogs. Not surprisingly, Kat asked again about the job.

What Kat didn't know was that Mia really had been thinking about it. Constantly in fact, but she also missed Chris terribly, which was not helping her decision-making process.

Mia stopped and readjusted her grip on the leash while Gizmo investigated an exciting patch of ground. "Part of me would love to take the job, but I'm not sure. Walking in the woods with you, even in all this rain, has been great. I have enjoyed being here."

Kat raised her eyebrows. "Then what's the problem? Is it the money? I know I can't afford to pay much, but if you get into grooming you can start making some serious cash. I'd just take a percentage for the use of the space and setting up appointments."

"That's not it. I think I told you that I have some money. It's enough to last for a while until I figure out what to do. It's Chris."

"And the problem is that he's in San Francisco."

"Yes! In fact, he actually wants me to *move* there." Mia raised her arms in a gesture of exasperation. "But that's insane. We've only known each other for a few days."

"How do you feel about him?"

"I don't know. We have a good time together and I really miss him. Way, way more than I thought I would. But maybe that's just because I've had no friends, much less a date, in who knows how long."

Kat looked thoughtful for a moment. "I have no idea what your relationship with him is like, but I can tell you that I invited Joel to move in here not too long after we met. It was probably the best decision I've ever made."

"Do you mean like *days* after you met?"

"I don't remember exactly, but there was a fire and his house smelled like smoke, so I suggested that he stay here." She grinned. "And the rest is history."

"So you think I should move to San Francisco?"

"Not at all. That's your decision. I think you should do what you think is best for you. I'm just saying that in my case, almost from the moment I met him, I realized Joel was like no one I had ever known before. So I made what was, to a lot of people, a really impulsive decision. But it was right for me. Only you know what's right for you."

"I'm completely confused." Mia sighed. "Didn't people think it was strange that Joel moved in here so quickly?"

"Sure they did. You've met Maria, so you can imagine her response."

Mia nodded. "I hate to think what she said."

"Yeah, she gave me all kinds of grief. My mother called Joel a gold-digger who was only interested in me because of my vast fortune." Kat chuckled. "Yeah, right."

Mia stopped short. She really did have a fortune. Okay, it wasn't like a multi-million-dollar fortune, but still, she had money. And Chris had made no bones about the fact that he was practically bankrupt. Was that really what was going on? If she moved to San Francisco to be with him, suddenly Chris would have lots of lovely lottery money available to pay his exorbitant rent. Would he really do that? How well did she really know him, anyway?

Kat looked at her. "Are you okay? Did I say something to upset you? When I talk about my mother, it usually only upsets me or other people who have actually met her."

"It's fine." Mia glanced at Kat and almost without thinking blurted out, "But yes, I want the job. We can try it out over the winter like you said. I just need to find a place to live."

"That's fantastic!" Kat stopped and gave her a hug. "Thank you! I know right now it's quiet, but next week, it's like the floodgates break loose and half the dogs in Alpine Grove are going to be here."

Mia was taken aback at Kat's enthusiasm. "I guess I should look into rentals."

"Well, Gwen wants to get out of here before winter. Maybe you could rent her place. It's kind of ugly, so I bet it would be cheap."

"Actually, the inside is cute. She fixed it up, so it's way nicer than the trailer I used to live in. I have to talk to her again anyway."

"Didn't you call her?"

"I got her answering machine and didn't leave a message. I couldn't figure out what to say. If I offer to rent her place, maybe she'll be more interested in talking to me."

"No doubt. According to Joel, she really doesn't like shoveling snow."

"I got that impression."

After leaving Kat's place, Mia stopped by the bookstore for more books and then returned to the H12. She tried to call Gwen again, to no avail. Maybe she'd be back after five when the workday was over.

In the meantime, it was nice to have some time to collect her thoughts, since Mia had just, somewhat impulsively, made a commitment to taking a job and living in Alpine Grove. And in the process probably just torched any type of future with Chris. But if her past track record were any indication, she probably didn't have a future with him anyway.

An opportunity to earn money doing something she liked to do didn't happen every day. In fact, it had never happened at all. The idea of learning how to groom dogs professionally and having an actual career was exciting. For once, the future looked promising and she finally had a plan for what to do next. Living in a motel room was getting old. Even if Gwen said no, she probably could find another place to rent somewhere in Alpine Grove.

Mia's thoughts were interrupted by the phone ringing. She reached to the nightstand to answer it. A little flutter of excitement swept over her at the sound of Chris's voice greeting her. She smiled. "I'm so glad you called. How did everything go today?"

There was a pause before Chris replied, "Well, uh, not very well."

"Was the meeting about the firm losing the library job?"

"Yes, and there was a lot of rah-rah talk about how we all need to work harder to ensure we are selected for the next project. Except me."

"What do you mean *except you*?"

"After the big meeting, my supervisor Bill pulled me aside and claimed that it's my fault they weren't selected."

"You're kidding. I thought you were working on a closet."

"More like the ceiling materials for a closet." He sighed. "I sat down in his office and Bill went over all my flaws in excruciating detail. If I could just work on those things and basically change who I am as a human being, I could be a great asset to the firm."

"That sounds awful, but I don't understand what your flaws or the closet you designed have to do with losing the contract."

"More or less that my flaws were represented in my work. I don't know. I started to lose focus as I got more and more pissed off at what Bill was saying."

Mia raised her arm in frustration. "I don't understand. It's a closet, for heaven's sake!"

"I know. I mean, I can deal with some constructive criticism. Nobody is perfect, and we all know I'm not. But I guess I must have looked upset, because he asked me what my problem was."

"I've had conversations like that." Mia clenched the receiver. "I think your problem is him. That's so unfair!"

"I think I said something like I can't change who I am. And then he said, 'Well, what are you going to do, quit?'"

"Uh-oh."

"Yeah. I said, 'You think I'm too much of a wimp to quit, don't you?'"

Mia didn't say anything, but it was pretty clear where this was going.

Chris continued, "He said, yes, I do think you're that much of wimp. So I said, 'Fine. Consider this my two weeks' notice.' And then I stood up and walked out of the office."

"Wow. What are you going to do?"

"I have no idea. I was so angry I was shaking. By the time I got back to my desk, I'd calmed down a little and it started to dawn on me what I had just done. I'm so screwed."

"You'll find something else. Something better."

"Maybe. And I realized that the other person who is going to be really screwed is Ben. I mean, he loved my design ideas for the lake house. They'll transfer the work to someone else, but I feel bad. We really got along great and our ideas just gelled. It was actually fun. Probably the most fun I've had in my entire career."

"I'm so sorry." Mia twisted the phone cord around her finger. "Can't you work for him and finish the job?"

"I can't. There's a non-compete clause in my employment agreement. You get in trouble if you poach clients from GTH, and I have enough problems. Right now, I'm sitting here trying not to freak out. The only good thing is that I applied for one of those zero-interest cards and worked on consolidating my student loans. Tomorrow I'll give back my car to the leasing company. Then, well, I don't know. More panic, maybe?"

"I have a lot of experience with losing jobs, and even though I know it doesn't seem like it right now, everything will work out. You'll see. You hated that place." Mia sat up straighter. "In fact, this could be the best thing that ever happened to you. So congratulations!"

He offered an ironic chuckle. "Thanks, but I think *you're* the best thing that ever happened to me. I miss you so much it hurts. Is there any way you can visit while I still have a place to live?"

Mia paused. Chris probably wasn't going to like what she was about to say. "Well, I, ah, have decided to stay in Alpine Grove. I accepted Kat's job offer."

"Already? Did you talk to your father? What did he say? I was so wrapped up in my own mess, I forgot to ask."

"No, the number was disconnected. But I looked at some of Kat's old photos. Gwen's daughter Heather looks like my dad. I decided to stay here because I like it here. Kat is great and I love the dogs."

"Those are good reasons. I'm happy for you. And I can't say I'm not envious."

Mia looked down at the ugly plaid bedspread and picked at an errant thread. "Maybe you could come back for a visit."

"I have to work on finding a new job. And saving the few pennies I have left."

"Maybe once you find something, you could visit."

Mia could hear the resignation in his voice as he softly replied, "We'll see."

~

After hanging up the phone receiver, Mia stared at the telephone for a moment. Chris had sounded so forlorn that now she had an overwhelming urge to cry. Every choice had repercussions and her decision to stay in Alpine Grove meant she probably wouldn't see Chris for a long time. Possibly never.

She felt guilty that part of the reason she didn't want to go to San Francisco was because of money. Was she really that selfish? That cynical? If she were brutally honest with herself, the answers weren't particularly flattering. But she didn't want to get more involved with someone who might end up using her. It wasn't worth the risk. The reality was that enough people had let her down in her life that she didn't trust anyone much at all.

Chris had said that he missed her so much it hurt. Unfortunately, that feeling wasn't one-sided. There was a little ache in Mia's chest whenever she thought about him. And every time something happened like Kat offering her the job, the first thing she wanted to do was run over to the Enchanted Moose and talk to him. But he wasn't there. When they were together, she'd told him anything and everything that she was thinking and he'd understood.

Mia shook her head. She was a lot of things, but one thing she was not was a sappy romantic. It was time to get over her little-girl fantasies and accept the fact that the time she'd spent with Chris was just a fling. Time to move on. In fact, right now she needed to call Gwen and get things moving. If she ended up getting the answering machine again, she was going to leave a message. No chickening out this time.

She sat up, straightened her shoulders, and picked up the handset again. The phone rang a few times and when the machine picked up, she took a deep breath and said, "Gwen, hi, it's Mia. Kat said you might be interested in renting out your place and I'm interested." She gave her number at the H12 and didn't manage to mix up any words or numbers.

After hanging up, she leaned back on the bed and let out a deep breath. Thank heavens that was over. Now that Gwen had an incentive to return the phone call, maybe she could get some answers about her father and possible half-sister. In the meantime, there was a big stack of novels sitting here waiting to be read. She might as well enjoy her last gasp of leisure time before she joined the ranks of the employed.

The phone rang, jolting Mia from her drowsy half-asleep efforts to read. Perhaps she was a little more tired than she'd thought. She was greeted by Gwen's stern voice on the other end of the line.

"Hi, Gwen. I was hoping I could talk to you about renting."

"I want to sell the place, not rent it."

"Do you have a buyer already?" Mia twisted the phone cord. Maybe she was too late.

"No, I don't."

"I'm guessing that winter is not a great time to sell real estate in Alpine Grove."

"Don't you think I know that?"

"Well, if I rented your place for the winter, you could visit your daughter. And then you could list it for sale again in the spring if you wanted. But I'd like to take a leak...I mean *look*...look at your home again first. I only saw the kitchen and living room."

Gwen paused for a moment before continuing in a softer tone. "I probably shouldn't ask, but *why* do you want to rent it? So far, the only people who are interested want the land. They tried to convince me to pay to have the trailer removed, which is ridiculous. If they want this mobile home gone, they can move the stupid thing themselves. The other calls have been from loggers and Abigail would roll over in her grave if I sold out to a logging company."

"Kat offered me a job at her kennel and living next door would be convenient. Your house is far larger than where I was living before or the motel rooms I've been staying in."

"You don't care that it's an old mobile home?"

"The last place I rented was an Airstream. I don't need much space and your place is gigantic by comparison."

"You're really serious about this?"

"I promise I'd take good care of the place for you."

"It's pretty isolated out here, you know."

"I know. But Kat and Joel are next door if I need anything. I'm a quiet person, but as you know, I do have a dog." Mia wasn't going to volunteer that Gizmo had an unfortunate habit of eating his way through his accommodations. "You could put your valuables in storage. Or rent the place to me unfurnished. It's up to you. I can be flexible."

"It certainly sounds like it. Okay, I think you talked me into it. This could work, and the idea of being in San Diego this winter makes me practically giddy. Let me talk to my daughter. Could you stop by tomorrow afternoon after work, so I can show you everything? You should know what you're getting into."

"That would be great. I'm looking forward to it."

After they worked out the details of her visit, Mia hung up the phone and clasped her hands together. Everything was starting to work out. She could have a job doing something she loved and an incredibly short commute if she lived right next door. Gizmo could even come to work with her. Maybe they could walk to work. He'd love that!

She looked back at the phone. Now she wanted to tell Chris. But he'd sounded so upset when they hung up that he probably wouldn't want to hear more about her plans for staying here.

Nothing was really settled, so she didn't really have anything new to tell him yet anyway. She just wanted to hear his voice. Depending on what happened with Gwen tomorrow, maybe she could talk to him afterward. Smiling at the idea, she curled up with her book again in an effort to settle her racing thoughts. Setting up an entirely new life required a lot of mental energy.

The next day, Mia got up and began making an effort to pack up her room. It was incredibly premature, since it wasn't like she could move into Gwen's house immediately. There could be some tragic flaw with the place. Or Gwen would be angry about Mia's suspicions that Heather was her half-sister and summarily throw her out of the trailer into the rain. And yet Mia kept puttering around folding clothes, trying to get organized.

At this point, Mia was a little desperate to stay some place that had a kitchen. The cafe food was okay, but eating out all the time was exhausting, and eating by herself at restaurants was depressing. She felt like everyone was watching her. The thought of sitting in her own space with Gizmo begging at her feet was incredibly appealing.

Mia peeked out the window and found the rain was starting to let up at last. If she went out to the kennel a little early, she could spend some extra time playing with Gizmo. Kat had said that they needed to go over start dates, times, and procedures. Mia was eager to get going with her new job, so getting there early would show initiative. Lenore at Round House Distributing would be stunned by Mia's work ethic.

Chapter 11

Secrets

Mia had an enjoyable afternoon tending to dogs with Kat and discussing what she'd be doing every day once she started working at the kennel. She also learned from Joel that an old trail ran through the woods from Gwen's house to Kat's. If she were able to rent Gwen's place, Joel promised he'd hack back the vegetation so she and Gizmo could walk through the forest to the kennel. But first Mia had to convince Gwen that she'd be the perfect tenant.

At the agreed-upon time, Mia drove over to Gwen's house. As she made her way down the driveway, she viewed the scene differently than she had before. What would it be like to live here? If she rented the trailer, this would be her route home. How would that feel? What would the area look like covered with snow?

She parked in front of the mobile home and walked to the door, casting her eyes over the dingy exterior. It certainly wasn't the prettiest abode, but that could work to her advantage when it came to negotiating.

Gwen opened the door and gave Mia a smile as she motioned for her to come inside.

Mia walked up the steps and turned her head to look around at the interior. Although it wasn't like she was walking into full-color Oz from a black-and-white Kansas, the difference between the interior and the exterior of the mobile home was striking.

Gwen walked to the stove and reached into a cabinet for a box. "Would you like some tea?"

"Yes, that would be nice."

After setting up the tea, Gwen turned around. "So are you ready for the grand tour? We can get through it before the water boils. As you can see, the living room is over there. The bedrooms and bath are down the hall."

"Okay, lead the way."

Gwen walked down the hallway and gestured as she passed each room, "Second bedroom, bathroom, master bedroom."

Mia walked into the rooms and peered into closets. There was a fair amount of storage space, which would be a novelty. "It looks fine to me. Did you find the squirrel hole in the bathroom?"

"I nailed an old board over it. Potty Mouth should be an outdoor-only varmint from now on."

Mia smiled. "I'm glad to hear that. So, what type of rent are you expecting?"

The whistle of the teakettle interrupted Gwen's answer and they hustled back to the kitchen area. Gwen handed her a mug and they sipped tea as they negotiated rent and deposits.

Gwen set down the mug. "I can be out of here pretty quick. I'd love to miss the first snowstorm."

"I'm staying at the H12, so I can move in whenever you're ready. When does it usually snow?"

"The first storm could be any time now. I called that mini-storage place and they have men and a truck. I'll pack up my personal stuff and put it in storage. My furniture, like the couch, is mostly crap, so I'll just leave it here if you don't mind."

"That sounds great. Thanks."

"All right, it sounds like we have a deal." Gwen grinned widely, which transformed her appearance. She was actually an extremely pretty woman when she wasn't wearing her typical frown.

Mia took a deep breath. Time to move to less pleasant topics. "I know we talked about it before, but if you have a few minutes, I was wondering if I could ask you a couple of questions about my father. His number has been disconnected and I can't reach him."

Gwen's frown returned. "I suppose."

"I'm not sure how to ark, asp...ugh, I mean *ask* this, but I saw a photograph of Heather, and well, she looks a lot like my father. And you said she was in fourth grade in 1975."

Gwen crossed her arms. "Yes. She turned thirty this year."

"So did I. I'm wondering if she's my half-sister."

"You're quite the little Nancy Drew, aren't you?"

"I liked *Harriet the Spy* better and I'm sure she could have figured it out. The math wasn't very hard." Mia raised her palms toward the ceiling. "Does my father know this? Does Heather?"

"No, and I'd rather they didn't."

"Didn't Heather ever ask about her father?"

"Yes, for a while. I just said he was dead. For all I knew, he could have been. If you must know, it was a shock to have him turn up here in 1975."

"Why didn't you tell him?"

"Because he told me about his wife and you. The whole story about how you were mad at him because of the dog. The man was distraught and had enough problems—and so did I." Gwen stood up and got some more tea. "It was just one night. He was nothing more than a sperm donor."

"But don't they both deserve to know?"

"I thought about that and came close to telling Dan about Heather once, but what purpose would it serve to tell them now? I can't think of any reason to rock the boat. Heather is happy. And when I talked to Dan recently, he seemed fine too."

"He didn't sound fine in the letter I got from him. In fact, I'm afraid he's about to die or something."

Gwen turned back toward the table. "Why do you say that?"

"It's just the way it was worded. Like a final goodbye to me. And now that I know he really didn't take my dog away, well, I really want to talk to him. I feel like I need to apologize. I've been so angry and spent so much time blaming him. I need to let it go and tell him I forgive him."

Gwen shook her head. "Heather is doing great. Her life is on track and she and her husband are thinking of finally having kids. I could be a grandma! I don't want to screw things up for her right when everything is going so well. And what will it do to our relationship with each other? She'll know I lied to her for *years*."

"I know she's a complete stranger, but I'd like to meet her. Now I know she shares my blood, and the whole idea of having a sister is amazing to me. Maybe we have similar interests. Maybe we even look a little like each other."

Gwen sat down with a sigh. "I can tell you that you do. The similarity is sort of hard for me to deal with, if you want to know the truth."

"Don't you think Heather would be just as curious about me as I am about her? Doesn't she deserve the chance to meet me and maybe her dad, assuming I can ever find him again?"

"I suppose."

"Will you talk to her? Please?"

"I'll think about it." Gwen put her forehead on her palms. "It was all such a long time ago. I can't believe this is really happening."

Mia placed her palm on Gwen's back. "I know. I can't either."

~

After the emotionally draining conversation with Gwen, Mia went back to the H12 and sprawled out on the bed. She needed some decompression time so she could think. How was she going to find her father, given that she had so little to go on? Almost nothing, in fact. Gwen didn't have any more information than she'd already provided. Dan Riggins had been in Santa Barbara, and now he wasn't. In a situation like this, people hired a detective, didn't they? Where was she supposed to find her own Sherlock Holmes in Alpine Grove?

Tired of her whirling thoughts, Mia rolled over and grabbed her novel from the nightstand. Maybe after a good night's sleep she'd have some idea what to do. Holding the book in front of her, she smiled. Whenever she'd had questions in her life before, the library always had answers. Why should this be any different? Tomorrow, her first stop would be the Alpine Grove library.

After breakfast, Mia set out to find the library. Two sets of steps led up to the imposing brick building, which sported arched doorways and windows. Mia wondered if Chris had seen this place. Architecturally speaking, it was a beautiful structure. He'd probably know exactly what style it was and if it was historic in some way. All Mia could say about it was, "it's old."

Because her thoughts had turned to Chris yet *again*, she frowned as she opened the door to go inside. She needed to stop thinking about him. Chris probably had figured out the same thing she had, which was that there was no way anything between them would ever work. It was a good thing she hadn't been more insistent on a visit. At least he hadn't leaped at the chance to freeload off her. That scored a few points. Maybe she was focusing too much on Kat's gold-digger comment. Obviously, the woman didn't think Joel was a gold-digger, or she wouldn't be marrying him.

Shaking off her scattered thoughts, Mia walked up to the counter, where a woman with curly reddish-blonde hair sat behind a computer monitor surrounded by piles of papers and books. She looked up and smiled. "May I help you?"

Mia said, "Um, I ah, am not sure this is the right plate... *place* to ask. But I need to find someone."

"What do you mean find?" The woman stood up and walked around the desk. "Are you doing genealogy research? If so, I can help with that. I love helping people find their roots. It's fascinating what you can uncover."

"No, not exactly. The person I'm looking for is still alive. Or I hope he is. I'm trying to find my father. I guess I might need to hire a detective. But I'm not sure how to do that or where to start."

The librarian looked thoughtful for a moment. "Interesting. Last year, the FBI's National Crime Information Center reported that there were more than nine-hundred-sixty-nine-thousand missing persons."

Mia raised her eyebrows. "That's, uh, detailed."

"You're right. That's not helpful. My name is Jan, by the way." The librarian put out her hand. "Don't mind me. I tend to remember facts like that. It's an occupational hazard. Do you have any information about your father at all?"

"His name is Dan or Daniel Riggins and he was in Santa Barbara recently. All I have is a post office box number and a phone number that's disconnected."

"Well, that's a good start. I could do an Internet search for you, but most records aren't available online. And even though some information might be publicly available from a legal standpoint, certain records can be accessed only by law-enforcement personnel or a licensed private investigator."

"How would I go about finding a private investigator?"

"Well, there is a state association for licensed investigators. I can contact them and see if there is anyone local. Also, lawyers often use investigators. There's a lawyer here in town that I could call and ask for a referral."

Mia's eyes widened. "Would you really be willing to do that?"

"Certainly. Research is what I do." Jan gestured toward the rows of shelving. "Do you want to browse while I do a couple of searches and make those calls?"

"I don't have a library card yet. I just decided to move here."

"I can help with that problem. Everyone should have a library card." Jan grinned. "Welcome to Alpine Grove."

Mia had a thoroughly enjoyable time roaming through the stacks and pulling out books. She'd spent so much time at the Windiberg library that visiting a different one was like going to a chocolate-truffle factory versus a candy store. Although the Alpine Grove library wasn't huge, it was full of books she hadn't read yet.

She returned to the desk with a big pile of books. "I might have gotten carried away."

"That happens to me sometimes and I work here." Jan handed her a piece of paper. "Please fill this out."

Mia filled out the form and handed it back.

Jan looked it over and began typing on the computer keyboard. "So I got a name from Larry Lowell, the lawyer here in town, and verified that the person is still a member in good standing with the association."

"Thank you." Mia took her new library card from Jan and tucked it into her wallet.

Jan handed her a slip of paper with a phone number. "Her name is Edith Moffitt and according to Larry, she's a bulldog who does it all—in addition to being a private investigator, she does skip-tracing, process-serving, and even bond enforcement."

"She's a bounty hunter?"

"According to Larry, she's extremely tenacious and works cases throughout the state. He also mentioned that she can be a bit gruff, so when you talk to her, don't be surprised if she doesn't seem particularly friendly at first."

Mia tried to ignore the twinge of anxiety in her chest. "I guess it's worth a try."

Jan pushed the stack of book toward her. "These are due in three weeks."

Mia carried the books back out to her car, got in, and set the pile down on the passenger seat. The idea of talking to Edith, the bulldog bounty hunter, was daunting. Gruff was one of those words that often was used as a euphemism for irritable, unpleasant, or downright nasty. People like that often had zero patience for Mia's tendency to mangle the English language.

She drove extra slowly back to the H12, trying to muster up her confidence and courage. For someone who had spent most of her life avoiding confrontation, she certainly had been given a lot of opportunities to engage in awkward and uncomfortable conversations lately. Even more annoying was that what she really wanted to do was call Chris and talk to him about it. And how sappy was that?

～

When she returned to the H12, Mia called Edith before she could dwell on it any longer and lose her nerve.

The phone rang several times and then a husky voice greeted her. Mia cleared her throat, "Yes, may I please speak to Edith Moffitt?"

"You found her."

Mia's jaw hung open for a moment. That was a woman's voice? "Well, um, yes, I got your name from a lawyer here in Alpine Grope...Alpine *Grove*."

"Yeah, Larry. How's that randy old boy doing?"

"Fine." Mia hoped he was fine, since she'd never met him. "I was told that you can find beagles."

"I'm not the dog catcher, lady. Call the SPCA."

"I'm sorry, I meant *people*. I'm hoping you can find my father."

"Maybe. You got a budget for this? Because I'm not cheap."

"Yes, I know it will cost money. I'm afraid he might be sick or dying and I really need to talk to him."

"All right. What's his name?"

"Dan Riggins."

"What else do you know?"

Mia went through the story of the postcards, Gwen, and anything else she could think of that might help. "Do you think you can find him?"

"Piece of cake. Wire me the money, and I'll get started tomorrow."

Mia thanked Edith and hung up the phone. She flopped back against the pillows on the bed. If the interrogation she'd just been through were any indication, there was no doubt that Edith would find her father. Jan's bulldog description was apt. Edith Moffitt was no demure shrinking violet.

Now she needed to go find a bank and wire her deposit to Edith. She grabbed her bag when the phone rang. Maybe Edith had forgotten something.

Mia stopped short when Chris greeted her. She sat down on the edge of the bed. "How are you?"

"I'm doing okay. Mostly, I wanted to let you know that I'm moving to LA. We promised not to lose touch, remember?"

"I do." Mia didn't want to say how much she missed him. "I'm still here, obviously. But I'll be moving into Gwen's house. I still almost can't believe it, but she agreed to let me spend the winter there."

"It sounds like everything is working out for you."

"I know! It really is for a change. I'm hiring a private investigator to find my father."

"That's a big step."

"It is, and I agonized over the decision because this woman, Edith, costs a fortune."

"Well, as I recall, you have a fortune."

Mia traced the ugly plaid design on the bedspread, skirting around a hole in the fabric. Why was Chris bringing that up? "I don't have a fortune, but yes, I do have enough money to pay her."

"Is something bothering you?"

"No, everything is fine." Except that she missed him. Why was she getting weird about money again? He hadn't asked her for a cent. "I'm sorry if I sounded…funny."

"It's okay. I miss you and I'm trying to get my act together so I can come visit. I'll be staying with my sister for a while. You have the number, if you want to call."

"What about your apartment?"

"I'm giving it up, selling my furniture, and getting out of here. Being unemployed gives you a lot of time to think. I decided it's time for me to start over somewhere else."

"You're lucky you have your sister. And you even get to see Lulu again."

"I know. My sister has been great about everything." Chris chuckled. "Although she says I spoiled Lulu so badly while I was taking care of her that in exchange for a room at her place, I have to take the uppity little poodle princess to obedience classes."

"Aww, but she's so cute. She'll probably win them over."

"We'll see. I'll give you a call once I've moved. I'm shutting off the phone here tomorrow."

"So soon?"

"Along with every other creditor in Northern California, the phone company isn't too happy with me."

"Oh." Mia's stomach started to ache. Now she wouldn't even be able to call Chris. "When will you be at your sister's house?"

"As soon as I can. I'm rounding up people in the building to have a group yard sale. We're hoping to do it this weekend, if it doesn't rain."

"I'm so impressed you're making all these changes. It's got to be hard."

"It's not as hard as I thought it would be. Like I said, I've had a lot of time to think. After beating myself up about getting myself into debt, I started wondering why."

"What do you mean why?"

"Why did I spend so much? Even while I was buying stuff, I felt guilty and anxious about it. Part of me kept thinking that buying whatever that next shiny thing was would make me feel better. But it never did."

"It sounds like you were unhappy about a lot of things."

"I think I was trying to use shopping as some kind of escape. But it didn't solve anything and made matters worse. Getting rid of all that stuff feels good. It probably doesn't make any sense, but I feel lighter."

"That makes perfect sense. I get it."

"You always do."

"I know." Mia tried not to sigh in his ear. "I really do miss you, you know."

"I'm glad. I was starting to worry."

"Don't. Call me as soon as you can, okay?"

"I will. Promise."

They said their goodbyes and after Mia hung up the phone, she flopped back on the bed again. Who was she kidding? No matter how she tried to fight it, just hearing the sound of Chris's voice made her insanely happy. Was it possible that she was falling in love with Chris? Really? The thought was so outside of her realm of experience, she wasn't quite sure what to do with it.

It reminded her of the old Christmas TV special with the Grinch whose heart was two sizes too small, and once he discovered the spirit of Christmas his heart grew. Maybe Mia's battered, shriveled little heart just needed a little love and encouragement for a change.

She propped herself up on her elbows and stared at the ugly curtains. By the time Chris had settled himself in Los Angeles, maybe she'd have sorted through her feelings enough to talk to him about it. If he felt the same way, it would be amazing. And if not, well, it certainly wouldn't be the first time she'd made a fool of herself. You'd think with all the practice she'd had, she'd be good at it by now.

But at the moment, she had other things to do. Like go send an obscene amount of money to the grumpy new private investigator she'd just hired.

~

Over the next two weeks, Mia learned more about dogs and dog behavior than she ever thought possible. Kat hadn't been kidding when she'd said that more dogs would be staying at the kennel. When Mia had brought Gizmo to stay, the kennels had been quiet, but the peaceful interlude was definitely over. With sixteen boarding dogs in residence, suddenly the dog walks became a much more complicated multi-excursion process.

Kat took her own five dogs out at lunchtime with a few boarding dogs, but Mia was in charge of walking the rest of the boarding dogs multiple times each day. She quickly learned which dogs walked well with each other and which did not. She also figured out how to walk multiple dogs on leashes without tying herself or the dogs into a gigantic knot.

During her first week, Mia thought her feet were going to fall off. Her whole body ached, but her feet were the worst. By the time she went back to the H12, all she could do was collapse in a heap and fall asleep. Years of sitting in a cubicle typing information about carrots and then sitting in her car driving around the state hadn't prepared her for such a physically demanding job.

The Saturday after her first week at work, she'd helped Gwen move and was finally able to check out of the H12. The first snow flurries had fluttered around, which seemed to fire up Gwen's enthusiasm for getting out of town as quickly as possible.

After giving Gwen a goodbye hug, Mia took her meager belongings to the trailer and enjoyed a trip to the grocery store. Gizmo seemed pleased with his new home and Mia acquired a large sky kennel for him to sleep in at night. The last thing she needed was for Gizmo to chow down on the house while her eyes were closed.

True to his word, Joel had cut back the vegetation on the trail and once she was staying at Gwen's house, it was an easy walk with Gizmo to the kennel. Because Gizmo went with her to work and on many of the walks, he was getting as much exercise as she was. Convincing him to curl up in his new crate at night was not a problem.

Having such a relaxed and well-behaved dog was a new experience for Mia. Now she knew that poor Gizmo had undoubtedly been such a problem child before because he wasn't getting enough exercise. She'd done the best she could, but life in Windiberg hadn't been particularly good for either of them.

Mia talked to Betty, the groomer in downtown Alpine Grove, and asked her about an internship or apprenticeship. The woman had been amenable to the idea, but not until after Thanksgiving. She was taking a trip to see her grandchildren then, but she admitted that after the holiday she was going to be swamped with people wanting to have clean dogs for Christmas.

Edith, the bulldog private investigator, had called with a status report. She hadn't tracked down Mia's father, but she was hot on the trail, so it was only a matter of time. Mia found she was impatient to talk to her dad, which was absurd. She hadn't spoken to her father in more than a decade. A few more days wouldn't make any difference.

Mia also was impatient to talk to Chris, even though she knew he was still working on his own move. He had the number at Gwen's house, but moving four hundred miles from San Francisco to Los Angeles was certainly more complicated than Mia's move into the trailer from the H12.

Because she had lots of time to think while she was walking dogs, Mia imagined sharing stories with Chris about silly dog antics and the cartoons he might draw to accompany the stories. She missed his sense of humor and especially his kindness. Few people had ever been as supportive and compassionate toward her as he had. Even though they hadn't known each other long, she missed him and the connection they had more than she ever would have expected. If she weren't so exhausted by the end of each day, she'd probably lie awake dreaming of him like some lovesick teenager. But as it was, she was just too tired, so she restricted her girly mooning to daylight hours.

After a long day of walking and tending to dogs, Mia was reclining on the sofa reading while Gizmo snored on the throw rug in front of her. The phone rang, causing both of them to jolt upright. Mia ran to the wall phone in the kitchen to answer it. "Hello?"

"Hi, it's Chris."

"I'm so glad to hear from you! It feels like forever and so much has happened. Are you in LA yet?"

"I made it, although it was way more complicated than I thought it would be to sell everything. But it's done and I paid off practically all my creditors, so I only have two bills: one credit card and my newly consolidated student loan. Now I can finally focus on finding a job."

"Do you think you might be able to visit?"

"There's the little problem that I don't have a car anymore, remember? I gave it back to the leasing company."

"Can't you get another one?"

"Not until I find a job. My sister is going to let me borrow her car to get to interviews, but with my credit and no job, I'm going to be spending a lot of time on the bus."

Mia nodded in sympathy. "Been there. I ended up buying an old junker I named Dottie."

"That sounds like the name for a horse."

"She wouldn't go much faster than a horse. It was unpleasant trying to get her on the freeway. Anything more than forty-five miles an hour was rough on her, but mostly we just puttered around town, so it wasn't that bad."

Chris chuckled, "You have a way of taking things in stride."

"I didn't have much choice."

"I suppose. I'm trying hard to accept my fate gracefully, but a lot of the time I find myself furious about everything that has happened. Losing my job has been demoralizing."

"You quit for good reason and you hated the job anyway."

"I suppose." He sighed. "Living with my sister is the next-best thing to moving back in with my parents. I feel like such a failure."

"At least you have a sister. Oh, wait, I guess I do too. Somewhere."

"Did you find your father? What happened?"

After Mia described her conversations with Edith, the bulldog PI, Chris asked, "So what are you going to say to your father once she finds him?"

"I have no idea. Mostly, that I'm sorry. I'm worried he's going to die thinking that I still hate him."

"Are you going to tell him about Heather?"

"Gwen doesn't want me to."

"Does Heather know about your father?"

"Gwen said she'd talk to her, but I don't know if she really will. I'm not sure what to do. If he's dying, shouldn't he know he has more than one daughter? Particularly, one who is actually successful?"

"You're successful."

"No, I'm not. I'm walking dogs in a little town in the middle of nowhere."

"But you like it. You just finished telling me how much you're enjoying learning more about dogs. And weren't you the one who told me I was lucky to have found something that I love to do? Now you have, so by your own definition you're successful."

"I didn't think about it that way."

"Maybe you should. You struggled for a long time doing work you hated. Enjoy the fact that you don't have to anymore."

Mia smiled. "You might want to take your own advice."

"Okay, yeah, point taken."

～

The next evening after work, Mia got the call that she'd been both anticipating and dreading. Edith said she'd found Dan Riggins at a hotel in Los Angeles. She passed along the phone number and the amount of her final invoice.

Mia sat on the old wooden kitchen chair staring at the notes she'd written on the notepad. After everything she'd been through to find him, finally talking to her father was inducing a little panic attack. Her stomach was churning, and Gizmo put his muzzle on her thigh, clearly aware that she was upset. She stroked the dog's soft ears. What was she going to say to her father?

Petting Gizmo made her feel better, but didn't give her any ideas. She was just going to have to suck it up and have yet another uncomfortable conversation.

She dialed the number and asked to be put through to the room. Hearing her father's voice for the first time in years was so surreal, Mia could barely manage to squeak, "Dad? It's me, Mia—Amelia."

"Is it really you, Mimi?"

"Yes, it's me. I've been looking for you for a while."

"I told you where I was. I thought when you didn't get in touch that you were still angry—that you still hadn't forgiven me."

"It's a long sorry...I mean *story*. But I'm sorry too." Mia tried not to burst into tears as memories flooded over her. "I said so many terrible things, and I'm sorry."

"I'm glad you said something. It's been so long. And I'm about to go."

"That's what you said in the letter. Are you sick? Is there anything I can do?"

"I'm not sick. What gave you that idea?"

"Your letter."

"I told you when I sent the postcards that I was joining the Crisis Corps."

"I didn't get *that* letter. I only got the postcards and lottery tickets. My dog ate whatever else was in there."

"I suppose that explains why I didn't hear from you."

"What's the Crisis Corps?"

"The Peace Corps just formed it. Returning volunteers can go help out in other countries on short-term assignments."

"You're a returning volunteer? Since when?" Mia put her palm over her eyes. "So you're really okay. You're not dying?"

"Not immediately, as far as I know. I had to get a physical exam and the folks at the Peace Corps seemed to think I'm in good enough health to travel."

"When do you leave?"

"In a few days."

"Is there any way you could come to Alpine Grove?"

"I don't have a car. I sold it after I found out I was accepted into the program and going overseas."

Mia sighed. "I really would like to see you in person. I, um, well, have a lot of questions about what happened with Mom and other stuff too."

"How is your mother?"

Mia couldn't believe what he was asking. He still had the same laconic, slow way of speaking that her mother used to say was what turtles would sound like if they could speak. "Dad…um, Mom *died*. She's been dead for years."

"*What?* No one told me. What happened? When?"

"Howard shot her and himself the day of my high school graduation. It was in all the papers. It was probably the biggest scandal in Windiberg in the last hundred years."

"I was in the Peace Corps then, and never heard anything about it. Didn't your mother tell you I was in Paraguay?"

"No. She never said anything about you after you left. Howard had a tendency to lose it if she talked about the past."

"Is there any way you can get to LA? I'd like to see you and discuss everything that's happened in person." He paused and added softly, "I really want to catch up on the last twenty years before I go back to Central America."

"I'll see if I can get a day or two off work."

After gathering a few details about the location of the hotel where her father was staying, Mia hung up the phone. The amount of things they didn't know about each other's lives was bizarre and upsetting. He really hadn't known his ex-wife was murdered more than a decade ago.

Mia called Kat and explained the situation. She'd need to take off two days of dog walking and board Gizmo at the kennel. Although Kat understood what was going on, she was obviously not happy about the short notice. Although it seemed like she'd apologized about three hundred times, Mia still felt terrible.

Grabbing the receiver again, she called Chris. "Guess what? I'm coming to Los Angeles tomorrow."

"When can I see you?"

"After I talk to my dad."

"So the bulldog found him?"

"Yes, and he's about to leave the country to be a volunteer in Central America, so he wants to see me."

"I guess that means he's not dying."

"Nope." Mia went on to explain that her dad was in fine health and was headed overseas. "I had no idea he was ever in the Peace Corps."

"Your father seems to have all kinds of interesting secrets."

"And I have a few more for him that he doesn't even know about."

By the time she hung up the phone, Mia felt vastly better about her impromptu trip, partly because she couldn't wait to see Chris again. He sounded so much more relaxed now that he was unemployed.

After settling Gizmo into the kennel, Mia left early the next morning for Los Angeles. As she descended from the mountains, her anxiety began to increase along with the traffic. The adrenaline from the nervousness of talking to her father was long gone. Now she was just slightly panicked. It had been such a long time since they'd seen each other. And he seemed to have no idea what had happened in the interim. Had he never communicated with her mother at all? Maybe he hadn't. What if she and her father discovered they hated each other now?

Explaining her appalling personal and professional failures of the last twenty years wasn't going to impress him. He wasn't exactly going to be wowed by the amazing life she'd lived since he'd left. Parents didn't dream that their child would end up trying to eke out a meager existence in a rundown Windiberg trailer park.

And then there was the whole question of Heather. Did Mia have the right—or the guts—to mention her newly discovered half-sister? Every potential way that meeting her father could go wrong rattled through Mia's mind as she drove toward the coast.

In an effort to get her brain to shut up, she turned on the radio. The Eagles' song "Take It to the Limit" blasted from the speakers, which reminded her of driving around Alpine Grove with Chris. She smiled at the thought of him telling her to relax and reassuring her everything would be okay, as he had so many times before.

With a deep breath, she made a conscious effort to push her negative thoughts aside, as if it were a big rock that needed to be dislodged. Visualizing her thoughts as something apart from herself led to an unsettling realization. The voice in her head that said she was worthless and would never be anything but a loser sounded a lot like Howard.

She shook her head, as if the movement could banish his voice. The man was long dead, and that part of her life was over. He had no power over her anymore. Whatever was going to happen with her father would happen. And then she could talk to Chris about it. Spending time with him would undoubtedly help her decompress from the whole ordeal. Maybe once she finally had dealt with her past, she'd be able to move toward a better future.

Chapter 12

Meetings and Greetings

The hotel Mia's father was staying at was fairly close to LAX and the traffic was horrible. As she pulled into the parking lot, she gripped the steering wheel even more tightly, but it was way too late to chicken out now.

When she walked into the restaurant, she turned her head to look around. It was a typical hotel eatery, with nondescript beige and maroon furniture and leafy plants strategically placed to try to make the seating seem more private than it actually was. An older man sat at a table with his hands clasped around a coffee mug, gazing out the windows. His short hair was completely gray and the glasses were different, but it was unmistakably Dan Riggins. Mia's heart was pounding so hard it felt it was going to leap out of her chest. After twenty years, everyone's appearance changed, but it was startling how much older her father looked.

He turned his gaze directly at her, and Mia realized he probably had no idea what she looked like, so she raised her hand in greeting. His eyes widened in surprise and he stood up as she walked over to the table.

He moved toward her and she looked into his eyes. "Dad?"

Enveloping her in a big hug, he murmured, "Mimi," then released her so she could sit down.

As he settled back into his chair, Mia stared at him and tried to organize her thoughts. "I'm so glad to see you."

"It's been so long, Amelia. You've turned into a beautiful young woman."

"Be glad you missed some of the more unpleasant phases." Mia smiled. "My teenage years weren't pretty."

"I'm not glad. You probably won't believe it, but I thought about you every day."

"Then why didn't you try to get in touch with me?"

"I did. Over and over." He shook his head. "You mother said you wanted nothing to do with me."

"I probably did say that, particularly at first. Then I figured you'd just written me off. She said you had moved on, and then she wouldn't say anything about you at all." Mia glanced toward the doorway. "My relationship with Mom deteriorated after you left. By the time I was in high school, we barely spoke at all. Most of the time when I wasn't in school, I hid out at the library or at Denny's."

"I'm sorry. I wanted to see you, but your mother wouldn't grant me any visitation rights."

Mia pointed at him. "Ever since I knew enough to understand, I've wondered how that was even possible. I mean, did you do something to make a judge think that you were unfit to see me?"

"Your mother thought so. But no, I didn't do anything." Dan ran his fingers through his hair. "It was a terrible divorce. I know no divorce is good, but ours was particularly acrimonious. Are you sure you want to hear this?"

Mia nodded. "I'm tired of secrets."

He took a deep breath. "You might remember your mother was easily bored."

"Among other things."

"Well, yes, her manic highs and lows didn't help. Everything was always an extreme. Living with another person can be difficult under any circumstances, but your mother needed constant entertainment. You know what she was like. Suffice it to say, I was too dull, and she said I didn't appreciate her. I…well…didn't react the way she might have hoped. Her constant disappointment in me and criticism caused me to pull away. I felt disconnected from her and spent a lot of time at work. I volunteered for every possible travel assignment so I could get out of that house."

"Well, you were an agricultural inspector. You were supposed to travel, weren't you?"

"Yes, I traveled all over the state. But that didn't help you or your mother. When you combine me being gone and her wanting someone to make her feel special, well, it wasn't a surprise that she eventually found someone else."

Mia made a face of disgust. "That would be Howard."

"You're really sure you want to hear this? It doesn't get any better."

"I know. Keep going."

Dan took another deep breath. "Okay, so things got worse. You were there, so you might remember this part. Fights, then silences, then the trip to the hospital."

"Dad, I know she overdosed on painkillers. She tried to commit suicide, didn't she?"

"All right, yes, she did. Not too long after that, she told me about the other guy, how she was miserable living with me, and that meeting me was the worst thing that had ever happened to her."

"I'm not sure what to say."

Dan leaned forward and put his elbows on the table. "She stood there in the kitchen, leaning against the counter waving her arms at me saying, 'It's different with him. He makes me feel special and I love him with all my heart. I really and truly do.'"

"What did you say?"

"What *could* I say? She wanted a divorce. In a way, part of me was relieved, I guess. I was exhausted from so many years of drama."

"That didn't get better after you left."

"I was hoping it would. I thought that if that guy Howard was as wonderful as she said, maybe that would be a good thing for everyone. She'd take her medication and things would calm down. Me being away from home didn't help and I hoped that having a stepfather who was around more would be better for you."

"It didn't work out that way. You were way off, Dad. *Way* off." Mia took a sip of water. "Did you ever meet Howard?"

"Not officially, but I did see him once. He was extremely good looking, so it was easy to see why your mother was so interested."

"Well, he certainly thought he was impressive. In his world, he was always the most important—with a capital I— person in the room. I hated his guts from the moment I met him."

A corner of Dan's mouth turned up in a half-smile. "Don't hold back, honey, how do you really feel?"

"There are no words that can express how much I hated that man." Mia took a breath, trying to calm down. "He killed Mom, although I've often thought that she wanted him to. It was the only way out."

Dan reached for Mia's hand across the table. "I'm so sorry, Mimi. I never would have left you in that situation, if I had known."

"You still didn't answer my question. How would a judge not let you have visitation rights?"

"Your mother claimed I was unfaithful and a bad influence on you."

"Did you really cheat on Mom?"

"I thought about it, but I swear to you I never did. When the marriage was completely falling apart, a woman—it was Gwen actually—called the house and your mother went ballistic."

"When was that?"

"Not too long after I took Rusty to Alpine Grove."

"I know you saw Gwen then and Abigail too."

"Yes, but nothing happened. I helped Gwen move. She was grateful to have the help. That was it. I never found out what she wanted."

"So Mom convinced a judge you were a cheater?"

"You know how charming she could be. I was painted as an absentee father who had ignored his child for years. And she was providing a stable family environment with her wonderful new husband."

"That's quite a fantasy she came up with." Mia looked down at the tablecloth, then into Dan's eyes. "I don't understand. Why did you take Rusty to Alpine Grove in the first place?"

"During the day while you were in school, Rusty kept getting out. Your mother never paid attention to the gate, or him, and the neighbors were angry. One day, I watched

Rusty almost get hit by a car, and it scared me because I loved that dog too, you know. I couldn't be there to keep an eye on him and I didn't want you to have to go through him dying on top of everything else." Dan shook his head sadly. "In hindsight, it was probably a mistake, but I honestly thought it was the best thing."

"I'm working at Abigail's place, so I see why you thought it would be a good home. Dogs love it there."

"You work at Abigail's house? Doing what?"

"Abigail's niece, Kat, has built a dog-boarding kennel there. She offered me a job walking dogs. I'm planning to do grooming too, once I learn more about it."

Dan squeezed her hand. "That's wonderful, Mimi. So you're living in Alpine Grove?"

"Yes, in Gwen's house. The trailer you moved her stuff into is still there."

Dan chuckled. "That's hard to believe. It was old then."

"It's older now. But it's cozy and nice on the inside. I like it."

"So how was college?"

"I didn't go."

"But I set up a savings account for you. The money was transferred, so I just assumed..."

"Howard got a new car right before he died." Mia offered a wry smile. "It was nice, even though it didn't last long. The creditors took everything."

Dan bent his head and rested his forehead on his palms. "I'm so sorry. I knew I should have tried harder." He put his hands back on the table and looked at her. "I felt like such a failure, as a husband and as a father. That's part of why I joined the Peace Corps. I wanted to do something right for a change."

"You might have a second chance on the father part, anyway."

"I'm so glad Mimi. Seeing you again is wonderful."

Mia leaned forward. "I almost forgot—the lottery! You know those tickets you sent me? One of them actually hit. I won! I've never even played the lottery before. It was amazing."

"When?"

"September. That's how I was able to get out of Windiberg. So thanks for sending them with the postcards. Leaving that place was one of the happiest days of my life."

"For years, I sent you tickets with the child-support checks. Didn't you get those?"

"I never saw them." Mia took a drink of water. "Although now that you mention it, Howard once said he had won twenty bucks."

Dan groaned. "You never got any of the letters? None? For ten years?"

"I didn't know you paid child support. Maybe that's what we were living on. No one really talked about it."

"This is unbelievable. Why would your mother do this?"

"I'm biased, but I think it was Howard. It's hard to explain, but he was incredibly manipulative. Honestly, I try not to think about him too much because I just get angry again." Mia gestured dismissively. "I think I know why Gwen called that time after you helped her move. She told me that you met during the 1965 New York City blackout."

He raised his eyebrows. "That's true. So what?"

"So at the risk of prying, did you do more than just talk during the blackout?"

Dan looked uncomfortable and squirmed in his seat. "What are you getting at, Mimi?"

"Sex, Dad. Did you have sex with Gwen in 1965?"

"Uh, well, yes, we did. It was a...well, an unusual night. People were thrown together due to extreme circumstances."

"Gwen mentioned that. You need to talk to her. She just moved to San Diego to be near her daughter. I have the number."

"Gwen has a daughter?"

"You need to talk to Gwen. Please promise me you'll call her."

"All right. I will."

"Thanks, Dad."

~

After having lunch with her father, Mia met Chris in front of the Ferris wheel in Pacific Park on the Santa Monica pier. Mia had never ridden a Ferris wheel before and they agreed that situation needed to change.

Chris had never been to the new amusement park, since it had just opened a few months earlier. Mia was looking forward to some plain old fun after all the emotional upheaval related to talking to her father. Although it had been enjoyable sharing some of her childhood memories with him over lunch, Mia kept thinking about Heather. Mia hoped that Gwen would finally tell her father and Heather they were related.

Mia got off the freeway and navigated to a parking lot near the pier. As she walked toward the sign that said Pacific

Park, she looked up at the roller coaster and Ferris wheel. The curving yellow metal of the roller coaster seemed to weave through the sky and the Ferris wheel was festive with its red and yellow gondolas. Nearby was a ride called the Sea Dragon, which was a huge ship that was swinging back and forth in an arc. Another ride called Rock and Roll was busy spinning riders in a circle. The amusement park area had a carnival atmosphere complete with arcade games and shops filled with souvenirs and t-shirts decorated with hideous designs that people bought anyway. The ocean breeze was tinged with the scent of sugary cotton candy, funnel cakes, and deep-fried foods. Mia couldn't help but smile at all the happy kids running along the pier to get to their next exciting ride.

Chris was standing with his hands in his pockets, next to the Ferris wheel entrance, looking up at the huge wheel as it methodically started and stopped so people could load and unload from the gondolas. Mia scurried up behind him and tapped him on the shoulder with her fingertip. He whirled around, grinned, and wrapped her in a hug, nuzzling his face into her hair.

She leaned back so she could look into his eyes. "I missed you so much."

With a smile, he pulled her toward him and kissed her in a way that made it clear he'd missed her too. When he released her, they stared at each other for a moment until Mia said, "Wow" and they both laughed.

Chris took her hand. "Are you ready for your first Ferris wheel ride?"

"It's huge."

"Isn't it cool? I read in the paper that it's nine stories high. I hope you're not afraid of heights."

"I guess we'll find out."

Apparently unwilling to let go of her hand, Chris led her to get tickets and they stood holding hands, waiting their turn to get on the ride. They clambered into one side of the octagonal gondola as another couple settled into the other side.

As the massive wheel turned and they rose up toward the sky, the view opened up, and from above it looked like the beach went on forever. Mia discovered that not only was she not afraid, she loved the perspective from high above the city. To the north was Malibu and looking to the south were LAX, Palos Verdes, and the ships waiting to port at Long Beach. Because it was late November, the weather was cool and the beach wasn't crowded. There were just a few tiny silhouettes strolling along the sandy shoreline.

Mia turned to Chris. "Let's do the roller coaster next. And we have to walk on the beach before we leave."

"Whatever you want."

After Mia had tried most of the thrill rides and smashed into Chris numerous times on the Sig Alert bumper cars, they walked out of the amusement park area and onto the fishing pier, listening to the waves crash and seagulls squawk. The whole area was crowded with countless tourists and the sound of street performers created a soundtrack in the background, as the artists attempted to entice people to part with their cash.

Hand-in-hand, Mia and Chris slowly strolled along, discovered the famous Route 66 sign that proclaimed it was the "End of the Trail," and stopped to watch a fisherman reel in his catch.

At the entrance to an arcade, Mia pointed to the far wall. "Skee ball! We have to play skee ball."

After several games, Mia cashed in her tickets for a cheesy prize. She held up the plastic frog. "I think I'll name her Thelma."

Chris examined his plastic dinosaur and pointed it toward her. "Obviously, this must be Louise."

Near the arcade entrance was a photo booth. Mia dragged Chris behind the curtain and kissed him before putting money into the slot. Holding up their plastic animals aloft proudly, they pressed the button and made faces until the red light began blinking and a bright flash meant the picture had been taken.

They stood and waited outside the booth for the strip of photos to emerge from the slot. Mia grabbed it and held it up to Chris with a giggle. "I'm pretty sure we can't show these to anyone, ever."

"That's an intriguing new look for the mushroom girl."

She gave him a playful hug and they went back out onto the pier to watch the sunset. After the sun sank into the ocean, they walked off the pier to the Third Street Promenade and found a restaurant for dinner.

As they sat down at a table, Mia grinned. "This is a little nicer than the diner at the Enchanted Moose."

"But there aren't any crayons."

Mia rummaged around in her bag and pulled out a pencil and pad. "I came prepared."

"Not only did you offer to pay for dinner, you're providing art supplies." Chris pressed his hands to his heart in a mock swoon. "I'm overwhelmed."

Mia laughed. "I've missed having conversations that include illustrations. I saved every single placemat."

"Even the one I spilled ketchup on?"

"The way you incorporated the splat into the drawing was extremely creative."

"That was the X-rated placemat wasn't it?" He grinned. "I was inspired."

"Is your sister expecting you back tonight?"

He shook his head. "I sure hope not."

"Good." Mia reached her hand across the table and Chris took it in his. She smiled. "I was hoping you'd say that."

"Did I mention how much I've missed you?"

"Maybe a couple of times. I've had so much fun today."

"It's not over yet.

During dinner Mia shared the highlights of her lunch with her father with Chris. He asked a few questions but mostly just listened.

Mia pointed her fork at him. "Now that you know every little thing about my whole family drama, I want to know what's up with you. How are things going with the job search?"

"Okay, I guess. I've been sending out resumes, but I feel like I'm throwing paper down a garbage chute. No one has called me for an interview, except for a sort of crummy drafting job that I don't want." He set his fork down on the plate. "I did get a call from Ben this week though."

"As in Ben, the developer building the opulent house in Alpine Grove? That Ben?"

"The very one. Before I moved, I sent him a thank-you card and gave him the number at my sister's place in case there were any questions that came up after they transitioned the project to the new architect."

"Wouldn't the architect call you?"

"Unlikely. Jonah would never stoop to talking to the likes of me."

"You're being a little hard on yourself, aren't you?"

"This guy thinks he's God's gift to architecture. He fancies himself an *artiste*." Chris sketched a somewhat exaggerated likeness of Pepé Le Pew, sporting a black beret and a cloud representing skunk stink. "It turns out, Ben can't stand Jonah."

"There's an oddly circular element to a caricature of a cartoon character."

"Don't show it to Warner Brothers. They'll probably sue me too."

"Who is suing you?"

"No one. But when I talked to Ben, he tried to talk me into working for him directly. But I can't because I signed a contract that says I can't work for clients of Gilbert, Tingler, Halberstam, and Associates Architecture for a year or they'll sue me. That's the last thing I need."

"Can't you make a deal?"

"You might recall I didn't leave on the greatest of terms. And it's not like I can afford a lawyer. I told Ben—nicely— that I appreciate the thought, but it wasn't going to happen. And that I have the interview next week, so I might have a new job here in LA."

"You mean working at the job you don't want?"

"Well, I didn't tell Ben that. It's an entry-level job, which is a pretty major step down, but if I get it, I could start paying off my debt. And move out of my sister's second bedroom."

Mia leaned forward, resting her elbows on the table. "We're never going to see each other, are we?"

"We're seeing each other now."

"I know, but with the holidays coming up, I won't be able to get away for at least a couple of months. Kat has a book she's writing, which is why she hired me. I felt bad leaving this weekend and it's just for two days."

"Well, you had to see your father before he left." Chris drew a stick-figure family holding hands next to a boxy, childlike rendering of a house.

"True, but I wanted to see you too." Mia pulled the pencil from his hand and he looked at her. "I think, I mean, I don't know. Um, okay, I'm mangling this, even for me. What I'm *trying* to say is that whenever I'm with you, I never want to leave. I think I love you."

His eyes widened. "I love you too. But to be honest, I was afraid to say anything because I didn't think you felt the same way."

"I do. So what are we going to do about it?"

"I have no idea."

∼

Later at the hotel, Mia was dozing next to Chris, listening to the sound of his breathing. It was so peaceful, she wanted to lie there forever and never return to real life. The phone rang, disturbing the serenity, and Mia jerked her head up off the pillow. "Ow, get off my hair!"

Chris leaped away and Mia reached for the phone on the nightstand and said hello as he curled back around her and stroked the hair along her temple in silent apology.

"Hi Mia, it's Dad."

"Hi, I um, didn't expect to hear from you tonight." Mia glanced at Chris, who raised his eyebrows in query. She shrugged and he moved over, reaching for a book that was sitting on the nightstand.

Dan said, "I talked to Gwen. Why didn't you tell me?"

"It wasn't my secret to tell."

"Have you met Heather?"

"No, but I'd like to."

"Okay, that's what I wanted to know. I'm going to see if I can push my start date back a couple of weeks. I want to spend Thanksgiving with you and Heather."

"I can't really get away. The kennel is booked solid."

"What if we came to Alpine Grove? Maybe I can work something out with them."

"Okay, Dad. You have my number. Let me know."

Mia hung up the phone and snuggled up to Chris again. "Dad wants to come to Alpine Grove for Thanksgiving. Do you think you can visit too?"

"Maybe. It depends on if I have a job and if I can figure out a way to get there. My sister is doing a big Thanksgiving thing with a bunch of her friends. I'm not sure I can ditch that either."

She hugged him. "I understand. But I'm feeling thankful I met you."

"I'm thankful for that too." He pointed at the book. "So, what are you reading here?"

"Just some trashy romance novel I picked up."

"This romance is a lot more…explicit than the one I read to you before. Check this out: they're doing it on a llama. Is that even possible? I didn't know couples rode llamas. Is that a thing? Are there llama saddles? And if there are, how would two people fit? Wouldn't that be uncomfortable?"

"I don't know." Mia sat up and looked at the text of the book. "Hey, I missed you. I was lonely and needed a distraction."

"Sex on llamas is definitely distracting. So is this." He pointed at a paragraph. "I mean, come on, that's gotta hurt. And what does *lave* mean?"

"Wash, I think."

"Isn't that's kind of gross? I mean what is this guy doing? Laundering her? Ick. I've got images of a drooling Saint Bernard stuck in my head now. That's *not* sexy."

Mia started to laugh. "I think you might be getting a little too literal with all that purple prose. It's just a book."

"What about this?" He flipped to the next page and pointed at a paragraph. "I know it's been a long time since I took biology class, but I'm not sure it's anatomically possible to do that."

"Well, maybe he's got an extra prosthetic-limb kind of a sex aid or something."

Chris grinned. "Well, that would sure help a lot of guys out."

"You're having a little too much fun with this."

"I'm just saying there are a whole lot of unusual flower parts and shafts and clenching and shattering. It all sounds pretty dangerous. I'm amazed anyone is willing to ever have sex again after reading this. I'm a little scared now."

"Don't be afraid." She put her arms around him and gave him a kiss. "I promise I'll be gentle with all my throbbing ecstasy."

"Cool." He tossed the book aside and pulled her closer to him. "That sounds promising."

The next morning, Mia came out of the shower with a towel wrapped around her chest and sat down on the bed next to Chris. "Have you seen my shirt?"

"No. When you took it off last night, I wasn't paying attention to where you put it. My mind was elsewhere."

"No doubt. What did I do with it? I've looked everywhere." She stood up, and then crouched in front of the dresser, peering underneath. "I can't believe this. I *liked* that shirt."

Chris stood up, walked over to her, and kissed her bare shoulder. "It couldn't have gotten far."

Mia moved away from him. "I need to get back to Alpine Grape...*Grove*. Kat is going to kill me. I'll probably get conned...*canned*."

"Hey, it's no big deal. It's just a shirt, and it has to be here somewhere."

Mia sat down on the end of the bed and pulled her towel around her more tightly. "I know. It's just everything was going so well all of a sudden, and now I have to leave you. But I don't want to. Then I'll probably screw up this job. Because that's what always happens. Just when I think everything is fine for a change, the other shoe drops and I'm back to being the mutant mushroom girl again."

Chris took her hand and pulled her up into a hug. He slowly unwrapped the towel from around her, dropped it onto the floor, and turned her to face the mirror. "Look in the mirror. What do you see?"

"A flabby, kind of weird-looking woman who, in addition to losing her blouse, also really needs to find her comb. And jeez, I think my cellulite is expanding its horizons. That's just fantastic."

Chris ran his fingers through the hair at the nape of her neck and bent to kiss her earlobe. "You are an amazing woman. The only one who doesn't believe that is you."

"I'm working on it." She smiled at his reflection in the mirror. "So what do you see when you look at yourself in the mirror?"

"A kind of goofy guy who is hopelessly in love with the mushroom girl. But it's all a little blurry because I'm not wearing my glasses."

"Well, that's not so bad. That means you can't see my cellulite either."

Chris wrapped his arms around her in a hug. "I'm going to miss you."

Mia rested her head on his shoulder. "Me too. I hate goodbyes."

"Call me when you get back home, okay?"

After finally locating her shirt under the bed, packing, and saying a lingering farewell to Chris, Mia got in the RAV and drove back to Alpine Grove. Although she tried not to cry, leaving was even worse than before. They'd had such a good time together, picking up right where they'd left off like no time had passed at all. Was it so wrong to want that every day?

The ugly reality was that there were no architectural firms in Alpine Grove. It wasn't that Chris couldn't get a job; it was that there were no jobs to be had. And she didn't want to give up the situation she had with Kat. To his credit, Chris didn't want her to either. He was thrilled that at last she'd finally found something she enjoyed doing.

They'd gone back and forth a zillion times on possible options, and Mia somewhat guiltily realized that Chris had never once suggested freeloading off her lottery winnings in any way.

At least for the short term, she'd just have to be satisfied seeing Chris for the occasional long weekend or holiday. Everyone said patience was a virtue. Maybe they'd work out something over time, but for right now, she had to accept the fact that they wouldn't be able to spend much time together. But she didn't have to like it.

Chapter 13

Karma

Mia returned to her daily dog-walking routine and looked forward to her after-dinner conversations with Chris. Although it sounded like the interview for the entry-level drafting job had gone well, they'd turned him down. Mia was well aware of how demoralizing the job-hunting process could be and she tried to help Chris keep his spirits up, even in the face of rejection and a lot of silence from prospective employers.

Two days before Thanksgiving, Mia was putting away groceries before she had to go back to the kennel for the afternoon dog walks and feeding. Somehow her father had been successful in talking the Peace Corps into letting him leave after the holiday and in convincing Gwen and Heather to meet Mia in Alpine Grove on Thanksgiving.

Mia was extremely nervous about the whole situation, even though it was basically all her fault that it was happening. The night before, while she was trying to convince Chris not to give up and get a job at the local 7-Eleven, he was trying to convince her that meeting her half-sister wouldn't be a complete disaster. She smiled at the memory of what he'd said. "I love you, so why wouldn't they?" A corner of her cynical little heart probably melted into sloppy, sappy goo right then and there.

The phone rang and Mia slammed the refrigerator door shut. She reached to grab the phone, picked up the receiver, and was surprised to find it was Chris. "How come you're calling so early?"

"I was thinking you might be at lunch. Do you have to go back to work right this second?"

"I'm just putting away groceries. My refrigerator is officially stocked now. I went to the grocery store to avoid the major rush tomorrow. Is something wrong?"

"No, but I need to talk to you. It could be really good, but I need a favor."

"What's that?"

"Could I crash at your place?"

"When?"

"Tomorrow."

Mia grinned widely, "Are you kidding? Yes! Does this mean you're visiting for Thanksgiving?"

"Maybe longer. Ben called and he wants me to finish the house on the lake. He fired the firm because he wants to work with me."

"I thought you couldn't do that, or they'll sic their lawyers on you."

"He talked to our good friends at Gilbert, Tingler, Halberstam, and Associates Architecture and got me out of my employment contract."

"How?"

"I'm not sure. But he says he has a signed piece of paper that asserts they have no claim on me in any way. The bottom line is that they won't sue me."

"That's fantastic. So you get to finish the house?"

"I do, but the best thing is that I'll be in Alpine Grove near you. That's what makes me happiest. Talking on the phone has been great, but I miss you all the time. I want to touch you and just be around you."

"I think it would be easy to do that if you moved in here."

"You mean for more than just a visit?"

Mia smiled. "I don't want you to leave again. But you can call it a really long visit if it makes you feel better."

"No way. I'll fill out change-of-address cards tomorrow. I can't wait to see you."

"How are you going to get here?"

"I'll rent a car. I still have the one credit card and I haven't hit my limit yet. It's just a one-day rental, so it shouldn't cost too much. And soon I'll actually be earning money again."

"That's great." Mia glanced at the clock. "I've got to go, but you know where the place is—it's right next door to the kennel. I'll leave the key under a white rock next to the door. Just come in and make yourself at home. Architecturally speaking, it's an ugly box, so try not to be offended."

"I don't care what the place looks like. It's what's inside that matters. If you're in the box, that's where I want to be."

"Drive carefully. I love you."

"I love you too."

Mia walked back to the kennel in a daze. Was it possible? She was really going to get to work at a job she loved, live with a man she loved, and even have a family again?

If someone had told her three months ago that any of this would happen, she never would have believed it. Talk about winning the lottery! Maybe there really was something to karma after all.

All those times she failed and picked herself up and started over again, she'd survived loss, humiliation, and countless hurts and never given up. Yes, she had flaws. Countless flaws. But when karma had circled around and finally given her a break at last, she'd taken the opportunity to change her life and run with it. She'd taken risks, had difficult conversations, and moved forward.

Even Gizmo eating the letter had been a lucky break. If he hadn't, she might never have found out about Heather. Maybe she'd give Giz an extra treat on the walk today.

She strolled along the forest trail, looked up at the tall trees, and took a deep breath. Although her life was more complicated now, there was no place she'd rather be and she was eager to find out what the future might hold.

Chapter 14

Epilogue

O n Thanksgiving Day, late in the afternoon, Mia and Chris exited the trailer to walk over to the kennel and tend to the dogs. A light snow had fallen overnight and the evergreens that surrounded the trailer were dusted with white.

As they walked along the densely forested trail, a commotion arose from the tree canopy above, and snowflakes fluttered around them, shimmering in the sunlight like a cascade of sparkling diamonds.

Mia looked up, where a squirrel was leaping from branch to branch. "I think Potty Mouth is angry that he can't figure out how to join us inside for dinner."

Chris stopped and took Mia's hand as the squirrel scolded and chattered above. "He's really annoyed with you."

"It's your fault. You're the one who fixed the hole after Gwen's patch fell off."

"I'm glad Joel has all those tools. Trying to cut anything with Gwen's old rusty handsaw was no fun. And when the handle broke off, it was over."

After the squirrel disappeared into the woods, they resumed walking. Mia glanced at Chris. "I can't believe you never told me you worked at a cabinetry shop in high school."

"It was just a part-time job. I haven't done any woodworking in years. The people in my apartment building used to frown on the use of power tools. I was too busy with work anyway."

"So you really made furniture?"

"Not by myself, but that's what they did at the shop."

"Did you enjoy it?"

"Working with wood can be satisfying. You make it fit together into something useful. I like sanding it, finishing it, and seeing the patterns of the wood grain appear. Sometimes you can transform even a cheap piece of wood into something beautiful."

"So if I ask nicely, will you build us a new kitchen table? As we discovered this afternoon, Gwen's ugly linoleum-and-metal thing is really rickety."

"Yeah, I'm glad it didn't collapse under the weight of all that food." He turned to smile at her. "I could be convinced, assuming you can get Joel to let me use some of the fine woodworking tools he's got."

"I'll get Kat to ask him. She's a lot more persuasive than I am, particularly with Joel."

The trail ended, opening up into the clearing where the kennel was located. The house sat off to the right and Kat and Joel were walking down the steps. Kat was carrying grocery bags that she handed to Joel, who was already holding a casserole dish. He walked to the green truck with the food while Kat waved at Mia and Chris and headed toward them.

Kat met them at the kennel and gave Mia a hug. "Happy Thanksgiving! You're sure everything will be okay, right? We'll only be gone a few hours. I learned during last year's Thanksgiving blizzard that it's better not to leave Joel and his sister together any longer than an afternoon."

Mia said, "Actually, coming over here is a nice break. The trailer isn't very big and having Dad, Gwen, Heather, her husband, Gizmo, and lots of food all crammed in there together is sort of complicated."

"It's nice to be outside in the fresh air," Chris added.

"I was going to bring Gizmo, but he refused to be separated from all the opportunities for snacking." Mia sighed. "Dad is supposed to be watching the dog, but really he's just sneaking food to him. I hope Gizmo doesn't get sick."

Joel walked up to the group and Kat took his hand. She turned back to Mia. "If anything happens, please call me. We'll come right home. You have the number at Cindy's house."

"If we have to come home early, it's okay," Joel said.

Kat gestured toward the house. "Our dogs are all fed and sleeping in the house. If you need to go inside, make sure that you don't go into my office. Maria's cat Scarlett is in there and you do *not* want to let her out."

Joel glanced over his shoulder. "You really don't."

Mia said, "Don't worry, everything will be fine."

"I know. You're not the first to point out that I worry too much," Kat said.

"I'll walk the dogs and they'll all go back to sleep. Have a good time. Enjoy your meal," Mia said.

As Kat and Joel walked to the truck, Mia glanced at Chris, who seemed to be lost in thought. "What are you thinking about?"

"All the plans we've talked about in the last day or so. It's kind of scary, but I'm excited. I suppose way back when Gilbert, Tingler, Halberstam, and Associates Architecture was just a twinkle in Leon Gilbert's eye, he felt the same way."

"I have no doubt that once people see the house you're working on for Ben, they'll be impressed and want you to design something for them too."

"It doesn't hurt that Ben seems to have already told a bunch of people about that lake house. He gave me a card for another friend of his who has land and wants to build a summer place. He wants me to call the guy after the holiday."

"Kat says she has about a hundred books on starting a business you can borrow too. And I can help you manage the money stuff."

"I can't believe this is happening."

"The only one who doesn't believe it is you."

With a laugh, he put his arm around her shoulder. "Gee, where have I heard that before?"

"I want to hire you too before your rates go up. If Gwen agrees to let me buy her place, you'll have another project." She turned to look at him. "I've seen the drawings you do when you think no one's looking, and I want one of those houses."

"When it's being built, if you let me do a little cabinetry work, I'll give you a really good deal on that too." Chris pulled her into a hug. "You know what else I can't believe?"

Mia looked into his eyes. "What's that?"

"How lucky I am to be here with you."

"I'm not sure how much luck has to do with it, but I'm glad you took a gamble on the mushroom girl"

"Sometimes you're lucky enough to meet the right person at the right time, I guess."

"I'm glad that person was me."

Chris bent to give her a kiss. "I am too."

Thanks for Reading

Thank you for dedicating some of your reading time to *The Luck of the Paw*. I hope you enjoyed Mia and Chris's adventures. I'll be writing more books that will feature Kat, Joel and various other residents of Alpine Grove who bring dogs to the new boarding kennel. The tenth book, *Daydream Retriever* is available along with ten other books in the series.

If you would like to be notified by e-mail when I release a new book, you can sign up for my New Releases e-mail list at SusanDaffron.com.

I know that not everyone likes to write book reviews, but if you are willing write a sentence or two about what you thought of *The Luck of the Paw*, I encourage you to post a review at your favorite book vendor site or share a message with your social networking friends.

If you would like to share your thoughts about the book with me privately, you can reach me through the contact page on the SusanDaffron.com web site.

I look forward to hearing from you!

~ Susan C. Daffron

About the Author

Susan Daffron is the author of the Jennings & O'Shea series and the Alpine Grove romantic comedies, a series of novels that feature residents of the small town of Alpine Grove and their various quirky dogs and cats. She is also an award-winning author of many nonfiction books, including several about pets and animal rescue. She lives in a small town in northern Idaho and shares her life with her husband and three really cute dogs.